"You underrate yourself."

Then Jonas stopped and said, "But there's something you should know about me, Miss Southeran. I play to win."

"And the prize in this case? Was it worth calling out such big guns?"

"It depends on what you mean by the prize. Victory over your aunt? An opportunity to dance with you? Or...what?"

Eleanor looked at him, which was a mistake. He was looking down at her with amusement and something more disturbing in his eyes.

* * *

Eleanor
Harlequin® Historical #232—March 2008

SYLVIA ANDREW

taught modern languages for a number of years, ultimately becoming vice-principal of a sixth-form college. She lives in Somerset, England, with two cats, a dog and a husband who has a very necessary sense of humor and a stern approach to punctuation. Sylvia has one daughter, who lives in London, and they share a lively interest in the theater. She describes herself as an "unrepentant romantic."

SYLVIA ANDREW

Eleanor

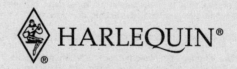

HARLEQUIN®

TORONTO • NEW YORK • LONDON
AMSTERDAM • PARIS • SYDNEY • HAMBURG
STOCKHOLM • ATHENS • TOKYO • MILAN • MADRID
PRAGUE • WARSAW • BUDAPEST • AUCKLAND

ISBN-13: 978-0-373-30541-4
ISBN-10:   0-373-30541-9

ELEANOR

DON'T MISS THESE OTHER
NOVELS AVAILABLE NOW:

#887 TAMING THE TEXAN—Charlene Sands

Clint Hayworth wants revenge—and he'll be damned if he'll allow
his father's conniving, gold-digging widow to take over the family
ranch! But something about her is getting under his skin....
This is one Texan in real need of taming—
and Tess is just the woman for the job!

#888 HIGH SEAS TO HIGH SOCIETY—Sophia James

Her ill-fitting, threadbare clothes concealed the body of an angel,
but what kind of woman truly lay behind her refined mask?
Highborn lady or artful courtesan, she intrigued him—
and Asher wanted to possess both!
Let Sophia James sweep you away to adventure
and high-society romance.

#889 PICKPOCKET COUNTESS—Bronwyn Scott

Robbing from the rich to give to the poor, Nora may have taken
more than she expected when she stole the earl's heart!
Sexy and intriguing, Bronwyn Scott's debut book heralds
an author to watch.

#890 A KNIGHT MOST WICKED—Joanne Rock

Tristan Carlisle will do whatever it takes to secure the lands and
fortune that will establish his respectability in the world and fulfill
his duty to the king. Even if it means denying his attraction to a
gypsy posing as a noblewoman....
Join this wicked knight on his quest for honor and love.

#231 THE LORD'S FORCED BRIDE—Anne Herries

When Catherine Melford sees a dark and handsome stranger
fighting in a town square, she is mesmerized. But she has no idea
that he's the lord she'll be forced to wed!

With love to my friends Joan and Brian Robinson

Chapter One

Eleanor had never seen anything so beautiful. The crystal drops in the huge chandelier splintered the flames from its candles into a million points of sparkling light. It was like…like fireworks frozen in the air, like all the stars in the Milky Way gathered together. It was worth coming to London just to see this. A fairy-tale enchantment…

'Eleanor, my dear, Lady Dorothy and her daughter wish to speak to you!' Eleanor was recalled to a more mundane reality by the sound of her aunt's voice. Without waiting for her niece, Lady Walcot had moved on a few paces in the direction of a dowager with a haughty air and an imposing turban, complete with feathers.

Eleanor gave a small sigh and started to follow, but stopped again when she became aware that a tall, broad-shouldered man with dark, hard features was staring at her from the other side of the room. He would have been an impressive figure in any circumstances, but what made him even more striking was the fact that in this crowded room he was standing quite alone.

As her eye caught his, he raised one eyebrow and smiled ironically. He was laughing at her! Of course, she had been behaving like the country bumpkin her cousins accused her of being, gazing like a moonstruck idiot at the chandelier, but she was not about to be put out of countenance by this creature's boldness! She raised her chin, gave him a cool stare, and then turned away to join her aunt and Lady Dorothy.

After exchanging civilities with Lady Walcot and agreeing, with every sign of pleasure, that the rooms were sadly crowded, Lady Dorothy said with a significant movement of her head, 'I see that he is back in London.'

'He?' said Lady Walcot blankly. Then her puzzled expression changed to one of disapprobation. 'Is he here now?'

'Come, Lady Walcot! You must have noticed him.'

'No, where?'

'Further down on the other side of the room—you passed him as you came in. He is quite on his own, of course. How he has the effrontery to show himself I cannot imagine!' The ladies turned and stared down the room. Eleanor looked too, but more discreetly. The tall man was gazing indifferently at the passing crowd, but when he became conscious of those two icy stares directed down the room at him he bowed ironically. Whatever the gentleman lacked it was not self-assurance, thought Eleanor with some amusement.

'The impertinence!' said Lady Dorothy as she turned back again, outraged. 'But, my dear Lady Walcot, there is worse. Mrs Anstey is here tonight, too. I only hope the poor woman is not brought face to face with him— that would be most unfortunate. In a moment I shall seek her out and warn her.'

'Indeed you must!'

Most of the sense of this conversation was lost on Eleanor, though it was certain that the two ladies were talking of the man who had smiled at her. Her aunt seemed to be genuinely worried by his presence, but beneath her display of righteous indignation Lady Dorothy was relishing the idea of seeking this Mrs Anstey out to warn her. Lady Dorothy had never forgotten that she was the daughter of a duke, and that marrying Edwin Rushton—a mere commoner—in no way diminished her right to order the lives of those around her. When they had last met, Eleanor had thought her an uncharitable busybody, and she now saw that the years did not appear to have mellowed or changed her. She sighed and waited patiently until the lady turned to her.

'Miss Southeran. How nice to see you in London again. Are you here for the season? I believe your mama is not with you?'

'I am a little old for that, Lady Dorothy,' said Eleanor with a polite smile. 'No, I merely came to take part in my cousin Bella's wedding celebrations. But I must go back soon—I have been away too long already. My mother is now something of an invalid, and I worry about her.'

Lady Dorothy's daughter, a pretty, fair-haired girl with doll-like features, cried, 'But how can you bear it, Miss Southeran? To be leaving London just as the season is beginning!'

'Be silent, Maria! Miss Southeran will do as she ought. No doubt she regrets having to leave London at any time, but it is not as if she were a girl in her first season. As I recall, you came out the same year as my

Charlotte, did you not?' said Lady Dorothy, turning to Eleanor again with a crocodile smile. 'Let me see, that must have been seven or eight years ago. How time flies! Has your aunt told you that Charlotte is now the mother of three charming little girls?'

'Indeed she has, ma'am. And how happy Charlotte is in her marriage.'

'It is fortunate. She was always a good, obedient girl, of course, and would never have dreamt of refusing Lord Crawford's offer. Her father and I would not have permitted it. But as it happens the match has turned out very well.' She turned to her youngest daughter. 'I hope you are paying heed, Maria! Miss Southeran here had just the same opportunities as Charlotte, but I am sorry to say that she wasted them all. Indeed your own brother Arthur was quite taken with her for a while. I dare swear she now regrets her foolishness and wishes she too had an establishment and children of her own!'

Eleanor replied calmly, 'If I could have been sure of making your son as happy as Charlotte is in her marriage, I would have accepted his very flattering offer, Lady Dorothy. But I am persuaded that his second choice of partner was a better one for him. As for the rest—you will perhaps remember that I had to leave London halfway through the season, when my brother died. I have not been back between then and now.'

Eleanor's voice might have been calm, but her aunt, observing the faint colour rising in her niece's cheeks, intervened hastily. 'I am sure that no daughter could have been more loving or more dutiful than Eleanor, Lady Dorothy. I have done my best to keep her in London a little longer, even pleaded with her to keep me company for a while now that Bella has left me, but she insists that her mother needs her.'

'I suppose that is understandable—London must seem strangely noisy after so many years in the depths of the country. For myself, I cannot imagine what it would be like to live so far from any really civilised society—very tame, I dare swear. Arthur and his wife live with me, of course, in the centre of town. They are forever entertaining and visiting. But now, if you will forgive me, I really must go in search of Mrs Anstey. Enjoy the rest of your stay, Miss Southeran! Perhaps we shall see you again. Come, Maria.' As Lady Dorothy sailed away with Maria in tow, Eleanor let her breath out in a long sigh.

'I had forgotten how odious that woman is.'

'Eleanor!'

'Well, she is, Aunt Hetty. I am willing to wager that Arthur is as much under her thumb now as he was seven years ago. I pity his poor wife.'

It was clear that Lady Walcot agreed with her niece, but was not about to say so. Instead she changed the subject. 'Would you like me to find you a dancing partner, Eleanor?'

'Do you think you could? At my great age? Lady Dorothy would think it most unlikely.'

'Eleanor, you let your tongue run away with you—you always did. It is not becoming in you to make fun of your elders, and especially not Lady Dorothy. In any case,' she went on, somewhat spoiling her effect, 'you are as handsome now as you ever were, and I am sure I shall have no difficulty at all in finding someone to dance with you.' As they walked up the room she went on, 'But I confess that I wish I could be happier about your future! Since you refuse to stay here in London, I suppose you must look for a husband in Somerset.' She sounded so doubtful about the idea that Eleanor burst out laughing.

'You are right to rate my chances low, Aunt Hetty! The young men of Somerset have younger, richer game to pursue—when they are not pursuing real game, or shooting pigeons, or…or…whatever they spend their time doing. Truth to tell, I find them rather boring! But pray do not concern yourself on my account. Mama and I are quite happy together. And you know that I have always loved Stanyards.'

Lady Walcot stopped by a quiet alcove. 'My dear, it isn't enough!' she said earnestly. 'A woman's best chance of security lies in a suitable marriage.'

'Such as one to Arthur Rushton, perhaps?' asked Eleanor with a slight curl of the lip.

'Why not? He is rich—or will be one day. And from what I hear young Mrs Rushton has a handsome allowance and any number of servants to look after her. And she has her children. It is a pity that her nerves do not always permit her to enjoy her advantages…'

'You see? No, Aunt Hetty. I think I am happier in my tame country existence than I could ever be in Clara Rushton's place.'

'Happiness is not the sole aim of marriage, Eleanor. Not even the chief aim.'

'Isn't it? I think it is the only one.'

'What nonsense you talk! Pray be serious for one moment! If you would only put yourself into my hands I could almost certainly find you a suitable husband here in London.'

'Well, then, I promise you, when I feel the need of

one I shall come to you first of all! But for now I shall look around me and enjoy the spectacle of London society amusing itself. The memory of it will console my tame country evenings.'

Lady Walcot shook her head at her niece's refusal to be serious, but decided to say no more, and they resumed their walk down the room. It was a magnificent apartment, lavishly furnished in red velvet with a richly decorated white and gold ceiling. Eleanor found it slightly overpowering—vulgar even, but dared not say so. The chandelier was lovely, though. She looked up at it as they passed, and nearly walked into her aunt as that lady suddenly stopped. The stranger from the other side of the room was standing in front of them.

'Lady Walcot—' Eleanor's aunt looked coldly at the gentleman but said nothing. He continued, 'We met at my cousin's house in Berkeley Square. My name is Guthrie. I should like to ask your companion to dance with me.'

'Thank you, sir, but my niece does not intend to dance this evening—not at the moment, at least,' said Lady Walcot frostily.

Perhaps the gentlemen saw Eleanor's astonishment, for he made no move to go, but said gently, 'Forgive me, but how can you possibly know? You haven't even asked her.'

'I would not dream of doing so, sir. I know that to have any closer acquaintance with a man such as yourself would be as abhorrent to her as it would to me, or to any woman of principle. And now you must excuse us, if you please. Come, Eleanor!' She took Eleanor's arm and almost dragged her niece away. Eleanor couldn't help casting a glance over her shoulder at the stranger to see his reaction to this massive set-down. He was gazing after them with the same ironical smile on his face. Then he shrugged and walked calmly towards the door to the rooms where the card tables were to be found.

'My dear aunt, you must, you really must explain! I shall explode with curiosity if you do not! Who is this monster called Guthrie? You and Lady Dorothy were talking about him before, were you not? What has he done that puts him so far beyond the pale? Tell me!'

Lady Walcot hesitated, then shook her head. She and Eleanor were sitting at one of a number of small tables which had been placed in the conservatory, and Lord Walcot, who had joined them for supper, was fetching some refreshment.

'That is impossible, Eleanor. The story is not a suitable one, but at the risk of setting your back up I assure you that that man is not a fit acquaintance for you.'

'Oh, come! I am not a simple schoolroom miss. As Lady Dorothy so kindly said, I am well past my first season! I need a better reason than that for not being allowed to dance with him!'

Lady Walcot looked even more determined. 'I am afraid that you must do without one, Eleanor. All I will say is that his treatment of the Anstey family has been wicked.'

'Can you tell me, at least, who these Ansteys are?'

'Mrs Anstey and her younger daughter, Marianne, are sitting over there in the far corner. The poor woman is trying to make herself inconspicuous.'

Eleanor turned her head a fraction and saw a pale, sweet-faced woman in black, almost hidden by the over-hanging branch of a potted palm. Next to her sat a very beautiful girl in a pale blue dress. 'Marianne Anstey is exquisite! She looks like a fairy princess!'

'Absolutely lovely, I agree. They have aroused a great

deal of attention since their arrival from America. The girl is certain to make a good marriage, although they are as poor as church mice, and totally dependent on their relatives.'

'What did Mr Guthrie do?'

'I cannot discuss it now—here is your uncle. All you really need to know is that the man is a scoundrel.'

'Who is this scoundrel?' asked Lord Walcot. 'No, let me guess. Jonas Guthrie, without a doubt. Why can't you leave him alone, Hetty? From what he says, Guthrie has decided to leave London soon and retire to the country. And I must say I don't blame him! Lady Dorothy and her cronies—'

'Cronies!'

'I beg your pardon, my dear, I forgot you were one of them—I should have said her friends! You've all been making life impossible for the poor devil with your scandalous stories about the Ansteys—not that he needs anyone's sympathy; he's well able to take care of himself.'

Eleanor, swift to seize her opportunity, asked, 'You do not agree with the stories, then, Uncle?'

'We don't know enough of the matter to judge, my dear. It's possible that Guthrie is a villain—I suspect he's no weakling, and he certainly isn't a fool—but I have found him to be perfectly straightforward in his dealings with me.'

'Are you suggesting that that sweet woman is not telling the truth when she says that Jonas Guthrie is the cause of all her misfortunes?' asked Lady Walcot, bristling.

'Not at all. I'm certain Mrs Anstey believes every word she tells you. How much she understands of business affairs is another matter. But this is the most idle speculation, and not fit for an evening of enjoyment! Come, Eleanor, if your aunt won't do her duty and find you a partner, I shall dance with you myself.'

Since Lord Walcot was generally considered to be the best performer of the waltz in London, Eleanor rose with alacrity and accompanied her uncle into the ballroom. Though she looked somewhat nervously around her in case Mr Guthrie should be watching, there was no trace of him. He had not, it seemed, found anyone else to dance with. Perhaps he had not tried?

They returned to her uncle's house in South Audley Street that evening without any further mention of Mr Guthrie. But her aunt's somewhat high-handed action had roused Eleanor's spirit and she was determined to find out more about him. She waited until Lady Walcot was in her bedroom and then went along to visit her. They discussed the evening for a moment or two, then Eleanor said, 'About Mr Guthrie, Aunt…?'

'Why are you so fascinated by the subject of Mr Guthrie? I would much rather forget him—he is an unworthy topic of conversation.'

'But you must see that I am consumed with curiosity! Now that we are private, can you not tell me why you refused to let me dance with him, when just a minute before you had said you would find me a partner? I am not Bella, Aunt Hetty. I am not accustomed to being treated like a child.'

Lady Walcot looked in affectionate exasperation at her niece. 'My dear Eleanor, you may be six-and-twenty, but you are still a young, unmarried woman! Oh, I know that you have been more or less in charge of Stanyards ever since you were a girl. I am sure anyone would admire the devoted manner in which you have looked after your mother—'

'There is no cause for admiration there, Aunt Hetty— I adore her!'

'—and managed the Stanyards estate—'

'I adore that, too!'

'Be quiet and let me finish, Eleanor!' said her aunt, smiling. But she quickly grew serious again. 'I have been thinking for some time that I should say something to you, and this seems to be a good occasion. Come and sit by me, my dear.' She thought for a moment, then, taking one of Eleanor's hands in hers, she said carefully, 'The…somewhat unusual circumstances of your up-bringing have given you an independence of mind which you do not trouble to hide. And of course this same independence has recently stood you in good stead while you have struggled to keep the Stanyards estate going. But, sadly, it is not generally regarded as a desirable quality in a young woman, and I fear it does not endear you to prospective suitors—nor to society in general.'

'Father always said I should think for myself, Aunt Hetty—'

Lady Walcot gave a small exclamation of impatience and said with sisterly scorn, 'Your father always had his head too high in the clouds to be a judge of anything. I don't suppose it ever occurred to him that that is the last thing to teach a young girl! Neither he nor your mother ever had the slightest idea of what goes on in the real world.'

Eleanor removed her hand. 'We were very happy, all the same.'

'But what now? Here you are—a very pretty girl, but six-and-twenty and no sign of a husband. Why on earth

didn't they insist that that brother of yours run the estate
if your father didn't wish to? Why leave it to you? It is
no occupation for a woman!'

'Since both my father and my brother are now dead,
it is difficult for them to reply, Aunt Hetty,' said Eleanor,
colouring up. 'I loved my father, and my brother, just
as they were. And I love looking after Stanyards—I
always have.' She got up and moved away. 'Moreover,
I came here to talk about Mr Guthrie, not about the
shortcomings of my family.'

Aware that she had overstepped the mark in criticis-
ing her brother to his daughter, Lady Walcot accepted
Eleanor's reproach with grace. She said gently, 'My
dear, I was trying to help you, believe me. I wish you
would abandon this interest in Mr Guthrie. It might be
well to think over what I have said about your own behaviour, rather than speculating on that of a known
scoundrel. I want to see you settled—married, with a
future which is secure, not tied to an ailing estate.'

'Ailing, Aunt Hetty? What do you mean? What do
you mean by ailing?'

Lady Walcot looked at her niece sympathetically. 'It
is time that you faced facts, Eleanor.'

'Stanyards is doing very well, and Mama and I are
perfectly happy to live there together. I do not need a
husband!'

'Then there is no more to say—tonight, at least. I
hope you will come to see things differently before it is
too late, my child. Goodnight, Eleanor. I shall see you
tomorrow.' She turned away and rang for her maid.

Eleanor went back to her own room with a distinct
feeling of grievance. How dared her aunt suggest that
Stanyards' future was not secure? It was true that it

was not as prosperous now as it had been in her grand-father's day, but it was still a handsome property. Eleanor dismissed uncomfortable thoughts of damp walls and decaying barns—they would soon be put right, just as soon as there was money for them. Quite soon, in fact.

And how could her aunt accuse her of not attempt-ing to hide the fact that she had opinions of her own? That really wasn't fair! Why, ever since she, Eleanor, had been in London, she had taken great pains to behave as Lady Walcot wished, though it had been far from easy. During interminable calls she had meekly listened to the vapid gossip which passed for conversation in Lady Walcot's circles, had attended innumerable routs and parties at which she had confined her remarks to the conventionally obvious, had danced with young men who, in spite of their town bronze, were as limited in their interests as the young men back home in Somerset. She had begun to doubt that she would ever find anyone interesting in the whole of London! Yet she knew that outside her aunt's narrow acquaintance there was a vast world full of interest and excitement waiting to be explored. It had all remained frustratingly closed to her. She thought she had been successful in hiding her im-patience. It now appeared she had not.

Her mind returned to the subject of Mr Guthrie. What had he done that was so disgraceful? It was flattering that he had braved an inevitable snub to ask her to dance, and his boldness had intrigued her. But her interest in him might have remained slight if her aunt's refusal to discuss him had not roused her curiosity and a feeling of rebel-lion at being treated like a child. She fell asleep with Mr Guthrie's dark features floating before her eyes…

* * *

The next morning Eleanor rose at her usual time and, since she usually kept country hours, this was very much earlier than the rest of the household. Lady Walcot had tried in vain to convince her niece that it was highly unfashionable to be up and active before midday, but when that had proved impossible her indulgent uncle had arranged both a horse and a groom for his niece's use, and Eleanor rode every morning. At this hour the park was usually pretty deserted, and the air comparatively fresh, and of all her activities in London these morning rides were her favourite. Lord Walcot, who sometimes accompanied her, was not up so early this morning, and Eleanor was alone except for her groom. This was a relief, for she was still wrestling with the spirit of rebellion which had been roused the night before. She made herself recall her aunt's many kindnesses, she told herself that her aunt was wise in the ways of London society, and she finally reminded herself that she would shortly be back in Somerset where none of this would matter.

As for Mr Guthrie—she would probably never see him again, and it was better so. She nodded to herself. That was right—she would forget him, remove him from her mind. She urged her horse to a brisker pace and rode forward, aware of a feeling of virtue and common sense. She was therefore slightly disconcerted when Mr Guthrie drew in beside her and raised his hat. He appeared to bear her no ill-will and greeted her cheerfully. 'Good morning, Miss Southeran. I see you are an early riser.'

The colour rose in Eleanor's cheeks as her composure deserted her. 'I am not sure, sir, that my aunt would approve of…of…' Her voice died away as he looked at her with such quizzical amusement in his eyes that she found herself wanting to respond.

'She wouldn't want you even to bid a perfectly respectable acquaintance good morning? I find that hard to believe. Your aunt is a stickler for the rules, I'm sure.' There was a dryness in his voice that roused Eleanor to defence.

'I doubt very much that she would describe you as "perfectly respectable", Mr Guthrie. My aunt may be a stickler, but I have never before heard her speak to anyone as she did to you last night.' She stopped short. She had almost sounded apologetic! She added coolly, 'I am sure she had good reason. Good day, sir.'

'So you're just a doll, a puppet without a mind of her own! When you're told to dance, you dance—oh, yes, I saw you last night! And when you're told not to dance, then you don't. I thought better of you.' Eleanor flushed angrily and moved on. Mr Guthrie moved with her. He said solicitously, 'You should not be riding alone in London, Miss Southeran. It really isn't safe, especially for dolls.'

'I am not alone, Mr Guthrie. I have my groom, as you see. Pray go away!'

'You certainly don't need both of us, I agree.' He turned round in his saddle and called to the groom, who had dropped back a pace or two, 'John! Be a good fellow and take a message to Colonel Marjoribanks at the Barracks. Tell him I've been delayed and will meet him shortly at Tattersall's. Miss Southeran will be quite safe with me—we'll see you at the end of this path in a few minutes. Off you go!'

Eleanor was both surprised and angry to see that

John instantly wheeled away. 'How dare he? I think he must have gone mad!'

'No, no, nothing of the sort!' he said soothingly. 'I ride a great deal with your uncle, you see. John knows me well. He knows I am to be trusted, even if certain others…' He looked at her again with that quizzical gleam in his eye, and once again she felt a strong wish to respond. He went on, 'But never mind him—I want to talk to you. Are you really a mindless doll? Tell me it isn't so. Tell me my first impression was correct—that you're a young woman with a mind of her own, that you don't judge a man on hearsay and gossip.'

Eleanor made one last attempt to obey her aunt's wishes. 'Mr Guthrie, I know it must seem feeble—as feeble-minded as gazing in such an idiotic manner at the chandelier last night—'

'I didn't find that idiotic! I thought it was enchanting! The look of wonder on your face, the reflections of those crystals in your eyes. I was bewitched!'

This was so totally unexpected that Eleanor gazed at him in surprise.

'Yes, that's something like the look,' he said softly. Eleanor snapped her mouth shut and made an effort to recover herself.

'P-please!' She was annoyed to find herself stammering.

He laughed and said, 'I'm sorry. I didn't mean to put you into such confusion. Forgive me. What were you about to say?'

'What was it…? Oh, yes! I believe I am not without a mind of my own. But I do defer to people whose judgement I trust. Tell me, why should I disregard my aunt's opinion of you—which is that you are not a fit companion for me—in order to pay attention to anything you might say? I met you for the first time last night.'

He was silent for a moment, then smiled wryly and said, 'You are right, of course. I seem to have caught the American disease of wanting to hurry things along too swiftly. You need time to get to know me. Well, that can be arranged. But dare I ask you to hold judgement until you do know me better?'

'I fear that may prove difficult. From what I observed last night, my aunt would never allow you to enter her house.'

'I agree with you—nor would most of the others! And I must confess that up to this moment I have not given a dam—'

'Mr Guthrie!'

'A dam, Miss Southeran, is a small Indian coin worth practically nothing.'

Eleanor was not wholly convinced of this, but let it pass, since her interest had been caught by something else. She asked eagerly, 'Have you been in India? Oh, how fortunate you are! I have always been fascinated by the stories I have heard of it, and of the countries in Asia.'

He smiled at the expression on her face. 'The romantic East? Don't get too carried away, Miss Southeran. There's a wealth of myth and legend about the East, not all confined to its history, literature and art. It's true that when I was young fortunes were there for those prepared to work for them, or, rather, fight for them. But the climate—and the life of most of the people—is very hard.' He looked down at her absorbed face. 'Would you really like to hear more about India? Come for a drive with me this afternoon in the park.' Eleanor hesitated. 'Unless you're afraid, of course.'

'Afraid?'

'Oh, not of me! You have nothing to fear from me.
No, of what the tittle-tattling matrons of London might
say. Any lady seen with me is automatically deemed to
be beyond redemption! It makes for a somewhat isolated
life.' When Eleanor still hesitated he said somewhat
grimly, 'I see. I am to be condemned without a hearing,
even by you.'

'I…I…' The battle with her conscience was lost.
'What do you drive, Mr Guthrie?'

'I normally drive a curricle. But if you were to
consent to a drive with me I would use something more
suited to a lady.'

'No! That is not what I want at all! I have always
wanted…that is, I should like very much… Do you
have a phaeton—a sporting phaeton, a high one?'

He stared at her, then his hard face broke into a smile.
'A woman of spirit! I knew it! I shall arrange to have
one this afternoon—but what will your aunt say?'

'I think my aunt would rather see me in a tumbril than
in any vehicle driven by you, Mr Guthrie. But you are
right. I am not a doll—nor a child! At what time do you
drive in the park?'

'Usually about five.'

'If I happened to be walking there at that time, would
you offer to take me up?'

'I should be honoured. At five, then?'

Eleanor took a deep breath and said, 'At five.'

They had reached the end of the path where John was
waiting for her. Mr Guthrie raised his hat again, gave
a nod to the groom, and rode off in the direction of
Knightsbridge. Eleanor returned to South Audley Street,
wondering if she had gone mad.

Chapter Two

By the afternoon she was sure she was mad. Hyde Park was crowded with the *ton* all taking their afternoon airing—walking, riding and driving in every form of vehicle. Gentlemen drove by in their gigs and curricles, ladies displayed their pretty dresses and parasols in open landaulets—the smarter set in handsome barouches—and Eleanor had the feeling that here was a world just waiting to watch her defy it. If she had not given Mr Guthrie her word she would have obeyed her strong inclination to go back to her aunt's house before the fatal hour of five.

However, when the gentleman stopped and offered to take Miss Southeran up, Eleanor interrupted her aunt's refusal, and accepted. In response to Lady Walcot's startled protest, Eleanor said firmly, 'Forgive me, Aunt Hetty. Half an hour only,' and climbed into the phaeton. She ignored the stares directed at her and put on an air of serenity which belied the pounding of her heart as Mr Guthrie drove off.

'Bravely done! Allow me to congratulate you.'

'I am not at all sure it is a matter for congratulation, sir! As you very well know, I run the risk of being sent to Coventry for this venture. However, since I have only a short time left in London I can bear that. Why do people dislike you so?'

'Because they mistakenly believe me to be dishonest and dishonourable.'

Eleanor blinked at this forthright statement. 'Have they cause?'

Mr Guthrie paused. At last he said, 'Matters are not always what they seem, Miss Southeran. They think they have cause.'

'You are fencing with me, I think.'

'You are right. Miss Southeran, there are reasons why I cannot be frank in talking of my own affairs. I do not intend to give you tedious half-truths. My hope is rather that if we could get to know each other better you would judge me more kindly than the rest of society does. But now you tell me that you have only a short time left in London?'

'I return home in a week's time.'

'At the very beginning of the season? Do you not regret that?'

'Not in the slightest. I love my home. I cannot wait to see it again.'

'Tell me about it.'

Eleanor never needed much encouragement to speak of Stanyards, and with that and stories of India the half-hour passed swiftly for them both. It was with regret that Eleanor noticed that they were leaving the park and making for South Audley Street.

'Where are you going tonight? Shall I see you there?' asked Mr Guthrie as they drew up at the Walcot house.

'Tonight? I think not. My aunt is taking me to a ball at the French ambassador's.' She paused, but curiosity got the better of her. 'Tell me, how was it that you were at Carlton House last night? I thought all doors in London were closed to you.'

'Not all, Miss Southeran, not all. There are still some brave souls who ignore Lady Dorothy and the other gorgons. The Prince Regent is one of them. Who knows—perhaps the French ambassador is another? But in case he isn't, shall I see you tomorrow morning?'

'I…I am not sure. I still have to make my peace with my aunt.'

'Come! It took a great deal of courage for you to make this afternoon's gesture on behalf of the underdog. Don't waste it!'

'Very well.' She smiled slightly. 'I'll see what I can do.'

Eleanor entered the house in a defiant mood. Mr Guthrie had proved a most interesting companion and she found it hard to believe he was the scoundrel her aunt had described. She could see, however, that he might not appeal to those who set great store by polished manners and the elegant niceties of polite behaviour, and was surprised that he apparently had the entrée to the Prince Regent's circle. But his abrupt style of address had not offended her, and she had actually found his directness curiously appealing. She felt a strong wish to see him again, and decided that she would do all she could to coax her aunt to agree. Meanwhile she would no doubt be faced with reproaches and some justifiable anger.

Lady Walcot was sitting in the salon on the first floor. When Eleanor walked in she said, 'I am relieved to see you back safely.'

'Aunt Hetty, I was never in any danger!'

'A high-perch phaeton! Driven at such a reckless pace! It only shows what disregard the man has for any lady's sensibilities—'

'No, Aunt! I asked Mr Guthrie to take me in the phaeton. And we went rather sedately, I thought.' Eleanor got up and went to sit beside her aunt. 'Truly, Aunt Hetty, Mr Guthrie is not the villain you have described. We talked of the most interesting things, and though he is not as polished as some of your acquaintance he was always the gentleman.'

'Really?' Her aunt was still annoyed. 'Allow me to tell you, Eleanor, that you have made a pretty spectacle of yourself this afternoon. What Lady Dorothy will say I cannot bear to think.'

'Pray do not worry yourself over such a trifle! I am not concerned with Lady Dorothy and her tales.'

'But you should be, Eleanor! She is not without influence in London, let me tell you.'

'Not with me, Aunt Hetty.'

Her aunt ignored her. 'I blame myself, of course. I should have remembered how wilful you can be, and told you more about him when you asked. What did he tell you? A pack of lies, no doubt.'

'I don't think so, Aunt. We didn't discuss Mrs Anstey, if that is what you mean.'

'I am not surprised at that—she would be the last person he would mention! Well, Eleanor, you have forced my hand. I shall tell you about Mr Guthrie. It is not an edifying story, as I think you will agree.' Lady Walcot paused, then began, 'Mrs Anstey is a widow. She is an Englishwoman, but she married a man from Boston in America, and lived there for many years. The family was a wealthy one and Mrs Anstey might reasonably have hoped for a comfortable and secure existence. However, some years ago her husband went into partnership in a business venture with the man Guthrie. Guthrie ruined them.'

'In what way?'

Lady Walcot said impatiently, 'How should I know what piece of chicanery was involved? I understand nothing of business or trade. But ruin them he did, and now Mrs Anstey and her daughter haven't a penny to their name. That is your precious Mr Guthrie.'

'How do you know all this, Aunt Hetty?'

'Everyone knows it!'

'Gossip, idle rumours, scandal. I am surprised you give so much credence to them.'

'It was Lady Dorothy who first told me, and she had it from Mrs Anstey herself.'

'But—'

'No, Eleanor, there is no "but"! What is more, I believe there is something else, which I am not at liberty to discuss. But if it is true, then I assure you on my life that the man is a dishonourable villain.'

'Mr Guthrie said people were mistaken in believing that he was dishonourable.'

'And you believed him?' asked Lady Walcot with contempt.

'Why should I not? Have you any proof to the contrary?'

'Eleanor, the proof lies in what we know to be facts! Henry Anstey shot himself because he and his family were bankrupt. The Guthrie creature, who was a full partner in the enterprise, remains a wealthy man. Whatever else may or may not be true, how do you account for that? Besides, Guthrie has never bothered to deny anything that has been said about him.'

'That is hardly proof of guilt! I agree it is tempting to believe Mr Guthrie to be the villain of this particular melodrama—he has all the appearance of one. And lovely Marianne Anstey looks like the very ideal of a damsel in distress. But is it not at least possible that appearances are deceptive?'

'Oh, it is useless to argue with you! It is just as I was saying last night—you are always determined to make up your own mind, determined to ignore the judgement of people who are older and wiser than yourself. And when you embark on one of your crusades you lose all sense of proportion. Now you are about to fling yourself at a known scoundrel. What am I to do?'

Eleanor drew herself up and said with dignity, 'Aunt Hetty, I promise not to fling myself at anyone—least of all a known scoundrel, whoever that is. But, unless you can give me more convincing proof of Mr Guthrie's guilt, I reserve the right to talk to the first man I have met in London whose company I enjoy—apart from that of my uncle. And that's another thing! My uncle is by no means sure of Mr Guthrie's villainy. I would trust his judgement sooner than I would that of Lady Dorothy!'

'Oh, your uncle is a man,' said Lady Walcot somewhat obscurely. She got up and went to the door. Here she stopped and said, 'I haven't finished with you yet, Eleanor. You have asked for proof. I shall see what I can do.' Then she left the room.

Eleanor was left feeling confused and uncertain. It was perfectly possible that Mr Guthrie had roused Lady Dorothy's enmity by nothing more criminal than omitting to give her the deference she imagined due to her rank. But Lady Walcot was another matter. Eleanor had known and loved her father's sister all her life—she could not dismiss her aunt's views on Mr Guthrie so lightly. She sighed.

'Good lord, Eleanor, don't look so glum!' It was her uncle who had just come in. 'Where's your aunt? Been giving you a lecture, has she? I'm not surprised, but don't worry—she'll soon come round again. Cheer up, my dear! Isn't it time you were thinking of your dress and so on for tonight? I'm taking you both to a ball, I believe. As for your aunt, by the time she's decided what she's going to wear, and what jewellery to put with it, she'll have forgotten about this afternoon. Come, let me see you smile, then you can go and pretty yourself up.'

Eleanor got up obediently and went to the door, but there she turned and came back to her uncle. She hesitated a moment, then asked, 'Uncle Charles, what do you think of Mr Guthrie?'

Lord Walcot shook his head in mock-reproof. 'Now, Eleanor, I'm too downy a bird to be caught by a question like that. What you're really asking is whether I agree with your aunt in discouraging you from having much to do with him. You should know better than to ask me what I think. You are in her charge, and I cannot oppose her wishes as far as you are concerned. That would never do.'

'I'm sorry.'

He looked sympathetically at her downcast face, and relented a little. 'He's a difficult fellow to know. A man who keeps his own counsel. Except for the stories about him, I've never had any occasion to distrust him—in fact, I would say that I quite like him. But your aunt and the others may well be right, you know. I believe Mrs Anstey tells a convincing enough tale, which he has

never denied. Give it up, my dear. You're upsetting your
aunt, and to what purpose? In a few days or so you'll
be setting off for Somerset and you'll probably never see
him again.'

Eleanor looked up and said with resolution, 'You're
right, as always, Uncle Charles. I shall be amenable
from now on.'

He laughed and said, 'Not too amenable, Eleanor. I
enjoy our discussions. Don't become like all the rest!'

That evening Eleanor found it impossible to remain
unaffected by the excitement and glamour of a really
large ball. The splendid rooms, lavishly decorated with
artificial fountains and fantastic pyramids, were impressive by any standards, and the dresses and jewels of the
cream of London society were a rare sight. Her own
dress, though modest in comparison, suited her very
well, she thought. It had been made originally by the
best dressmaker in Taunton, and had a bodice made of
blue-green silk, with a skirt of white sarsnet. Her aunt
had looked at it thoughtfully, pronounced it delightfully
simple and had then taken it away. It had appeared a few
days later with an overskirt of blue-green gauze, em-
broidered round the hem in blue, green and gold, and
caught up at the side with a knot of matching ribbons.
Her efforts had turned a pretty dress from a local dressmaker into a garment worthy of the highest London
circles. The result was eye-catching and very flattering.

But, lovely as the dresses were, impressive though
the rooms looked, to Eleanor's mind nothing could
outshine Marianne Anstey. The fairy princess was stun-
ningly beautiful in a very simple white silk dress. Her
pale gold hair was caught back on top with a knot of pale

pink roses, and fell in graceful curls to the nape of her neck. More pale pink roses were clustered at her waist, matching the delicate colour in her cheeks. Eleanor, along with many others, could hardly take her eyes off the girl, and no one was surprised when the ambassador kept more important guests waiting while he greeted this exquisite creature.

'The embodiment of every man's dreams, wouldn't you say, Miss Southeran? A lovely damsel in distress, waiting for her knight to rescue her. And what a prize!'

Eleanor turned round with a start to find Mr Guthrie immediately behind her. She looked round for her aunt, but the Walcots were some distance away, having been separated from their niece by the crowd. Mindful of her promise to her uncle, Eleanor said, 'If report is true, her face is her only fortune, sir. The knight in question may not have to rescue her from dragons—only her own, undeserved penury.'

'Yes, of course. I am cast as the dragon in this fairytale, "if report is true", is that not so, Miss Southeran? Well, it looks to me,' he swept on without waiting for her reply, 'as if the knight is about to make his appearance. More than a knight—a viscount, no less!'

The French ambassador had finally released Miss Anstey, and she had rejoined the group of fashionably dressed people with whom she had first arrived. Among them was a young man who was now talking most earnestly to her.

'Robert Morrissey, heir to an Irish earldom. A very worthy candidate, don't you agree?'

'Since I know neither the lady nor her knight, I cannot tell, sir,' said Eleanor coolly, disliking the thread of mockery running through Mr Guthrie's words.

'Well, I think it will do very nicely—it will at least relieve the worst of her fond mother's anxieties.' He bowed and disappeared as abruptly as he had come. Eleanor didn't know whether to be angry or pleased, but saw that her aunt and uncle were about to join her again, and was glad that awkward explanations had been avoided. She asked her aunt about the Ansteys' party.

'They are with their cousins, the Verekers—the ones who live in Berkeley Square. And the young man who is paying such particular attention to Marianne Anstey is Lord Morrissey. Would you like to meet them?'

She took Eleanor over to the other side of the room and made the introductions. Mr and Mrs Vereker were an amiable couple, who were clearly enormously proud of their beautiful protégée. Mrs Anstey was soberly dressed and stayed quietly in the background, pleased to let her cousins take charge. Eleanor, who was guiltily aware that she had spent half an hour in the park that afternoon with Mrs Anstey's reported enemy, was prepared for some coolness, but when they were introduced the lady smiled pleasantly enough, if somewhat timidly. Marianne proved to be as amiable as she was beautiful. Her manner was a delightful mixture of modesty and charm, and Lord Morrissey's attentions had brought an appealing flush to her cheeks and a sparkle to her lovely eyes. He was obviously well on the way to falling in love, and Eleanor privately agreed with Mr Guthrie's words that it might do very nicely.

After a few minutes Lord Morrissey made his excuses and took Miss Anstey off towards the ballroom. A young man Eleanor had met at a previous party came up and took her off as well, and soon the ball was well on its way. Though she did not quite dance every dance,

Eleanor was seldom without a partner, and received a good many compliments on her appearance. She found herself enjoying the evening. She had just returned from a set of country dances and was standing with her aunt and uncle when she saw that the ambassador himself was approaching them. She stood back modestly in order to allow him to speak to her uncle, but then saw that Mr Guthrie was with him. She looked anxiously at her aunt. Lady Walcot was smiling at the ambassador, and though the smile faltered a little when she saw his companion she quickly recovered.

'Lady Walcot, I am enchanted to see you so well,' said His Excellency. 'I see that you have lost one daughter only to gain another—and such a pretty one! *Mademoiselle*?'

Eleanor curtsied low and blushed as the ambassador took her hand and kissed it. He glanced mischievously at Mr Guthrie. 'And now, Lady Walcot, I see that your niece is not dancing at present. That is quite wrong. May I present Mr Guthrie to you as a most desirable partner for the young lady?'

Eleanor had difficulty in suppressing a smile. Her aunt was undoubtedly outraged by a manoeuvre which made it impossible for her to refuse, but no one could have guessed it from her demeanour. She smiled graciously, then inclined her head.

'How can anyone refuse you, Ambassador? My niece would be delighted, of course.'

'Excellent! And I shall take you and Lord Walcot to the refreshment tables—I have a champagne there which will please you, I think. Come, my friend Guthrie will take good care of the pretty niece, *n'est-ce pas*, Jonas?'

'Lady Walcot may have every confidence in me, Ambassador,' said Mr Guthrie smoothly, whereupon Lord Walcot made a curious noise which he was able to turn into a cough. Mr Guthrie raised an eyebrow, then turned to Eleanor. 'Miss Southeran?' he said, offering his arm, and Eleanor, with an apologetic glance at her aunt, moved forward. Lady Walcot exchanged a long look with Mr Guthrie and then turned to accompany the ambassador, and Eleanor's uncle, still amused, shook his head and followed his wife.

'That was not well done, sir!' said Eleanor severely as they walked towards the ballroom.

'Not well done? Well, upon my word, I wouldn't know how a man could do it better! To get His Excellency himself to plead my case…what more would you expect? The Prince Regent?'

Half laughing, Eleanor said, 'You know very well what I mean, Mr Guthrie! It was to pay my aunt back for refusing you last night, was it not?'

'You underrate yourself,' he said with a smile. 'There were other merits in the idea.' Then he stopped and said, 'But there's something you should know about me, Miss Southeran. When I play, I don't take chances. I play to win.'

'And the prize in this case? Was it worth calling out such big guns?'

'Well, now,' he said softly, 'it depends on what you mean by the prize. Victory over your aunt? An opportunity to dance with you? Or…what?'

Surprised by his tone, Eleanor looked at him, which was a mistake. He was looking down at her with amusement and something more disturbing in his eyes. She said uncertainly, 'If you are trying to flirt with me, Mr Guthrie, I must tell you that I don't appreciate it. I prefer sensible conversation such as we had this afternoon to…to silly compliments and empty phrases.'

'I assure you, I was not trying to flirt with you. And if I were capable of flattery—which I am not—I would tell you that you outshine every other woman in the room, that that entrancing dress is a perfect foil for your sea-green witch's eyes, and the dark gold of your hair—'

'Mr Guthrie!'

Undeterred by her angry exclamation, he went on, 'That, lovely though your features are, they are rendered yet more entrancing by your animation, the liveliness of your expression—'

'Mr Guthrie, stop this at once or I shall leave you instantly!'

'But I am not saying such things, Miss Southeran,' he said earnestly. 'They are quite clearly false, the merest flattery. You are pretty enough, but far from being the prettiest woman in the room. Miss Anstey, for instance, is a star!' After a brief pause he added, 'I grant that you're livelier than she is—and much more intelligent.' He gave a delighted laugh at her indignant expression. 'What sensible things shall we talk about, Miss Southeran?'

Eleanor had never known such a man! Never before had she experienced such a mixture of feelings— anger, amusement, puzzlement, sympathy. Never had she felt so alive.

'You shall tell me more about the East. But first we shall enjoy your prize, which,' she said firmly, 'is a dance.'

They didn't talk about the East, but after the dance was over he took her to supper, and they talked of other things. They walked through the crowded rooms and at one point found themselves among the plants in the winter garden, still talking. Eleanor had objected to something disparaging Mr Guthrie had said about life in England, and was arguing her case passionately. But her voice died away as she saw him looking at her as she spoke, his eyes focused on her lips. She was overcome with a feeling of panic and turned away from him. 'We…we must go back,' she said nervously. 'My aunt will be looking for me.'

'No, wait a little. How can we talk sensibly out there among all those people—?'

'I cannot stay here—it is most improper. My aunt would be very angry if she saw me.'

'The devil take your aunt!'

'Sir!'

'Oh, I'm sorry, I'm sorry. It's just that I have something I want to say to you, and there never seems to be a suitable moment. I keep putting it off…' He gave an exasperated laugh. 'I think I'm afraid!'

'Afraid?' she echoed, looked at him wide-eyed.

'Yes, and when you look at me like that it all goes out of my head. You have a most extraordinary effect on me—like no other I have ever known. How do you do it?'

Eleanor suddenly became aware of the very strange effect this conversation was having on her breathing. 'You are talking nonsense, Mr Guthrie—I must go back,' she said with determination, and started for the entrance to the ballroom.

'Wait! Eleanor—' he called, but stopped abruptly as he saw Lady Walcot standing at the entrance.

'At last I've found you! What on earth do you think you are doing?' Lady Walcot's voice was sharp, and one or two bystanders cast curious glances in her direction. She forced a smile, whispering to her niece, 'Don't bother to tell me. You've been with that man!'

'Aunt Hetty—'

'We'll talk when we get home, Eleanor, not here. Now come with me—several people have been asking to meet you. Ah, Lady Marchant, there you are! We've been looking for you—this is Miss Southeran, my niece…'

Eleanor did not see Mr Guthrie again that evening. Her aunt kept her close at her side until the carriages arrived to take them home. But she would not have looked for him in any case. Her feelings were much too confused to face him again so soon. This same confusion of feeling made it difficult for her to discuss the matter with her aunt afterwards, and Lady Walcot, drawing her own conclusions, was most concerned. 'I blame myself,' she said unhappily. 'I should never have agreed to your dancing with him—I know what he is. Heaven knows how he manages it, for he is not at all handsome. But he is a dangerous man, Eleanor. I beg you to forget this attraction he has for you.'

'He…he seemed sincere,' said Eleanor hesitantly. 'As if he too felt the same…attraction. Could I be so wrong?'

Lady Walcot exclaimed, 'The devil! The scheming, contriving devil! He has bewitched you, Eleanor, just as he bewitched Ev—But no, I mustn't say any more.' She appeared to be debating with herself, and then to reach a conclusion. 'You must go to bed, Eleanor,' she said slowly. 'And in the morning I shall see what I can do.'

Eleanor slept badly that night. She tossed and turned, reliving the moments with Jonas Guthrie, especially the time in the winter garden. One moment she wanted to meet him the next morning, and then, after another debate with herself, she had decided that it would be better if they did not see each other again. Was he a dan-

gerous philanderer—all the more dangerous because
he did not appear to be trying to charm? Or was he the
straightforward man he appeared to be? And what was
it that he had been afraid to tell her? She eventually fell
into an uneasy slumber, still debating the question.

She woke late the next morning to find that one
question at least had already been decided. It was far too
late for a ride in the park. When she eventually came
downstairs she found her aunt waiting.

'I have someone I wish you to meet,' she said briskly,
'and we are late. Put your bonnet on and come with me,
Eleanor. Don't delay—the carriage is waiting.'

A few minutes later they arrived at a modest house
in a street off Cavendish Square. Here they were taken
into a small parlour, where a lady was waiting to receive
them. It was Mrs Anstey. She greeted Lady Walcot in a
soft, well-spoken manner and then turned to Eleanor.
'Miss Southeran, you are very welcome, though I am
sorry the occasion is…is such an awkward one…' Mrs
Anstey paused and looked to Lady Walcot for help.

'Mrs Anstey has agreed, at my urgent request, to talk
to you, Eleanor. I am very obliged to her—the matter is
a painful one, as you will see, and I would not have asked
her to speak of it had I not been so anxious for you. I am
sure you will give her your earnest attention—it concerns
Mr Guthrie and his behaviour towards the Anstey family.'

'Surely this isn't necessary, Aunt Hetty—'

'In view of your refusal to accept my word for Mr
Guthrie's character, and especially in view of your behaviour last night…'

'I wanted to explain—'

'Forgive me, Eleanor, but Mrs Anstey's time is
precious. We must not waste it.'

Good manners silenced Eleanor. She sat chafing under her aunt's disapproval, convinced that this whole visit was an unnecessary exercise. Lady Walcot said, 'Mrs Anstey, would you mind telling my niece how well you know Mr Guthrie?'

'Jonas and I were brought up together, Miss Southeran. His mother was a Vereker, too. That is to say…I mean his mother was a Vereker before she was married. As I was.'

'You were sisters?'

'No, no! Oh, dear, how stupid of me…Caroline, his mother, was my cousin.'

'From what you have told me,' said Lady Walcot, casting a glance at Eleanor, 'you practically brought him up?'

'Well…yes, I suppose so,' said Mrs Anstey uncertainly. 'I was so much older than he was, and he had no mother… He was a dear little boy when he came to us.'

'Came to you? In America?' asked Eleanor, somewhat puzzled.

'No, no. This was over thirty years ago—Jonas was a baby… I was a girl and still living in England then.' She looked anxiously at Lady Walcot, then said nervously, 'Perhaps I had better explain. You see, Richard Guthrie, Jonas's father, abandoned poor Caroline before Jonas was born. She came back home to have the child, and died soon after. I think it must have been of a broken heart, don't you? Jonas and I…we were both orphans living with relatives. We were very close, though I was ten years older.'

'But what happened to his father?' asked Eleanor.

'He was a bad lot, I'm afraid. I think he eventually went into the army and was killed. But Jonas never really knew him. It is surprising…' Her voice drifted away.

'He must have felt very alone in the world.'

'Oh, no! He knew he always had me to turn to—until I left England and went to live in America…' Mrs Anstey's voice trailed away weakly again, and Eleanor felt a sudden impatience with her. The woman is a born martyr, she thought, and then reproached herself for her lack of charity.

Lady Walcot said, 'And later, I believe, your husband took Mr Guthrie as a business partner on your recommendation?'

'Well, partly. Jonas left England for India when he was still quite young. I'm not sure how, but he made a fortune out there. Then he came to see me in Boston. He was looking for a suitable investment, and my husband happened to need some new capital for his family concern and…and they helped each other. It worked very well to start with. I was delighted to see him again, and Henry and the girls were all devoted to him. For a while Henry and I even thought that we would be more closely related to Jonas. But then the engagement was broken off…'

'Engagement? Mr Guthrie has been engaged? To Marianne?' asked Eleanor, growing pale.

'No, no. Jonas was engaged to my other daughter. But then it was broken off. And things went wrong after that.'

'What went wrong?'

'Miss Southeran, I am not precisely sure what went amiss. I took no part in the business, of course. But Henry—my husband—and Jonas suddenly seemed to disagree a great deal, and though Mr Oliver did his best to keep the peace there were frequent arguments.'

'Mr Oliver?'

'My husband's other partner. He is now married to

Evadne.' Mrs Anstey's hands were twisting in her lap. She said suddenly, 'Oh, Miss Southeran, if you only knew how wicked Jonas Guthrie has been, how like his father!'

The sudden passion in this timid little woman's voice was startling. Eleanor was impressed, and, dreading what more was to come, she asked slowly, 'Why do you say that?'

Mrs Anstey looked uncertainly at Lady Walcot, who leaned forward and said softly, 'Please, if you can, tell her! I give you my word that it will go no further.'

'I… I…am ashamed to tell you that Jonas Guthrie is the father of my daughter's child!' This was said in a low voice, and at first Eleanor thought she had not heard correctly. She looked blankly at Mrs Anstey, who added in a clearer, louder tone, 'He seduced my daughter Evadne, and gave her a child.'

Chapter Three

Eleanor found herself without a word. The morning's revelations had been a shock and she was experiencing great difficulty in retaining her outward appearance of calm. She wanted to leave that neat little room, to refuse to listen to the ugly story which was being unfolded in it. But this was impossible. She must stay.

Mrs Anstey mistook her silence for embarrassment and said nervously, 'I'm sorry—your aunt did ask—'

'In her own words, my niece is not a child, Mrs Anstey! And I wish her to hear everything,' said Lady Walcot grimly.

Eleanor rallied and found her voice. 'But she is married to Mr Oliver?'

Mrs Anstey lowered her head and said, 'Yes. It is shameful, is it not? He…he agreed to marry her in return for a sum of money—paid by Guthrie.'

'Why didn't Mr Guthrie marry her himself? Why didn't your husband insist?'

'By the time her condition was discovered my husband was dead, and we were on the verge of bankruptcy.' Mrs Anstey's voice faded again and Lady Walcot took over the story.

'Mrs Anstey found herself without anyone to advise or help her and the one man who might have been her support proved to be her worst enemy. He refused to marry Miss Anstey—at first he even denied that the child was his! Then, when he was forced to admit the truth, he paid another man to shoulder his responsibilities.'

'How did Mr Oliver come to agree to this dreadful scheme? He was a partner in the firm, too. Why did he not take up your defence?'

'Jonas was…was more masterful. He knows how to get people to do as he wishes—I can't explain how,' said Mrs Anstey, 'and Mr Oliver was in severe financial difficulties himself. He had always been fond of Evadne and he was happy to marry her—but without the money it would have been out of the question.'

'It has proved impossible to find out why the firm foundered, Eleanor,' said Lady Walcot. 'The books disappeared after Henry Anstey shot himself. But Mrs Anstey saw them in Guthrie's possession the day before they vanished and she believes he still has them—or has destroyed them. And is it not significant that he seems to have survived the firm's collapse with his own fortune intact?'

'Conscience money,' said Mrs Anstey sadly. 'He paid conscience money. He made a fool of my husband, and a paramour of my daughter, and he thinks that he has solved everything when he buys a husband for Evadne. But how could he do it to us—to Evadne, to me? We loved him! We trusted him!' She shook her head mournfully. 'He was such a dear little boy!'

'Are you absolutely certain that Mr Guthrie is the villain?' Eleanor heard the slightly desperate note in her own voice and tried to speak more calmly. 'It seems so strange. Is there no one else?'

'It was strange, Miss Southeran! At first I refused to believe that he had cheated us, I refused to believe that he could be so wicked—so like his father! I begged, I pleaded with him to explain what had happened.' Mrs Anstey dabbed her eyes with her handkerchief and continued, 'But he pushed me away. He said we could think what we liked, that he had found a husband for Evadne, and enough money to pay for a passage to England for Marianne and me. That should be enough. His manner was so…so hard! It was as if he couldn't bear to look at us…' She paused, then added, 'The only other person involved was Mr Oliver, who was as poor as we were until Guthrie paid him to…to marry Evadne.' She shook her head obstinately. 'In the end he was just like his father. No, Miss Southeran, Jonas Guthrie is the cause of all our troubles. What else can I think?'

'Indeed, what else can anyone think, Eleanor?' said her aunt sternly.

'I… I'm not sure… He left you entirely without resources?'

'He must have had some vestige of feeling. He paid for our passage to England, he arranged for someone to meet us when we landed and take us to our Vereker cousins in Berkeley Square. They have been very good to us. But we have not spoken to Jonas since we arrived in England. Indeed, we have avoided meeting each other since we came to London, and, though I understand he was a frequent visitor at Berkeley Square before Marianne and I came from America, he has not been there since.' Mrs Anstey blinked down at her hands. 'I… I still find it difficult to believe…'

She stood up. 'I'm afraid you will have to excuse me. I must go and fetch Marianne from her lesson; she will wonder where I am.' She hesitated and then said timidly, 'Miss Southeran, I agreed to talk to you today because Lady Walcot has been so very good to Marianne and me. I do not know what I would have done without her. Thanks to the help from my cousins and your aunt's kindness in sponsoring Marianne in London, I now have hope that one of my daughters at least will make the marriage she deserves. Lord Morrissey has been so very attentive. But any scandal… I know I can be sure of your discretion.'

'Of course,' said poor Eleanor, pulling herself together. 'And I see now why my aunt wished me to hear your story. I am grateful to you for being so frank with me, Mrs Anstey.'

'I saw it as my duty,' said Mrs Anstey simply.

As they got into the carriage again Eleanor was conscious that her aunt was waiting for her to say something. But what was there to say? Mr Guthrie was a complete villain, it appeared—there was no mistaking the sincerity of Mrs Anstey's feelings. Before talking to her Eleanor had thought, hoped even, that the woman might be a charlatan—it wouldn't be the first time that a poor widow with a beautiful daughter had tricked her way into society. But unless Mrs Anstey was a consummate actress, which Eleanor very much doubted, she had been telling the truth. This was no scandalmonger, no vindictive gorgon—this was a woman patently sincere in her distress and shame. Mrs Anstey was completely convinced of Guthrie's guilt, and very unhappy that it was so.

'Well, Eleanor?' said Lady Walcot finally.

'Please, Aunt Hetty, could we wait till we are back in the house? I feel…I feel a little dazed at the moment. It was a shock.'

'Of course, my child. We'll soon be there, and you shall do just as you wish—talk to me, or spend some time in your room.'

The rest of the journey passed in silence, but this gave Eleanor a chance to recover her equilibrium and she was quite ready to talk to her aunt when they arrived. They went into the little parlour, and here Eleanor sat down, gave a great sigh and said, 'You were right, Aunt Hetty, and I was mistaken. I am sorry to have put you to so much trouble.'

'I am to take it that there will be no further tête-à-têtes in secluded spots with Mr Guthrie?'

'I… I cannot imagine why I was so indiscreet.'

'When you are on one of your crusades, Eleanor, there is no knowing what you might do! However, I think this particular crusade is finished, is it not?'

'It is finished, Aunt Hetty.'

Something of her niece's misery must have communicated itself to Lady Walcot, for she gave Eleanor a hug, then got up and said briskly, 'Come, you must now try to put it all behind you. You must enjoy what is left of your time in London. Would you like to rest now, or shall we go shopping? Have you bought a present for your mother yet?'

Eleanor pulled herself firmly together and declared that she was ready to do some shopping. She and Lady Walcot decided that a note should be written to Mr Guthrie which made it clear that she did not wish to see him again. This they did, and once it had been dispatched she felt as if a burden had been lifted from her, though she still felt a secret regret. If Mr Guthrie had been the man she had thought him, she would have enjoyed his company, and fought to maintain her right to it. But as it was she need never have anything more to do with him. She sighed and then consoled herself with the thought that in a few days' time she would be returning to Stanyards. She was looking forward to it more and more.

However, Eleanor was mistaken in thinking that she had finished with Mr Guthrie. She was to meet him again before she left London, and in very odd circumstances.

On the day before her departure she went out for one last ride. Ever since the conversation with Mrs Anstey she had taken to riding at a later hour than before, in order to avoid the embarrassment of meeting Mr Guthrie. Thus far she had been successful. It meant, of course, that she and John had to venture further in order to find less frequented areas of the park, since at the later time more people were abroad. On this occasion they had ridden almost to the western edge, and they were just about to return when they heard a faint groan coming from the bushes at the side of the path. John slid off his horse and went to investigate. He returned, saying urgently, 'It's Mr Guthrie, Miss Southeran. He's lying groaning something horrible! I think 'e must 'ave fallen off 'is 'orse.'

Eleanor dismounted and followed John. Mr Guthrie was apparently in the process of regaining consciousness. He was trying to sit up, then groaning again and holding his head in his hands.

'Fetch help, John. I'll stay here. Do as I say; I shall

be perfectly safe. Mr Guthrie needs urgent assistance, and I cannot be sure of finding the shortest way back. Go quickly—you know the way better than I do.'

John hesitated, but saw the sense of what Eleanor had said. He ran to his horse and rode off. Eleanor looked down at Mr Guthrie. He was now lying with his eyes closed. She knelt down beside him. His eyes flew open, and he said, 'What the devil are you doing here? Where's John?'

'He's gone for help.'

'He shouldn't have left you alone… Did you see anyone else?'

'Here? I don't think anyone else was here—'

'Of course there was! Why else do you suppose I'm lying flat on my back like this?' His tone was irritable, but that was perhaps understandable. His head was obviously hurting quite badly, and she could see a huge bruise developing over one eye.

'I thought you might have taken a toss. People do,' she said calmly.

'I am not so careless. And "people" don't usually ride into a piece of wire stretched across the path, do they? Look!' He struggled to sit up and pointed at a length of wire lying beside the path. Eleanor got up to examine it. 'I came off when the horse stopped dead. There was someone else here, though—I saw him standing a short way off before I fell. He looked as if he was waiting… He started coming towards me—and then the next thing I knew John was there. Confound it, you must have seen him! I wasn't out for more than a minute.'

Eleanor looked nervously about her. 'I'm afraid I didn't see anyone, nor can I see anyone now. Do you think it was footpads, or highwaymen?' Her voice had risen slightly.

'Oh, for God's sake, don't start getting hysterical! I'm perfectly capable of defending us both, if necessary.' With some difficulty Mr Guthrie drew a pistol out of the capacious pocket of his riding coat.

Eleanor said tartly, 'I have no intention of indulging in hysterics. And if you will permit me to say so, that pistol wasn't of very great help a moment ago—nor is it reassuring to watch you handle it now!'

'Don't talk rubbish. I was off my guard. And you are perfectly safe from it. What is more to the point—have you seen Captain?'

'Captain? Captain who?'

'My horse, my horse! He must be hurt, too. That wire caught him right across his legs.'

'Is that him? Over there?'

'Go and fetch him, there's a good girl. I'll have a look at him.' He started to get up, but stopped on one knee. Eleanor could hear him swearing quietly to himself. She went to help him, but he waved her away impatiently. 'Don't twitter over me! Make yourself useful by getting the horse, woman!'

Eleanor refrained from comment, though there was much that she would have liked to say. The man was clearly in great pain. She went slowly over to Captain. He was in a highly nervous state and it took her some minutes to calm him sufficiently to catch hold of his bridle, which was fortunately still in place. She led him slowly over to Mr Guthrie, who by this time had managed to stand.

'That was very well done,' he said with reluctant approval. 'You have a way with horses as well as with men, that's obvious. Now, Captain, my beauty, what have we here?'

Fortunately the wire had not been well anchored at one end and had given way before doing the horse any serious damage. By the time John returned with help, Mr Guthrie was leading Captain along the path, exhorting Miss Southeran to ride on without him. She had up to this point ignored him, merely continuing to walk alongside, leading her own bay. In any case, how on earth did he expect her to mount a fully grown horse without the benefit of groom or mounting-block? But when she saw John and the others approaching she breathed a sigh of relief and turned to her companion.

'Goodbye again, Mr Guthrie. I hope you have not suffered any lasting damage.'

'I am obliged to you, Miss Southeran. I think you might have saved my life, albeit unintentionally.' Eleanor looked at him doubtfully, but he was serious.

'If you think so, then I am happy to have been of service.'

'I've missed our rides,' he said abruptly.

Eleanor coloured, but said nothing. He gave a wry smile and went on, 'Well, I look forward to our next meeting—in more auspicious circumstances, I hope!'

'As I think my aunt said in her note, Mr Guthrie, I don't think another meeting is at all likely. I have now heard Mrs Anstey's story, you see—the full one. I shall take pains to avoid you in future.'

'You may try, by all means. Don't count on success, however,' he said coolly. 'I suppose you have no doubts, no uncertainties about my guilt?'

Eleanor felt a sudden flicker of hope.

'Do you…do you deny the truth of what she said?'

He hesitated for a moment, then he drawled, 'Since I wasn't there, how can I possibly know what she said?

She may well have been right. In any case, ma'am, why on earth should I deny anything? What business is it of yours, I should like to know?'

Eleanor was so incensed that she almost ran towards John, requesting him to help her to mount. Then she rode off without waiting to hear any more.

Eleanor went on fuming about Mr Guthrie throughout that last day in London—when she wasn't puzzling over the curious circumstances of the morning's meeting. In spite of everything, she still found it very difficult to reconcile the black-hearted villain of Mrs Anstey's tale with the man she had met. Her feelings were so confused that she was heartily glad to be leaving for Somerset the next day. She told herself she would forget everything to do with him once she was back at Stanyards.

On the day of her departure the whole household, including her aunt, rose early to see her off. She was fortunate enough to be able to travel with some friends of Bella's new husband, who lived near Lyme Regis, and who had hired a post-chaise. When they appeared in South Audley Street, Eleanor thanked her uncle, embraced her aunt warmly and prepared to climb into the carriage. Her aunt held her sleeve.

'I have done my best to change you into a conformable young lady, Eleanor, but I cannot pride myself on my success.'

'And I, for one, am glad of it,' said her uncle, embracing his niece.

'Well, there have been times when I could have shaken you for your behaviour—but we shall miss you. Life is never dull when you are there,' said Lady Walcot, smiling at her niece. 'Remember! When the time comes, you have only to say the word and I shall still spare no effort to find you a suitable husband!'

'Thank you, darling Aunt Hetty! But I'm afraid the task would be too difficult, even for you! Besides, there's too much to do at Stanyards! Come down and see us when you grow tired of the season. I shall miss you both! Goodbye!'

The chaise rolled off, and Eleanor waved until they turned the corner and the Walcots were lost to sight.

The journey passed pleasantly enough—the roads were dry and the weather favourable. But by the end of the second day she was heartily glad to stretch her legs at the posting house in Axminster, say goodbye to her kind friends, and join the carriage from Stanyards which would take her the rest of the way. Within an hour she was at the beginning of the long avenue of chestnuts which led to the house. She was home!

As soon as the carriage drew up at the door, Eleanor jumped out, ran up the low flight of steps and clasped her mother in her arms. After a rapturous greeting, Eleanor stood back and surveyed her. 'I ought to scold you for standing in the evening air,' she said. 'Why didn't you stay inside?'

'Daniel saw the carriage and told us you were coming. I couldn't wait to see you, Nell—and anyway I'm feeling very well at the moment, so you needn't scold me at all! Oh, it's delightful to have you home again! Cousin Louisa has been very kind, but I've missed you a great deal. Come in, come in!'

Eleanor followed her mother across the huge, stone-flagged hall into a room which opened off to the side. Here the low ceilings, ingle-nooks and casement windows set in thick walls proclaimed the great age of the house. But the log fire in the handsome fireplace and the books and tapestries around the walls gave it an air of warmth and comfort.

'I hope you don't die of a heatstroke, Nell. Cousin Louisa insisted on the fire.'

'Your mother hasn't enough flesh on her bones to keep her warm even on the hottest day of summer! And this room never really gets the chill off it, you know that. I am glad to see you, Eleanor. How was your journey? No, don't start talking before you have some food in you; I dare swear you have had nothing sensible for the past month. I've told Betty to bring a tray and we'll put it on the table by the window—the dining-room is far too damp unless you have a fire there, too, which would be wickedly extravagant.

'Anthea, I've drawn your sofa nearer the fire. It was foolish of you to stand outside in the night air for so long. Eleanor could well have waited another two minutes to see you; you look quite chilled. I'll ask Betty to bring you something warm, too— Drat the woman, you may wait till Domesday for what you want. I'll just see what she is doing.' Cousin Louisa went bustling out. Her cry of, 'Betty!' echoed through the hall as she went.

'She means well,' said Mrs Southeran with a wry smile.

'I know she does. Has it been very hard?'

'Not at all. But tell me about the journey, and when Cousin Louisa returns you can tell us both about Hetty and Bella and the wedding. Did you like the Wyndhams? It's a long journey to be cooped up with strangers.'

They spent the rest of the evening exchanging news and gossip. Candles were necessary quite soon, for day-light always faded early in the house, even in summer, and the three ladies sat cosily in the soft light till the tea-tray was brought in. But in all her descriptions of her life in London Eleanor never once mentioned the name of Guthrie.

The following day Eleanor woke early, and wondered for the moment where she was. There was a totally different quality to the air, and in the distance she could hear sounds of the country. She was home! She rose quickly, and quietly took herself out into the early morning sunshine. She had forgotten how lovely Stanyards was. For the next half-hour she wandered over the familiar paths and fields round her home, finding herself at length at the end of the chestnut drive.

'Good marnin', Miss Nell!' It was Daniel driving the cart up from the village. 'Would 'un like a lift up to the house?'

'No, thank you, Daniel—I'm enjoying the walk. The chestnuts look magnificent this year!'

'You be careful of 'un, Miss Nell! There's a good few as needs chopping down, I reckon. You have a look at the branch that's lyin' up by the bend. Nearly got old Betty last week, 'un did. Had to skip a bit, did Bet!' He grinned, showing blackened teeth, and drove on.

Eleanor refused to be daunted. The trees were said to be over a hundred years old—it was natural that they should be feeling their age. But they were beautiful. The early morning breeze caused the leaves to whisper and flutter in the summer air, now revealing tiny glimpses of a pale blue sky or the slanting rays of the morning sun, now closing over her head like a heavy canopy. It had always been airless in the city. Here at Stanyards it was cool and fresh. She felt a sudden uplift of spirits as she realised she really was home! Stanyards was where she wanted to stay for the rest of her life, and if the choice was to be between this house and a husband, then Stanyards was what she would choose. Her aunt was wrong to pity her, for she was a fortunate woman.

But as she reached the bend in the drive she stopped and stared. How could she have missed this last night? A huge branch was leaning drunkenly between two of the trees, just off the drive, its leaves drooping and a great jagged, bleached wound at one end. There were signs that the branch had been dragged a few feet, presumably to keep the drive clear. It was an unwelcome reminder that time was taking its toll of her beloved avenue of trees. Daniel was right—some of them at least would soon have to be chopped down.

She stood staring at the branch for some minutes, her happiness at being home again slowly seeping away, tempered by a small shadow of uncertainty. Stanyards was in desperate need of repair and restoration. It wasn't just the drive—the whole estate needed attention. For a black moment she began to doubt her own strength and determination. For years she had done what she could, jiggling account books, robbing Peter to pay Paul, trying to be in three different places every hour of the working day, but suddenly she was terribly afraid that she was slowly but inexorably losing the battle.

What nonsense! she chided herself. It only needed a little more patience, a touch more perseverance and energy. She was still tired after her long journey, but she would soon find the necessary energy and hope. Things would be better this year, she was sure. She threw back her shoulders and marched on up the drive.

* * *

In the afternoon Cousin Louisa returned to her own home, in the next village, and after she had gone Mrs Southeran told Eleanor several times how kind, how good, how very helpful Cousin Louisa had been.

'I'm sure she was, Mama—but why are you protesting so much? I already know how worthy Cousin Louisa is!'

'That's it! She's worthy! Oh, Nell, I have been so bored! And I haven't written a line since you left!'

'Now that is serious. Well, I am back now and you must start immediately—where are your things? I'll fetch them and you shall not leave your sofa until you have written at least ten lines! I shall be neither good nor kind until you comply!'

Mrs Southeran was a poet with quite a reputation in the West Country, and even beyond. She wrote under a pseudonym and few of her neighbours knew of her talent, but writing was as necessary to her as breathing. The news that she had been neglecting it was worrying.

'Don't be too concerned, Nell. It wasn't just because of Cousin Louisa or your absence. I've been doing some serious thinking and have even taken some action. Sit down, my dear. Now that we are alone again, I want to tell you something.'

Her mother's voice was so earnest that Eleanor's heart missed a beat. Had the doctor been making gloomier prognostications again? 'I knew I shouldn't have left you! You're feeling worse?'

'It isn't my health, it's you! I've been worried over you for some time now, and while you've been away I've decided that we must do something about it. Running this house and estate is sapping all your energy…all your youth. Your life is taken up with worry and work and little else—'

'Mama! I have just spent four weeks doing little else but enjoying myself!'

'And when was the last time you left Stanyards before that? Or went to a ball or a party? Wore pretty dresses? You have forgotten, and so have I. Well, it must not continue—and I have taken steps to see that it does not.'

'But I am quite happy living here and running Stanyards! I don't want to change anything—except perhaps to see you in better health again!'

'Stanyards is destroying your youth and looks, Eleanor, and it is taking away my health. I know, I know what you are about to say! Stanyards has been in the Southeran family for four hundred years or more, and is steeped in tradition and history. But Tom's death—' Mrs Southeran's voice faltered.

'Don't, Mama! Don't talk about it! It will make you ill.'

'I must! I have refused to face the consequences for far too long! When Tom was killed, Nell, the family name died out. You are not a man, however much you have played the man's part since Tom died.'

'And before,' muttered Eleanor.

'Yes, and before. It was a matter of regret to all of us that your brother never had your interest in Stanyards.' Mrs Southeran paused again, but this time Eleanor made no effort to speak. How could she say anything, when her feelings were so hopelessly tangled? Even after seven years she still felt love and grief for her handsome, laughing brother, was still angry at the recklessness which had caused his death and still resentful that he had cared so little for his heritage. Tom had only ever taken, never given.

Mrs Southeran looked at Eleanor's stormy face and sighed. But then she continued in a more determined voice, 'When you marry, or die, there will be no more Southerans of Stanyards.'

'What are you trying to say, Mama?'

'Not even you can claim that this house is comfortable to live in. Not in its present state. It is old, dark and damp. And we don't have the resources to change it. I have done what I must.'

Eleanor's throat was dry. She said in a strained voice, 'Mama, what have you done?'

Mrs Southeran looked at her with pity in her eyes. 'You will not like it, Nell, but it was for us both. I seized an opportunity which came out of the blue, and I cannot be sorry. I have sold Stanyards.'

For a moment Eleanor sat in stunned silence. Then she whispered, 'No, no! It's not true!' She threw herself down by her mother's sofa and her breath caught on a sob as she pleaded, 'Tell me it's not true, Mama! You can't have s-sold it!'

Mrs Southeran's face was troubled as she gazed at her daughter. But she said steadily, 'It is true, Eleanor. In two weeks Stanyards will have a new owner.'

'How could you? How could you, Mama? You must cancel the sale at once!'

'I did it for us both, Nell,' repeated Mrs Southeran. 'And I will not change my mind.'

Eleanor got up. Without looking at her mother she said, 'I feel…I feel sick, Mama. Excuse me, please.' She ran out of the room.

Chapter Four

Eleanor could never afterwards remember what she did for most of that day. For the first time in many years she had no thought for her mother, nor for the duties which needed her attention. She wandered through fields and woods, over stiles and ditches, unseeing and deaf. It was a miracle that she ended the day unscathed. She finally came to herself on the top of the hill which overlooked Stanyards, and stood there for a long time staring down at her home. At one point she imagined she might take hold of it, and she stretched out towards it, but then she let her arms drop hopelessly to her sides. Stanyards was lost, and she felt as if a stone had settled on her heart. She stood there for a little while longer and then stirred and turned away. Old habits reasserted themselves—she must go back—her mother would be worried about her. Slowly she set off down the hill.

But Eleanor could not bring herself to talk about the coming move, and spent a great deal of the next day going about her ordinary duties in silence. Finally her mother sought her out and took her firmly to task.

'We have much to do, and I cannot do it alone, Eleanor. I know you feel strongly—'

'You are wrong, Mama. I do not feel anything.'

'What nonsense!' Mrs Southeran looked at her daughter's wan cheeks and heavy eyes and said more gently, 'You have suffered a great shock, I know that. But do you think it is easy for me to leave my home?'

'I would not have thought so.'

'Eleanor, my dear, you must know in your heart that we could not have continued as we were!' Mrs Southeran paused, but when Eleanor merely turned away and looked out of the window she sighed. 'Perhaps I should have said that I could not have continued as I was? Perhaps I have made you pay too great a price for my own selfish comfort?'

Eleanor could not hold out against the note of uncertainty in her mother's voice. She ran to her and held her tight. 'Forgive me, Mama! I don't wish to hurt or worry you. It was a shock…but I will honestly try to understand your reasons, and of course I will help. How could I possibly do otherwise?'

'Believe me, Nell, I would not have done it if I had thought for one moment that it was not better for both of us.'

'Yes, yes. Anyway, it is all finished now.' Eleanor paused, and then said more cheerfully, 'I haven't yet asked you where we are going to live. Somewhere near?'

'Somewhere very near,' said her mother with a smile. 'In the Dower House.'

'But that is part of the Stanyards estate!'

'We have a lease on it. It was agreed in the sale.'

Eleanor got up and walked about the room. She was not sure what to think about this. On the one hand she would still be part of Stanyards, still have her friends and the countryside she loved so much within easy reach. On the other, how could she bear to be part of Stanyards and yet not part? She continued to pace the room, conscious of her mother's anxious gaze. The Dower House. Compared with the main house, it was modern and well-equipped—her mother could be very comfortably established there, with her friends also close at hand. She wondered about its state of repair—it had been empty for years. And, though no expense had been spared in building it, its rooms were pretty rather than large. 'What would we do with Father's books? There isn't a room that would hold them in the Dower House.'

'They…they are included in the sale. I expect the new owner will keep them where they are.' Her mother sounded apprehensive, but Eleanor could see the force of this. Her father, and his father and grandfather before him, had all been keen book collectors and one of Stanyard's largest rooms had been made into a handsome library some sixty years before.

'Shall I tell you about Stanyards' new owner?'

'No!' said Eleanor violently. In reply to her mother's look of astonishment, she went on, 'Thank you, but I do not wish to know anything about the man, not even his name. I cannot at the moment tolerate the thought of strangers in what was my home, Mama.'

'But, Nell, you will have to know more! Or are you going to refuse to meet him? That would be extremely difficult—the two houses are within a stone's throw of each other. I assure you he is a man of honour and integrity—he will do well by Stanyards—'

'No, Mama!'

'I cannot allow you to bury your head like this…'

'I know,' said Eleanor nervously, but with determination. 'Please be patient with me. I will come round, you'll see, but I need time. Give me a day or two, then you may tell me all you wish about the usurper!' Eleanor gave a slightly tremulous smile as she said this. Only she knew how much the effort she was making was costing her. Only for her mother would Eleanor have made this attempt to reconcile herself to losing Stanyards.

The Dower House lay a short distance from Stanyards itself, at the end of a branch from the main drive. It had been built about a hundred years before for the widow of an earlier and more prosperous Southeran. It was on a small scale but very pretty, built of brick, which was a rare luxury in this stone-based countryside, with a miniature pediment and sash windows. Behind was a small stable block and a path, decorated with ornamental urns and benches, which connected it with the main house. Here Eleanor and her mother were to live.

Having promised to do all she could, Eleanor threw herself into preparations for the move. She would normally have been out and about the estate, catching up with all the tasks which had fallen to her since the two men in the family had died. But now she stayed at home and directed the servants, supervised the packing of china and linen, consulted her mother on what should go and what should stay, all without once displaying the slightest interest in Stanyards' new owner.

Apart from her mother, no one seemed to know very much about him anyway. The negotiations had been concluded surprisingly swiftly—few had even caught a glimpse of the mysterious stranger who had apparently won Mrs Southeran's trust so easily.

One thing Eleanor could not help noticing. The Dower House was being given a thorough renovation, and its garden, which had become a wilderness, was being restored to flowerbeds and lawns. Even the small stable block, which had been out of use for years, was being made ready for occupation. She could not help knowing that a vast amount of money was being spent on all this refurbishment, and asked her mother about it.

'I cannot tell you!' said her mother with a small twinkle in her eye. 'The new owner is doing it all, and you do not wish to know about him!'

Eleanor was obstinate enough not to ask further. Later, of course, she wished she had.

A day or two before the Southeran's move to the Dower House, Eleanor, who had been inspecting yet more cupboards there, was making her way towards the path back to Stanyards. A large black dog, hardly more than a puppy, bounded round the corner from the stables and greeted her with all the warmth of an old friend. The dog was a complete stranger.

'Down, Becky! Down, I say! You must forgive her, Miss Southeran. She has yet to learn her proper place in life, I'm afraid. Did she frighten you?'

Eleanor had recognised the voice at once, of course. Who could mistake those deep, resonant tones? But she still stared at Mr Guthrie as if he had been conjured up by the devil himself.

'Miss Southeran? Are you all right? Becky hasn't an ounce of harm in her, I assure you.' He sounded concerned, and Eleanor made an effort to find her voice.

'It's not the dog! Why are you here?' she croaked.

'I beg your pardon?'

'Why are you here?' she repeated in a stronger voice.

'No, no, Miss Southeran! Even in the Colonies we know better than that. You must bid me "Good morning", say that it is pleasant to see me and then ask if I had a comfortable journey from London. Only then do you work round, by devious methods, to finding out why I am here. However, I should have thought you would know that.'

Eleanor still had no idea. The thought that Mr Guthrie had sought her out here in Somerset seemed ridiculous—but what else could it be? She must make the position quite clear. Curiously enough, it was his in-civility at their last meeting, not his perfidy, which came first to mind.

'Your final words to me when we last met were un-pardonably rude. I believe I have already told you once—I have no wish to continue our acquaintance, Mr Guthrie. If you are here to see me, you have wasted your journey.' She started off towards the main house, her dignity somewhat hampered by the dog, who danced around her feet as she went.

He strode after her and caught her arm. 'I suppose you think your lack of civility to me is allowable. That I don't merit any consideration? But that's neither here nor there—what I'd like to know is what the devil you're talking about—coming to see you indeed! As you very well know, I've come down here to take over the estate!'

'Take...?' Eleanor sat down rather suddenly on an or-namental bench. 'Take over the estate?' she said slowly. 'Oh, God! *You're* the one who has bought Stanyards?'

He looked at her white face. 'You didn't know, did you?' He sat down beside her and would have taken her hand, but she snatched it away. He sat for a moment watching her as she struggled with this new blow. 'I'm sorry if I gave you a shock,' he said, more gently. 'The negotiations for the house were conducted discreetly—for reasons of my own, I didn't wish the world to know where I was about to live—but why on earth hasn't your mother told you since you came back from London?'

'I wouldn't let her,' said Eleanor, her mind still reeling at the identity of the new owner. 'I didn't wish to know anything about the man who was taking Stanyards away from us.'

Mr Guthrie sighed and stood up again. 'Purchasing it, Miss Southeran. For a fair price. A more than fair price, considering the state it is in.'

Eleanor fired up at this criticism. 'Stanyards is a jewel! More than you could ever have hoped to aspire to!'

'Too good for me, eh?' This time his voice was full of mockery. 'Well, we shall see. Now, since I cannot see this conversation serving any useful purpose, and as I have a thousand other things to do, I hope you will excuse me. Or—would you like me to escort you to the house? I thought not. Your servant, Miss Southeran.' He turned to go.

'Wait!' cried Eleanor. 'These negotiations—did my mother take any advice before selling Stanyards to you?'

'Now what are you suggesting? That I cheated her?'

'She is under one misapprehension at least, Mr Guthrie. She assured me that the new owner of Stanyards was a man of integrity and honour!'

Mr Guthrie stood quite still for a moment. Then he took a deep breath and said softly, 'And you think you can prove differently? Prove, mind you! I warn you, Miss Southeran, if I find you are repeating here in the country the kind of scurrilous gossip which made London happy,

I shall take steps to silence you. Good day, ma'am!' He turned swiftly and walked away. After looking doubtfully at Eleanor, Becky trotted after her master.

Eleanor sat looking at his retreating back in a daze. How could it have happened? She had been truly glad to have seen the last of Mr Guthrie in London, for she had not enjoyed the confusion of feeling he had caused her. Now, it seemed, she was to see him every day, to be reminded every day of the unpleasant revelations in the interview with Mrs Anstey. And this was the man her mother trusted absolutely! What was she to do? She was desperate to talk to her mother, but waited until she saw Mr Guthrie's carriage go down the drive towards the village before hurrying up to the main house.

'You should have told me, Mama!' she cried. 'You should have told me that Guthrie was the man who had bought Stanyards!'

'My dear child,' said Mrs Southeran, justifiably perplexed. 'You said quite categorically that you did not wish to know anything about Mr Guthrie! How was I to know that you did not mean it?'

'I did mean it! That is to say, I meant it at the time, but if had known that this man Guthrie was the new owner I would have wanted to know!'

'Eleanor, I am not sure I perfectly understand you. Did you or did you not say that you wished to hear nothing about the new owner, not even his name? Oh…I see! You met Mr Guthrie in London? Is that what you are trying to tell me? You have never mentioned him to me, surely?'

'Yes, I… I met him in London. Oh, he's a deceitful wretch! He knew all the time we were talking that he had bought my home, he even asked me about it, yet he never said a word! Why did you sell our home to such a man, Mama?'

'I am convinced he will be good for Stanyards. Nothing you have so far said has changed that opinion.'

'How can you be so blind? He is far from being the honourable man you think him!'

'My dear child, it was perhaps not well done to conceal from you the fact that he had purchased Stanyards, but it was not dishonourable! Mr Guthrie has very good reason to keep his future home a secret from all but a small number of people.'

'But how can you be so sure? Surely this passion for secrecy is, to say the least, suspicious? How long have you known him? A few weeks!'

'I have known Mr Guthrie for most of his life.'

'I beg your pardon, Mama?'

'Perhaps I exaggerate a little. I knew Jonas when he was a boy. Our families lived quite close. I have heard from him occasionally—he wrote when your father died, and then again when Tom was killed. And then, just after you had left for London, he visited me here and made an offer for Stanyards. In all that followed he has behaved impeccably. Oh, he has no time for compliments and courtesies—but he has been very generous. You will not easily persuade me to change my opinion of him, Eleanor!'

Eleanor was in a dilemma, and left her mother without saying any more. For the rest of that day and through much of the night that followed she debated what she ought to do. Finally, though she was desperate to tell her mother the story concerning the Ansteys, she decided for a number of reasons to remain silent. She paid no heed to Guthrie's threat—that alone would

not have deterred her. But she had given her word that
she would not betray the most damning aspects of the
Anstey affair to anyone. And, most important of all, she
concluded that, for the moment, no useful purpose could
be achieved by revealing the true nature of Stanyards'
new owner. The deed was done, Stanyards was sold, and
it could only distress and worry her mother to know how
grossly she had been deceived, how sadly the boy she
had known in her youth had changed.

So she resolved to say nothing, but to keep a close
watch on Mr Jonas Guthrie and all his activities in this
part of Somerset. She was no timid widow, no delicate
eighteen-year-old to be used and brushed aside. Mr
Guthrie would find her, Eleanor Southeran, a foe to be
reckoned with! And woe betide him if he caused her
mother the slightest, the minutest difficulty!

But, far from causing difficulties, Mr Guthrie seemed
to be exhibiting every desire to help in any way he could
in the weeks that followed. He treated Eleanor with
careful courtesy, but he had a special manner, an uncere-
monious friendliness, for Mrs Southeran, which delighted that lady. It was not long before the Southerans,
together with Betty and Daniel, were established in the
Dower House, and Mr Guthrie was a frequent visitor.
Eleanor made sure she was present whenever anything
remotely like business was discussed, but she found
little to satisfy her suspicions. And she had to admit that
life was very much easier than it had been for years. The
Dower House had been built for comfort, and its light,
airy rooms were a refreshing change from the dim
dampness of Stanyards. As for Mrs Southeran, she
seemed to flourish in the new regime, and spent hours

at the little desk in her pretty sitting-room composing some very fine poetry.

Eleanor, however, was far from happy. At first there had been plenty to occupy her, for any move involved a great deal of work in the weeks following. But after a while time began to drag. She went for long rides, she visited friends, she invited visitors to call. After years of hard, satisfying work on the estate it all seemed rather trivial. Besides, the ladies of the village, the occupants of the large houses in the neighbourhood—all were unanimous in their praise of Mr Guthrie. Her only allies, if they could be so termed, were the farmers and their wives on the Stanyards estate. These good people rapidly developed a dislike of their new landlord.

Eleanor acted very properly. She listened to what they had to say when they came to see her, or stopped her on her outings, but she refused to comment on what was no longer her business, and advised them to take their complaints to the new master of Stanyards. But in her soul she rejoiced. Here were some people who were not deceived by Mr Guthrie's apparent benevolence. And, though she was careful not to say anything, she was in truth shocked at the ruthlessness he was showing in his dealings with the farmers. They were being subjected to a vigorous inspection of how they ran their farms, to largely unfavourable criticism of their practices, and were made to listen to blistering comments on the state of their farm buildings. This last was so patently unfair that Eleanor felt she had to intervene.

When Mr Guthrie next called, Eleanor met him in the hall and asked him if she might have a private word with him afterwards. He raised one eyebrow and asked mockingly, 'Are you sure that is wise, Miss Southeran? Are you not afraid to be private with such a dishonourable man as myself?'

'I can be brave when the need arises, sir.'

'You have the light of battle in your eye. Something tells me that, whatever it is, it is not to my advantage. Very well, I, too, can be brave when the need arises. Will you walk up the drive with me? There's something I wish you to see.'

Eleanor agreed stiffly, and they went into Mrs Southeran's sitting-room together.

'Good afternoon, Jonas! How very nice to see you and Eleanor talking to each other at last! Is your feud over, then?'

'Feud, Mama? Whatever do you mean?'

'I may be elderly and infirm, Nell, but I am not yet in my dotage. It has been quite obvious to me that you and Mr Guthrie have hardly exchanged two words in all the times you have met here.'

'But your daughter has not missed a word of our conversations, Mrs Southeran, especially when we talk of Stanyards and its affairs. She is the most attentive listener of my acquaintance. How do you go on? You are looking well.'

Eleanor grew pink with confusion. So he had noticed her silent watchfulness?

'I have often thought you would do well to consult Eleanor more often, Jonas. She more than anyone knows about the running of Stanyards. She could be a great help to you.'

Mr Guthrie looked sceptical. 'Perhaps she could,' he said dismissively. 'If she wished. But I prefer to see things as they are, ma'am, and as far as the estate is concerned your daughter wears rose-coloured spectacles.'

'Come, come, Jonas! If you are going to be unkind about Nell, then I shall not invite you here again.'

Eleanor could not keep silent. 'If seeing things as they are means that you threaten to evict people who through no fault of their own are unable to meet your high standards, then I prefer to keep my "rose-coloured spectacles", Mr Guthrie!' she said before she could stop herself.

'Ah! Now we have it! I thought as much—you've been gossiping with Threlfall and the others.'

Eleanor said scornfully, 'I do not "gossip". Nor did I seek them out.'

'But you have been talking to them?'

'And why shouldn't I? I have known them all my life. They appear to need someone to defend them, Mr Guthrie.'

'Miss Southeran,' said Mr Guthrie in biting tones, 'when I need help in dealing with *my* tenants, *my* labourers and *my* affairs I shall ask for it. Stanyards is no longer your concern. Meanwhile—'

'Stanyards is my concern!' There was sudden silence. Eleanor turned away and went to look out of the window. 'Was my concern,' she said bitterly. 'Oh, why did you have to come here?'

'Eleanor! Jonas! Stop this at once! I will not allow you to talk to each other like this—not in my sitting-room at least. Jonas, I should like you to apologise to Eleanor for your harsh words to her. It was cruel to bait her with talk of Stanyards.'

Guthrie said stiffly, 'I did not intentionally bait her, ma'am.'

'You have upset her, however.'

'I think my very existence upsets your daughter, ma'am, not anything I say.'

'Jonas,' said Mrs Southeran in a warning tone.

They both looked at Eleanor's unreceptive back, then Guthrie gave Mrs Southeran a wry smile and went to the window. He said, 'Miss Southeran, I beg pardon for my harsh words. My only excuse is that I have had a hard time of it since I took over the running of the estate. Country folk are very resistant to change.'

Eleanor turned round on him.

'But you—'

'Eleanor! Mr Guthrie has apologised handsomely. Now it is your turn.'

'But—'

Mrs Southeran continued firmly, 'If you *have* been responding to Threlfall's complaints, then Mr Guthrie has good reason to be annoyed. You must not stand between master and man, my dear, however hard it may seem. It is your turn to excuse yourself.'

Eleanor could see that her mother meant what she said.

'It is true that I listened to Threlfall. But I have always—always, Mr Guthrie—told him and the others to speak to you, not to me, about their grievances.'

'This is an explanation, not an apology, Eleanor. You were very rude to Mr Guthrie.'

Eleanor said carefully, 'I am sorry, Mr Guthrie, for…saying that I wished you had not come here.' She looked up at him to see how he would take this somewhat double-edged remark and then wished she hadn't. To her annoyance, the quizzical expression on his face once again made her want to laugh.

'Now come and have some tea, both of you,' said Mrs Southeran with a sigh of relief. She had been no more deceived than Guthrie by Eleanor's 'apology', but thought it better to ignore its deliberate ambiguity.

By accident or design, Eleanor was not quite sure which, Mr Guthrie entertained the two ladies over tea with talk of India and his travels there. Eleanor almost forgot her antagonism towards him as she lost herself in the exotic world of the East India Company and the Raj, and her eager questions kept him talking until it was time for him to leave. Her mother watched them both with a small smile on her face.

When Mr Guthrie got up to go Eleanor rose, too. 'Will you excuse me, Mama? Mr Guthrie has something to show me, I believe. Is that so, Mr Guthrie?'

'Er…quite so. I shall be delighted.'

'I shan't be long, Mama. Do you need anything before I leave you?'

'No, no, my dear! You go with Jonas.' As they reached the door she added with amusement, 'And try not to quarrel with each other!'

Chapter Five

Eleanor and Mr Guthrie walked for a few moments in silence. As they reached the beginning of the path to Stanyards Mr Guthrie said, 'You wished to say something, Miss Southeran. Was it about Threlfall? I warn you that I will not listen patiently to accusations of injustice.'

'But you have been unjust! Threlfall tells me that you blame him and the others for the state of their buildings. But the buildings are the responsibility of the Stanyards estate, not the farmers. I do not expect you to understand that landowners have responsibilities as well as privileges, Mr Guthrie, but to threaten eviction—'

'You will doubtless be disappointed to hear, Miss Southeran, that I have so far threatened no one with eviction.'

Eleanor stopped dead. 'No one?' He shook his head. 'No one at all?'

'Not one,' he said slowly and emphatically.

'But Threlfall said—'

'Threlfall's capacity for understanding what is said to him is as limited as his capacity for hard work! And

in spite of your scorn, Miss Southeran, I do understand my responsibilities—better perhaps than you!
All the buildings on the estate, including Stanyards
itself, are in a poor state of repair. I intend to put them
all into good order again, but it will obviously take
time and money. A lot of time and money. No, don't
fire up at me. I apportion no blame—I knew when I
took it over what it was like, and rather like the idea
of the challenge.'

'Challenge?'

'Yes, Miss Southeran. The challenge of making a
beautiful, potentially rich house and estate, which
through neglect and ignorance has been allowed to fall
into ruin—'

'How dare you?'

'For God's sake be realistic, woman! Stanyards could
not have survived another two years! Oh, I know
everyone tells me what a heroine you've been—the
hours you've spent, and the dedication you've shown.
I've been told how much everyone loves you, how
generous, how kind you are. To what purpose?'

Eleanor cried desperately, 'Stop this! I don't wish to
hear any more!' She turned to run down the path again
but he caught her back and held her by the arms.

'You started this discussion. You told me what a
landowner's duties are. Now you shall hear what I have
to say!' He sat her down firmly on the bench near by and
stood over her while he went on slowly and clearly,
'Your tenants are a crowd of lazy good-for-nothings
who would rather let their farms fall down about their
ears than stir themselves. You have tamely accepted
their stories of small harvests and poor returns—'

'They weren't stories!'

'Don't interrupt! I agree, they weren't stories. The returns were indeed poor. The farmers could never afford the higher rents the estate needed, so you, and your family before you, never attempted to raise them. But did you never ask why the returns were poor? The land here is some of the richest in the West Country. So why couldn't your farmers—including you and your own employees—make a decent living? Laziness, Miss Southeran! Laziness and mismanagement. Stanyards has been idling along, content with the old ways, the old methods for far too long, and it was about to die, stifled by its own inertia.'

'You're wrong!' cried Eleanor, putting her hands to her ears. 'I won't listen to you. I loved Stanyards, and I wasn't lazy!'

Mr Guthrie squatted down so that his face was on a level with hers. 'No one is suggesting that you were lazy. But how could a young woman—a girl, when you started looking after Stanyards—possibly hope to run an estate like this without help? What made you think you could tell rascals like Threlfall how to run their farms? Your father or your brother, now—'

'Neither my father nor my brother ever showed the slightest interest in running the estate,' said Eleanor, trying hard to keep her lips from trembling.

'Then why the devil didn't you employ a manager?'

'We did. B-but we found him to be dishonest. And…and I thought I could take over…' Eleanor's feelings overcame her and she got up and turned away from him, unwilling to let him see her tears. 'I was wrong,' she said forlornly. 'All that work, all those years—all wasted.'

'Miss Southeran…Eleanor! Please! I didn't mean—

Oh, confound it, I did!' His honesty produced a reluctant laugh, which ended in a sob. He swore softly and then, turning her round again, he gathered her into his arms and held her tightly. 'Don't cry! Whatever else I meant, I didn't mean to hurt you.'

'Heaven help me, then, if you ever do wish to!' She looked up at him.

'I…I…I cannot imagine the occasion arising,' he said slowly, holding her eyes with his own. Eleanor was suddenly afraid and made an attempt to set herself free. 'No, don't go yet. I let you go once before against my better judgement.'

'In the winter garden…'

'I wanted to tell you about Stanyards then, but…but we were interrupted.' His arms were still round her, holding her fast. 'Don't go!' he said again. 'I haven't finished. I want to ask if you would help me.'

'In what way?' asked Eleanor, still feeling strangely breathless.

'I need you…' He cleared his throat. 'I need your help in talking to the people on the estate. So that they understand what I'm trying to do, and give it a chance. Believe me, they will all be happier and more prosperous for it.' He was still holding her.

'I… Yes, I think so. But you must explain it to me first.'

He smiled. 'Of course I will.' He slowly, very slowly, bent his head and kissed her. Eleanor had never before experienced the excitement which now filled her. She found herself returning the kiss, reluctant to let it end. But then she came to herself and was shocked at her behaviour. She tried to push him away.

'Mr Guthrie! Sir!'

'Call me Jonas,' he murmured, and kissed her again.

'Mr Guthrie!' She broke away and stood on the path a few yards away. 'How…how dare you kiss me?'

'It was to seal our bargain,' he said, as if that explained it. 'Was it very unpleasant?'

'Yes, of course!' He raised a quizzical eyebrow. 'Well, no,' she replied more honestly. 'But it mustn't be repeated, or I shall have to refuse to see you alone again.'

'That would be a pity,' he murmured, looking at her lips, just as he had in the winter garden.

Eleanor felt her knees go weak, but said firmly, 'I mean it!'

He laughed and said, 'I can see you do. And you are right. It is too soon.' He grew serious again. 'Much too soon. There are matters which have to be cleared up first. I have no right to…involve you in my private difficulties.' Then he smiled again and said, 'Are you prepared to come up to the house? I've drawn up plans and suggestions for managing the estate. It's early days yet—they mostly lie in the future, but I thought you might like to see them. It might explain a few things. And…I promise to behave.'

Eleanor put her head on one side and studied him. Mrs Anstey's account of his behaviour had been graphic, and his actions a moment or two ago gave absolutely no reason to suppose that he had changed. She would be mad to trust him. 'Yes,' she was astonished to hear herself say. 'Yes, I'd like that.'

They walked up the rest of the path in a slightly guarded silence. Becky met them halfway and greeted them both rapturously.

'Down, Becky! Will you get down, dog?'

Eleanor laughed at her companion's efforts to restrain Becky. 'The estate may go in fear and trembling of you, Mr Guthrie, but that dog has your measure. What are you going to do with her?'

'She's young yet, but I think she's intelligent. She'll soon learn who is master here. Meanwhile, let her have her fun. I enjoy her spirit,' he said, with a look. Eleanor wanted to object to that look, but decided in the end it was better to ignore the hidden meaning, and she kept silent.

They went into the house, through the hall, which looked much as it had always done, and up the stairs to the room on the first floor which had been made into a library. As they went, Mr Guthrie explained, 'I've started on some of the rooms—there's a lot of damp. This side of the house seems to be worse than the other.' Eleanor nodded without comment. She wasn't yet ready to voice any criticism of Stanyards. He went on, 'I don't know how your mother survived it so long. She isn't strong—she never has been.'

'You knew her before, didn't you?'

'Yes, we lived near one another when I was a child.'

'Does my mother know Mrs Anstey?' They had reached the library. He stopped with his hand on the door-latch.

'Yes,' he said expressionlessly. 'Yes, she does. We all knew each other.' Suddenly the atmosphere was different. The warm feeling of confidence which had been flowing between them vanished as if it had never been, and the chill of the house surrounded them. Eleanor shivered. Could she really trust this man?

'Shall we go in? The plans are in here.' He opened the door and they entered the room.

The room was in darkness, for the heavy tapestry curtains which covered a series of small windows were still drawn. Mr Guthrie said, 'Stay here by the door.

There are things on the floor and you might trip. I'll let some light in.'

She could hear him making his way to the windows as she stood there absorbing the smell of her father's library—a mixture of leather and candles and mustiness, remembered from her earliest childhood. Her father had spent most of his time here, poring over his books. Recent Southerans had all been scholars, preferring the world of their library to the harsh realities of life. They had amassed a wonderful—and very valuable—collection of books from all ages. But, however pressed for money the estate had been, it had never entered Eleanor's mind to suggest that they should sell any books. They were a part of Stanyards itself. Allowing Mr Guthrie to buy them along with the house had merely been her mother's way of keeping the library intact and at Stanyards.

When the first curtains were drawn she could see that the room was being reorganised. The shelves nearest the door, where the most valuable books had been stored, were bare and boxes were stacked on the floor beneath them. She wondered what the new arrangement was to be. But then, as more curtains were drawn and more light was let into the room, she could see that all the shelves were bare and some had been dismantled— indeed, one bookcase lay in jagged pieces in the middle of the room. What was happening here? She took a step forward and nearly fell over one of the boxes. She looked down. This one was already sealed and labelled, and when she examined the label more closely she saw the address of a prominent London dealer in rare books.

The vandal! The treacherous, ruthless vandal! Oh, now she could see how he intended to pay for his improvements! She should have known he wouldn't use any of his own money—the estate must pay for itself; he had said so. And he was now stripping Stanyards of its priceless, irreplaceable library to pay for the repair of a few farm buildings! Her father's and grandfather's treasures, collected and loved for over half a century, were to be shipped off to market like so many cattle? Not if she could help it!

Mr Guthrie drew back the last curtain at the far end of the room, then turned and said, 'I'm sorry about the mess—I had forgotten what a state the room was in when I asked you to inspect the plans. They're here on the table. What is wrong?'

Eleanor's eyes were burning. She was so choked with rage that she could hardly speak.

'I…I… You… My aunt and the rest were right! You are a heartless, dishonourable villain! Commerce and avarice have so corrupted you that you are not fit to live among honest people! I hate you! But you haven't heard the last of this. I won't let you destroy Stanyards as you destroyed the Ansteys. I won't let you ruin Stanyards' library as you ruined Evadne Oliver! I'll fight you every inch of the way, Mr Moneybags Guthrie!' She ran out, sobbing with fury. Jonas Guthrie had at first listened to Eleanor's tirade with astonishment. What was this girl-woman so furious about now? Then, as the meaning of her words became clear to him, his own face grew dark with anger and he strode to the door, intending to haul her back and make her eat her words. She wouldn't get far before he caught her. But at the door he stopped in disgust. He made no further attempt to follow her, but stood in silence listening to the sound of her fleeing footsteps.

He turned and went slowly back to the centre of the

room, staring down at the plans on the table without seeing them. How dared she? How could she be so unjust? Out there on the walk up to the house they had seemed to achieve a sort of understanding—an understanding which promised to help them in the many difficulties which lay ahead. Indeed, he had felt for a moment that there was more than that between them. Much more. But, whatever he had felt, there was obviously no answering feeling in Miss Southeran's soul.

In a sudden gesture of rage, he swept the plans to the floor. So much for help and confidence, damn her! So much for the stupid idea that he could win her over! To hell with her! He would manage without her. With her soft heart and impulsive ways, she would probably have been a liability anyway.

He moved over to the window-seat at the far end of the room and gazed out at the view. To the left was the long drive of chestnuts—he would soon have to do something about those; they were a daily danger. To the right was the Dower House. She'd be back there now, pouring out her heart to her mother. What would be the response? Not that it mattered—Eleanor was so set against him that she wouldn't listen to any defence, however hard Mrs Southeran tried.

His expression lightened briefly as he thought of Mrs Southeran. There was one person at least who was on his side—a rare feeling these days. All the other women he had met recently condemned him out of hand... It was the Anstey affair, of course. He had hoped that the full story would not become generally known in England—after all, it might not reflect any credit on him, but some of it didn't reflect any credit on Evadne Anstey, either. Evadne Oliver, he supposed he should call her. With a cynical smile he wondered how that marriage was faring. Probably quite well—they were two of a kind. All the same, he would have thought that Evadne's fool of a mother would have been more discreet. He smiled wryly—when had sweet, silly Amelia Vereker ever been discreet?

He couldn't really blame her. All the same, it was a pity. He could have lived down the question of the money—especially as he had seen to it that Amelia and Marianne had got back to England with a secure future. From what he had observed, Marianne would make a good match quite soon. But the seduction of Evadne— that was the story which stuck in their throats. That was the story which had dished him.

He got up again and moved restlessly round the room, and eventually his eye lighted on the sealed box of books. Those books should be sent off to the restorer as soon as possible. He bent down to check the label. 'Wilkes, purveyor of rare books'. Purveyor… Of course! Wilkes was a *seller* of books, as well as a restorer. That was why Eleanor had leapt to such an unflattering conclusion. She hadn't given him much benefit of the doubt. If she had asked, he could have told her why the books were being taken to Wilkes, why the bookcases were being dismantled. However much her damned family might have loved their precious books, they hadn't thought to look after them properly—or the shelves that housed them. The room was riddled with worm and damp. He wasn't at all sure that Wilkes could save some of the volumes he was sending.

The discovery of the labelled box had cheered him somewhat. It didn't remove his strong sense of injustice, but it did at least explain why Eleanor had been quite

so vehement. But he wasn't about to go after her,
begging her to listen to the truth about Wilkes' parcel!
Oh, no! If Miss Southeran chose to ignore all he had
done since coming down to Stanyards, and continued
to believe only the worst of him, then it was not up to
him to convince her otherwise. It would in any case be
a waste of effort.

Mr Guthrie returned to the centre of the room, picked
up the plans and put them back on the table. He stood
there for some minutes staring at them, then he gradually became more absorbed. He pulled up a chair and
sat down... It was a considerable time before he looked
up again. Yes, they would work. Stanyards could
become self-supporting quite soon, given reasonably
favourable seasons, and the co-operation of the people
concerned. That was where Eleanor might have helped,
had she chosen to. For a short while, a very short while,
he had visualised a time when together they would
create something worth having out of Stanyards. But her
stupid prejudice against him had put an end to all that.

He looked at the doorway and in his mind's eye he
saw her standing there. How lovely she had looked,
even in her rage—almost as lovely as when he had first
seen her in London, the candlelight turning her dark
gold hair to flame and her sea-green eyes reflecting the
lights of the crystals. When she was angry the eyes
darkened to blue...and when she was kissed... This
was pathetic! To hell with her! He jumped up impatiently and strode out of the room.

Mr Guthrie was not seen at the Dower House for
some time—at least not when Eleanor was there. He
would have been surprised to learn, however, that his

eanor responded to this small joke with a wan
. 'You are teasing me into doing as you wish—you
 I would never leave you for such a ridiculous
n.' She sighed. 'Can you arrange a meeting? I have
ven caught a glimpse of him since that day. I think
ust have been avoiding me as much as I have
ded him.'
 think that is highly likely.' Eleanor gave her mother
picious look. 'No, you need not look at me like that.
s has been to see me while you have been out, but
as said nothing. I have, of course, drawn my own
clusions. It would have been difficult for me not to
ect that you had fallen out again, but I had no idea
as over such an absurd matter. I'll see if he will come
 tomorrow. Would you like me to see him first?'
Eleanor assured her fervently that she would, and
 Southeran promised to do her best for her.

The next afternoon Eleanor stood back from her
room window and watched as Jonas Guthrie came
n the path to the Dower House. The expression on
 face was not particularly agreeable and her heart
k. She had a sudden feeling of panic at the thought
acing him—how could he possibly forgive her?—but
 forced herself to be calm. It had to be done, though
er own mind she was very doubtful of success. She
uld not have been reassured, either, had she heard the
versation between Mr Guthrie and her mother.

'I am glad you decided to come, Jonas. Eleanor will
relieved. I think she wishes to say how sorry she is
 her stupid mistake.'
'Really, ma'am? Which one?'

picture of Eleanor pouring out her troubles to her
mother was quite wrong. Eleanor had been too frightened by the turmoil of her feelings to confide immediately in Mrs Southeran. For years it had been her
aim to protect her mother from any form of unpleas-
antness, and her instinct now was to hide what she felt
until she was in control of it. So she avoided any
lengthy conversations at home and took to riding out
more frequently, and further afield. She avoided the
people on the estate, too.

She didn't want to have to think about what Guthrie
had said on the walk up to the house. Of course she
thought about it just the same, most of the time—and
about her reactions to him. From the beginning her
feelings about Guthrie had always been confused, but
now they were chaotic. Her head and her heart were at
odds completely—and even her heart was divided. How
could she still feel anything for a man who was destroying all she held most dear? What could she do to stop
herself? And what could she do to stop him? However
hard she racked her brains, she could think of nothing.
Thanks to her mother's unaccountable faith in Guthrie,
he had absolute control over Stanyards and everything
in it. She had never before felt so helpless and so lost.

But eventually the time came when Mrs Southeran
thought that Eleanor had been battling alone for long
enough. It was early evening and they were enjoying the
last of a glorious day's sunshine. Mrs Southeran's
chaise-longue had been drawn up between the doors on
to the terrace, and Eleanor was seated on a low chair
outside. She made a very pretty picture, framed against
the evening light, with her dark gold curls tumbling
down below the wide straw hat, but there was a weary

droop to her shoulders and she had spoken very little over the meal they had just finished.

'Eleanor?'

'Yes, Mama? What is it? Would you like me to get you a shawl?'

'No, sit down again! Please. Don't go away—I want to talk to you.'

Eleanor said nervously, 'Isn't it rather late for you to be in the air, Mama? Shall we go in?'

'Ah, don't, my dear! Don't shut me out.'

'I… I don't know what you mean.'

'Of course you do. I want to know what is causing you such trouble. Do you miss Stanyards so very much?'

'No, it's not that. It's nothing…' Mrs Southeran shook her head slowly at her daughter and Eleanor could hold out no longer. 'Yes, it is! Oh, Mama, it's what is happening to Stanyards! Did you know that Mr Guthrie is selling off Father's library?'

Whatever Mrs Southeran had been expecting, it was not this. 'Selling it off? What nonsense!'

'He is! I saw it—all the books were packed up, and the shelves had been taken down, and—'

'And this is what has been causing you so much anguish? Really, Eleanor, I could be angry with you if I were not so worried! Listen! Mr Guthrie, far from trying to destroy the library, has, with my full knowledge, been doing his best to save it.'

'Save it! How?'

'Some of your father's most valued books are seriously damaged with damp and mould. The room needs a thorough overhaul.'

'And what about the package for Mr Wilkes? Wasn't he one of Father's suppliers? Does he not sell rare

books? I tell you I saw it, Mama! M
off Father's library!'

Mrs Southeran's face was seriou
disappointed in you, Eleanor. I had
clear-headed than this. Pray forg
against Mr Guthrie for one momen
what you have just said. If it were a
you jump to such a hasty and ill-co
sion? I think not. You might rememb
does not only *sell* books.'

Eleanor stared blankly at her mot
eyes widened as she took in what she
restores them. They were being sent of
Southeran nodded. There was a short
Eleanor buried her face in her hand
muffled voice, 'Oh, Mama, I've been
never entered my head… Why didn't
spoke? I said such awful things to him

'What did you say?'

'I cannot tell you; I am too ashamed.
walked about the terrace restlessly. 'W

'The first thing is to see Jonas. You
peace with him. Shall I arrange it?'

'No! I cannot face him.'

'Nell, you must. If what you said
then you must offer him an apology.
anything else. I'm sure he will forgive

'Truly, Mama, what I said was unfor
much rather not see him again.'

'That is clearly impracticable—unles
forever and go to live with your aunt i
own I should miss you. In those circum
fall out with Mr Guthrie myself.'

'Has she made so many, Jonas? Surely not. In any case, you know which one we are speaking of here, of course. You are merely trying to be difficult, which is not kind of you.'

'I must confess, ma'am, I do not feel very kindly disposed towards your daughter.'

'Nor to me?'

His voice grew warmer, though his expression remained set.

'I always feel kindly disposed to you, Mrs Southeran.'

'Well, then, for my sake will you see Eleanor and hear what she has to say? It would be very awkward if we had to go on as we are, would it not? You cannot continue avoiding each other forever. It is most difficult. And… Eleanor is in some distress.'

'Forgive me if I say that it is no more than she deserves.' He took a look at his hostess's anxious face. 'It is almost impossible to refuse you anything, as you are well aware. Very well, I shall see Miss Southeran and listen to her apology.' His features relaxed into a faint grin. 'Though if it is at all like her last attempt I'm not sure it would satisfy me.'

'No, no. The case is quite different. This time she is honestly repentant. Tell me, Jonas, why did you not tell her the truth about the books straight away?'

'I was given no opportunity— No, that's not the real reason. It's true that I had no opportunity, but I would not have taken it anyway.' His face darkened again and he walked away from her to look out of the window. 'I told you when I first came to Stanyards earlier this year that there were…difficulties in my life—that not everyone would regard me with favour, and that I was not in a position to defend myself.

London was full of scandalous stories about me when your daughter was there.'

'You assured me that there was nothing in your past of which you were ashamed. Your word was good enough for me, Jonas. I knew you.'

'I… I am deeply grateful for your trust, and I swear I will not betray it—neither with Stanyards, nor with Eleanor.'

'Ah, there we have the crux of the matter, have we not? Eleanor.'

'She hasn't the same confidence in my honour. She has good reason for this—the tales in London were very convincing, and Lady Walcot warned her against me. But I had hoped with you down here she would learn to trust me as you do. It is clear to me that she never will.'

'Perhaps she needs more time?'

'That may be true, but I doubt it. And I do not intend to justify myself to anyone—least of all to someone who regards anything I do with instant suspicion!'

'Of course, you cannot entirely blame Eleanor, nor the stories in London, for her prejudice against you. It was a great shock to her to find out that her home had been sold over her head—and to you. I was wrong not to consult her beforehand, but I thought at the time it was better to take that decision from her—and it all happened so swiftly! But why didn't you tell her in London about Stanyards?'

'Yes, that was a mistake. I can see that now. But I thought I had good reason. At first, as you know, I didn't wish to publish my future whereabouts. Then…to be frank, when your daughter first described her home to me in such loving terms, I couldn't bring myself to tell her that she was going to lose it. After that, the right moment never seemed to come. I suppose I was always afraid of destroying what friendship she had for me. I was deceiving myself, of course. She has none.'

'That must be the first time I have heard you admit either to a mistake or to cowardice! What has happened to you, Jonas?'

'A slight madness, which I now regret.'

After a short pause Mrs Southeran said, 'You are wrong about Eleanor. She is not usually so unreasonable.'

'No? You know her better than I, naturally.'

'Will you see her?'

'Of course,' he said politely.

'And you will be kind to her?'

'That may be more difficult, but I shall try.'

When Eleanor came into the sitting-room, Mr Guthrie was standing with his back to the window, his face in shadow. Her mother gave her an encouraging smile and said, 'Eleanor, Mr Guthrie is here to listen to what you wish to say to him. I think he can see what brought you to misjudge him so badly, and I know he understands how difficult it has been for you to relinquish your claim to the Stanyards estate.

'I am largely to blame for that, of course. I should have consulted you. I hope you will forgive me, my dear, as I am sure Mr Guthrie will forgive you. And now I am going to leave you to sort things out between you. I shall make my peace with you later, my child.' She went out, shutting the door quietly behind her.

Chapter Six

There was an awkward silence in the room after Mrs Southeran had left. In the friendly privacy of her bed-chamber Eleanor had practised what she was going to say and it had sounded elegant and appealing. Now she couldn't think how to begin, and the man in front of the window didn't appear to be about to help her. Finally she said, 'I am not sure what I can say to persuade you to forgive me, Mr Guthrie. I wouldn't blame you if you had refused to come.'

'I am not so unreasonable, Miss Southeran. And I am here to listen.' His tone was neutral.

Eleanor took a deep breath and said, 'I am sincerely sorry for my over-hasty judgement of you in the library last week. I was completely in the wrong, and am ashamed of what I said to you.'

'You now believe that Lady Walcot and the others were wrong, too?'

'It is unfair of you to ask me that. How can I possibly know? But I was wrong to accuse you of selling the books, and I do believe that you mean well by Stanyards.'

'This is progress indeed!' Mr Guthrie's voice was still cool.

'What else can I say?'

'It would be foolish to expect more, I agree. Very well, Miss Southeran, we will forget the matter.'

Eleanor felt uncomfortably close to tears. In all her encounters so far with Mr Guthrie, whether they had been friendly or otherwise, she had been aware of a current of feeling running between them, a kind of extra line of communication. This was now noticeably absent.

'I... It is also my opinion that Stanyards will fare better in the future under your management than it has in the recent past.'

'More progress!' A mocking smile accompanied these words.

'And if I can be of any help...'

This time his response was swift and decisive. 'Thank you, but I think not. There must be no divided loyalties among the people on the estate.'

'There wouldn't be! If I gave you my help it would be whole-hearted. Do you believe me incapable of loyalty?'

He drawled her words of a few minutes before. 'How can I possibly know?'

She caught her breath. 'You haven't really forgiven me at all, have you?'

A faint pink appeared in his cheeks. 'Miss Southeran, I do not blame you for thinking ill of me, though I had hoped... We'll forget that. I suppose I do understand. And in return I hope you will understand why I cannot accept your offer of help. How can you persuade my tenants and workers to have confidence in me, to trust me, when you yourself do not trust me?'

'But I do! Where Stanyards is concerned, that is. Your life before you came here is another matter.'

'Trust, Miss Southeran, is complete or not at all.'

'But how can I trust you completely knowing what I do about your past—broken-off engagements and… and worse?'

'Engagement?' He looked blank. 'What engagement? Oh, yes, of course! My engagement! You need not consider that. It was of no consequence.'

'Perhaps not to you, sir!'

'Nor to the lady concerned, either, I assure you. You may forget my engagement. The rest is different, I agree, and more difficult to explain.' His manner became even cooler. 'Not that I propose to. I accept your apology in the spirit it was given, Miss Southeran. And now I think we should ask your mother to come in to hear that we have made up our differences.'

Eleanor saw that any further attempt to heal the rift between them would be useless. And what more did she want? Mr Guthrie had already done more than she had dared to hope. Her words to him had seemed to her to be unforgivable, and yet he had forgiven them. She could not reasonably expect him to forget her insults so quickly—especially when she was incapable of saying that she trusted him in the same whole-hearted manner as her mother did. But she was filled with a deep regret, all the same, for something that was lost, though she wasn't quite sure what it was.

That night Eleanor found it impossible to sleep. After tossing and turning for what seemed like hours she eventually got up and sat by the window. The night was warm and the stars were bright. She stared up at them as they slowly moved through the sky, and found herself wishing that she had never listened to the wretched Anstey woman! Could she really reconcile the Jonas Guthrie she knew—a man who was prepared to shoulder all the responsibilities of a large estate, who wanted to create, to make up for the neglect of previous generations—with the Jonas Guthrie of Mrs Anstey's account—a heartless monster who had shuffled off his obligations in exchange for a sum of money? Hardly. But, on the other hand, Mr Guthrie had never attempted to deny the story, or justify himself in any way. He had merely demanded that she should trust him—against all the evidence. How could she do that?

Eleanor got up and paced the room. She had liked this man from the first, but what did that mean? What did she know of the wider world—she, who was so in-experienced? Yes, she had felt a sense of kinship with him. But wasn't it just possible that Evadne Anstey had experienced the same delightful sense of kinship, before discovering, too late, that she had been deceiving herself?

Eleanor came to a halt as she remembered Mr Guthrie's view of his engagement. Of no consequence, indeed—the consequences had been dire for poor Evadne Anstey! She turned impatiently. There were so many questions about this man, and no answers.

The debate which had started that night in Eleanor's mind continued throughout the following week. Her instinct was to trust him but, try as she might, she could not simply reject Mrs Anstey's story, nor could she forget Mr Guthrie's careless dismissal of his engagement. Her mother was unable to help her with any facts which might throw light on the question.

'Jonas engaged? Well, I never heard of it, but that is not to say it wasn't so. I don't know all the details of his life in America. I can tell you that he isn't engaged now. As for Amelia—yes, I knew Amelia Vereker when she was a girl. She was a few years younger, so I cannot say I was a bosom friend of hers. She was a pretty little thing.'

'Is she…? It may seem a curious thing to ask, Mama, but would you say she was honest?'

'Completely.'

'I see.'

'She wasn't clever enough to be anything else! No, don't look at me like that, Nell! One has to face facts. Amelia Vereker was everything that was amiable and kind, but not at all clever. She had an air of helplessness about her which some found very appealing, though I was not one of them. Henry Anstey apparently fell in love with her at first sight.'

'How did she meet him?'

'She was visiting the London Verekers, and met him at a ball. They were engaged almost immediately and married very soon after that—his time in Europe was limited and he wanted to take her back to America with him. We were surprised at the speed with which it all happened, but her life with the Thomas Verekers had not been particularly happy—she was an orphan, you know. So was Jonas. I think that is why they were so devoted to each other.'

'Did you know Mr Guthrie's mother, too?'

'Caroline Vereker? Oh, yes. Now there was a character!'

'Oh? I am surprised. I had the impression that she was rather like Mrs Anstey.'

'Good lord, no! Whatever gave you that idea?'

'Wasn't she deserted by her husband? And didn't she die soon after?'

'Yes, but not of a broken heart, whatever Amelia may have said! She was a spirited, courageous creature. Absolutely straight, scornful of any weakness or subterfuge, but very headstrong. She was probably too headstrong for her husband's taste—he was fond of his own way, too. No one ever knew exactly what happened between the Guthries—certainly not Amelia, who wasn't much more than a child at the time. But Caroline came back to Somerset without her husband, Richard. She had the baby, and then, typically ignoring all advice, went riding too soon afterwards, developed a fever and died. They tried to trace Richard Guthrie but he had vanished. They found out later that he had gone into the army.'

'This is a different picture altogether!'

'Just what I was saying—Amelia Vereker would always tell what she believed to be the truth, but might well not understand the facts.'

'My uncle said much the same thing,' said Eleanor thoughtfully.

'Why on earth was your uncle talking about Amelia Vereker? And, Eleanor, why do you want to know all this history now?'

'When I was in London Mrs Anstey told me something about Mr Guthrie—Jonas Guthrie. If it is true, then he is dishonourable.'

'Eleanor! Are you still trying to prove that Mr Guthrie is a villain? I thought we had finished with all that nonsense!'

'On the contrary, Mama. I am trying to find out if he could possibly be the victim of some kind of plot.'

'I see.' Mrs Southeran thought for a moment, then

shook her head. 'Amelia Vereker wouldn't be clever enough to invent a plot. And she certainly wouldn't harm Jonas—she adored him. You cannot have understood her properly, Nell! What did she say about him?'

'I'm afraid I can't tell you. I gave my word.'

'Well, then, I'm afraid we cannot go much further. But I would never have sold Stanyards to Jonas if I had not had absolute confidence in him. Have you never asked him to explain the matter?'

'His "explanation" was that it was none of my concern.'

'Oh, dear! Not very helpful, but very typical! He was always a touch too arrogant for his own good, just like his mother. But wait! When he first came to see me here he did say that he was unpopular in London—presumably because of the stories you heard. He assured me that he was not ashamed of anything he had done—'

'Not ashamed!'

'And if Jonas said that, then there was nothing to be ashamed of, Eleanor,' said her mother firmly. 'The fact that he hasn't defended himself must be because he is protecting someone—and I would say that was Amelia. He was always very protective of her, even though she was some years older.'

'But that just doesn't fit, Mama!' said poor Eleanor. 'It doesn't make sense! Mrs Anstey was one of the people who suffered because of what he did!'

'*Amelia*? That is inconceivable. There must be some mistake.'

They both sat frowning. At last Mrs Southeran said, 'The whole affair is most puzzling and I don't think I can help you any further, Nell. Since I do not know what crime Jonas has been charged with, I cannot produce a defence for him. Except that I trust his word—and so should you.'

But, in spite of her doubts about Mrs Anstey's story, this was not yet enough for Eleanor.

Life continued quietly enough at Stanyards and the Dower House. When Mr Guthrie and Eleanor met they were civil to each other, and if Mrs Southeran was present they even conversed. But there was an invisible veil between them which prevented any real communication, and Eleanor did not know how to get rid of it—even had she wanted to. She tried to behave circumspectly. If, when out riding or walking, she met the tenants and workers on the estate, she took care to confine her interest to questions about their families. But Eleanor could not avoid hearing that Mr Guthrie was pressing on with reforms on the estate, and she could see the farmers slowly beginning to respond—especially when they saw that their landlord's unfavourable comments on their buildings had been followed by practical measures to repair them.

Then one day Eleanor was drawn by the sound of sawing to investigate the drive. She was horrified to see that a team of men were at work cutting down her beloved avenue of chestnut trees. She waved her arms and shouted to them, but they were intent on their work and the sound of the saw drowned her voice. She started to run towards them, but suddenly stopped after a few paces. What was she thinking of, telling the men to stop? But that was just what she must not do—the trees, the drive itself, no longer belonged to her, and she must not interfere.

She stood for a moment in a state of indecision, battling with a strong desire to tell them to stop all the same. She thought what it would mean to her to lose her trees—their chestnut candles in spring, their stately green canopy in summer, their brightly polished nuts in the autumn—and the thought gave her courage. How dared he remove them?

She turned on her heel and swept up the drive towards the house, intending to challenge Mr Guthrie. But once again she had not gone very far before she came to a halt. Could she be wrong? Was the episode of the library about to be repeated? Were the men perhaps merely removing those trees which were a danger? Perhaps she should find out before storming in on Stanyards' master.

She started back towards the men only to stop yet again when Becky came running out from behind the trees to greet Eleanor with her usual uninhibited enthusiasm.

A man's voice called, 'Becky! Down, girl!' Becky stopped as if pulled on an invisible lead. 'Sit!' With an apologetic look at Eleanor, Becky came no further but sat down where she was. Eleanor looked round and, with dismay, saw Mr Guthrie leaning against one of the trees on the other side of the drive. From his stance, it was obvious that he had been there some minutes.

'Good morning, Miss Southeran,' he called, and came over to join her. She saw that he was regarding her with some amusement.

Eleanor went scarlet as she realised that he must have been observing her stops and starts. He might even have been able to divine the course of her thoughts from them, and had been laughing at her inability to make up her mind. 'Good morning,' she said abruptly, and turned to leave him. Then she turned back again. 'No, I *will* ask you!'

He burst out laughing. 'Good!' he said. 'We have a decision at last.'

'What do you intend to do with the chestnuts?' This came out more truculently than she had intended, and she added in a more conciliatory tone, 'If you don't mind my asking, that is.'

He looked at her speculatively. 'What do you think I intend to do?'

Eleanor felt this was some kind of test. She hesitated before answering and considered the men at their work. Then she turned to him, an expression of uncertainty on her face. She had come to a surprising conclusion. 'I think…I think you are trying to preserve what you can of them.'

'Not selling them for their timber?'

'Chestnut timber isn't worth much,' she said absent-mindedly. 'No, I don't mean that! I mean, it's true that it isn't worth much, but I don't think you would cut the trees down in order to sell them, anyway. No, I think you are getting rid of the dangerous ones and will try to keep the rest. Is that…is that right?' In a way, this was a declaration of some faith on her part, and she waited anxiously for his reply.

'And if I decide that I cannot save any of them? They are all very old.'

Eleanor's answer came swiftly and instinctively. 'I think you will plant new trees.' She had succeeded in surprising him. Indeed, she had surprised herself. He looked down at her with a faint smile.

'Well done! It seems I am making progress—real progress.'

'They won't be the same as the old trees, of course,' said Eleanor, reluctant to concede too much.

'No, indeed they won't. That is why I am keeping as much as possible of the old stock. I shall plant a new.

line some distance back and, when the last survivors of these stalwarts finally succumb, the young trees will be ready to take over to form a new, wider avenue. But I won't plant horse chestnuts again.'

'Why not?' Eleanor demanded, her hackles rising at any criticism of Stanyards. 'They are beautiful.'

'They don't last long enough.'

'What do you mean? These are over a hundred years old!'

'That is nothing in terms of an estate such as this. I want Stanyards to be beautiful still in two hundred years, Eleanor—and more yet. I shall plant lime trees.'

Eleanor gazed at him in bemusement. Who would have thought that such a visionary dwelt behind those dark, hard features? How far removed was this man from the callous adventurer of Mrs Anstey's tale, and how could she ever reconcile the two?

He grinned at her. 'You are making me feel somewhat like a chandelier, Miss Southeran.'

'A chandel… Oh!' Eleanor grew pink and said in confusion, 'Forgive me. I was staring.'

'You were, but I enjoyed it. It is some time since you regarded me with anything but a basilisk glare.'

Eleanor burst out laughing. 'How unkind! And how unjust! I have merely been reflecting your own cockatrice looks at me!'

They laughed together, and then suddenly became serious. He said quietly, 'Shall we try again, Eleanor?'

Eleanor was filled with a sudden exhilaration. 'Yes!' she said shyly. 'Yes, I should like that.'

'Do you approve of my plans for the drive?'

Eleanor was anxious not to assume too much. 'My approval isn't necessary—but I do.' She said with a touch of sadness, 'I knew the chestnuts would have to go soon—I just hate the thought of losing them.'

He smiled at her. 'A woman of spirit and intelligence, and a sentimentalist, too. What a rare mixture you are, Eleanor Southeran!'

'No rarer than you, Jonas Guthrie!' she flashed. 'I find it impossible to fathom you! What has this lover of the countryside, this designer for the future to do with the business cheat—and worse—of Mrs Anstey's tale?' She stopped short, aghast at her own outspokenness. 'I'm sorry,' she faltered. 'I shouldn't have said that. Forgive me.'

Jonas was frowning as Eleanor waited anxiously for him to reply. She cursed her wayward tongue for spoiling what had promised to be a reconciliation. But finally he said, 'No, it is you who should forgive me. Eleanor, there is an explanation for it all, but I cannot give it to you—not yet, at least.'

'Why not?' asked Eleanor, conscious of the importance of this moment.

'Because the happiness of other people—people to whom I owe a great deal—is at stake. In a few weeks' time it might be different, and then, believe me, I shall tell you everything. Are you willing to wait a little? Or must we go back to our former state of armed neutrality?'

'My mother trusts you,' said Eleanor slowly.

'She, too, is a rare woman,' he said with a smile. 'Eleanor, can you not do the same? I won't deny that there are episodes in my past of which I am now ashamed. I've led a hard life, and a dangerous one sometimes, and I cannot pretend that I have always played according to the rules.' He paused, then added, 'And I always play to win. I have said that once before, I believe, but it is true of big things as well as minor ones. If you don't like it, then I am sorry, but there it is.'

She frowned, but once again his honesty disarmed her. 'I'll wait till you can tell me the truth about yourself,' she said impulsively. 'And meanwhile we shall be friends, I think?'

He smiled, and her heart gave a little jump as he took her hand and kissed it, looking all the while into her eyes. His own eyes darkened and, putting his hands on her shoulders, he pulled her towards him...

'No!' whispered Eleanor, more feebly than she would have liked. 'No, Jonas. The men...they'll see us.'

For a moment he seemed not to pay any attention, but then he gave a deep sigh and released her. 'What is it about you, Eleanor Southeran? From the first moment I saw you looking at that damned chandelier, I've been bewitched. I've never known anything like it! And now...I know very well that I must not do or say anything that we might later regret. And to kiss you in full view of my own workmen would be the very height of idiocy! But you have only to look at me with those sea-green eyes and I am lost! Why do you do it to me?'

'I...I don't—not deliberately!'

'That's the hell of it,' he groaned. 'You're not even trying!'

Eleanor's lips twitched as she said demurely, 'You are presenting a picture of a siren which I find very difficult to associate with myself! I have never excited such uncontrollable passions in anyone else, sir!'

'Have you ever felt uncontrollable passion, Eleanor?'

She grew serious immediately. 'I...I don't think that is a question you have a right to ask. But the answer is no. Not yet.'

'Then don't joke about it! However, my passions are not yet uncontrollable, thank God! I have enough sense left to know that I must make do with your friendship until…until certain matters are cleared up. I have no right to ask for more. Will you forgive me for my behaviour just now and be my friend?'

She was puzzled, but said calmly, 'If uncontrollable passion is the only alternative, then I should prefer it.'

'Good!' Then he nodded in the direction of the drive. 'Now, about these trees… You were saying how you loved your chestnuts. We'll plant some in the park. Would you like that? I had intended to put a number of specimen trees about the grounds. Why shouldn't there be a humble horse chestnut among the more exotic samples?'

This was an idea which caught Eleanor's imagination immediately. It was a plan she had cherished for some time, but had never had the resources to carry it out. 'What else are you planting? Are you importing any?' she asked eagerly.

'I have some lists at the house—perhaps I could show them to you? I'll bring them down to the Dower House,' he said deliberately. 'My contacts in India and North America are going to send me some samples—I don't know how many are suited to this climate, of course, and I thought I might engage an expert to advise me. There's a man in Exeter—'

'Mr Lucombe. I have his list.' Eleanor's eyes were glowing with enthusiasm, and Mr Guthrie laughed as she took his arm quite unselfconsciously and started to urge him in the direction of the Dower House. 'You must tell my mother about your plans. She will like them.'

* * *

From then on Mr Guthrie was as good as his word, and Eleanor was able to feel completely at her ease with him. Though he showed her in all sorts of ways that he valued her company, he never once overstepped the boundaries of friendship, and she, accepting the limits he had set, had never been so happy in her life. She was once again involved in the work for Stanyards, but, more than that, she was working with someone who shared her interests, whose enthusiasm for Stanyards and its estate rivalled her own.

She learned a great deal, too. Mr Guthrie brought a fresh approach to management of the land, and it was a revelation to her to see the effect his new methods were having on the farming community. Their former attitude of resigned apathy, their previous hostility to the new landlord were swept away by his energy and his eagerness to make a success of the new enterprise, his willingness to listen to any idea which looked as if it might work, his readiness to finance new ventures. The neighbourhood was finally at one in applauding Mr Guthrie.

It was unfortunate, therefore, that this state of affairs did not last very long. Cousin Louisa brought a foretaste of the coming storm when she arrived at the Dower House one afternoon for tea with the Southerans. Eleanor came in to hear her say, 'Well, of course, Anthea, we were most intrigued. I mean, it isn't often that we have a newcomer in Combe St James—not that she's a newcomer exactly, but… Ah, Eleanor, there you are. How do you go on?'

'Well, thank you, Cousin Louisa. I'm sorry I wasn't here when you arrived. How are you?' An account of the state of Cousin Louisa's health followed, to the general effect that she was very well.

'And I have to say, Eleanor, that your mama is blooming! Your company certainly does her good—or is it the move to this house? I was completely astonished to hear about the sale of Stanyards. Why, I said, why didn't Anthea say anything about it while I was staying with her? I could have helped! But there—I know you, my dear. You didn't want to cause me any trouble—as if I would worry about a little extra work!'

She smiled affectionately at Mrs Southeran as she continued, 'Fancy Mr Guthrie turning up like that and offering to buy! It was providential, was it not?' She paused for breath, then said, 'And now his cousins are coming to stay in Combe St James.'

Eleanor caught her breath, and her mother gave her a warning glance. It was not necessary. Very much on her guard, Eleanor asked casually, 'Cousins?'

'Yes, Mrs Anstey and her daughter. She was a Vereker, and so was his mother, but you know that, of course. Is that not delightful?'

'Delightful,' echoed Eleanor. 'When do they arrive?'

'Oh, any day! Now that the season is over, there is little reason for them to remain in London. They are not, I think, very rich—at least that is what I have been told, and Mrs Desmond is usually right in her information, though where she gets it from is a mystery to me. Did you meet her when you were in London, my dear?'

'Mrs Desmond? I don't think—'

'Dear me, no, Eleanor! Mrs Desmond hasn't left Combe St James for the past twenty years or more. You'd never believe it, for she always appears to know all the London gossip. I think she has a niece who writes to her quite often.' She paused for thought, then added judiciously, 'Well, not perhaps all that often, but two or

three times a year. But no, I meant Mrs Anstey. If you
do know her it would be pleasant for her if you were to
come over to visit soon after she arrives, would it not?
She will probably find herself quickly at home—she
comes from these parts, they tell me. That would be
before I came to Somerset, Anthea, because I don't
think William and I ever met her…'

'Amelia Vereker left Somerset just before you married
my cousin,' said Mrs Southeran, stemming the flow.

'And now she is coming back a widow, to the home
of her youth! I did tell you that she is a widow, did I not?
Oh, how stupid of me, of course you knew that already,
too. Really, you must think me very silly. Oh, how nice!
Here is tea!'

After Cousin Louisa's departure the two Southeran
ladies sank back in relief. 'Mama, I have never been so
full of admiration for you as I am at this moment,' said
Eleanor, not altogether joking.

'I'm delighted, of course. Admiration is always
welcome to a lady of my advanced years. But why
particularly?'

'How you lived with our worthy cousin for six weeks
without murdering her I shall never know!'

'Eleanor! She was very kind, and you must not talk
so extravagantly. Though I must admit…'

They both laughed and then Eleanor grew serious.
'You realise what Mrs Anstey's arrival must mean to
Mr Guthrie?'

Her mother said, 'It will certainly be awkward if
what you say is true—that Amelia believes she owes her
misfortune to him. Though she is surely mistaken.'

'It hardly matters whether she is mistaken or not. If
the story told in London gains ground here in Somerset

and Jonas still refuses to deny it, then he will be ostracised here, too.'

'Jonas?'

'I mean Mr Guthrie. It is because you always refer to him as Jonas that I forgot.'

'Of course,' her mother murmured, watching with interest as the colour rose in Eleanor's cheeks. 'But I cannot believe that the neighbourhood will pay any attention to such tales. Mr Guthrie—or Jonas, as we call him—has surely gained too much credit in the district.'

'I hope you are right, Mama.'

'Really?' asked her mother, opening her eyes wide. 'Am I to infer that you have had a change of heart about Jonas's behaviour to Amelia Anstey?'

'No! Yes! I don't know!' Eleanor got up and walked round. Then she said more calmly, 'Yes, I do. I am now virtually certain that Mrs Anstey's story—stories—are wrong. I could not be so mistaken in his character. But there *is* a mystery. And Mr Guthrie refuses to help himself or others.'

'Then we must see what we can do,' said her mother briskly. 'I now realise how important it is. Tell me as soon as you hear any news of Amelia Anstey's arrival.'

Chapter Seven

This news was not long in coming. Just a few days later a note from Cousin Louisa announced that Mrs Anstey had arrived in Combe St James, and had settled in a house in the middle of the village.

> And, whatever one may say, Church Cottage is not a suitable place for dear Mrs Anstey. It is large, but in a very bad state of repair. What a pity she is so poor! I am sure she has an interesting history, she is such a charming lady, but it must be a sad one. The whole neighbourhood feels for her situation. What I find strange is that she was surprised when she heard that Mr Guthrie lived near by. Why didn't she know? She remembers you, Anthea, quite well, and, of course, she met Eleanor very recently. She says she would like to see you both again. Do come and visit me soon, and I will arrange a meeting.

'I think you must have misunderstood what Amelia Anstey told you about Jonas, Eleanor,' said Mrs South-

eran. 'You haven't told me what it was, so I am somewhat in the dark, but it cannot have been as serious as
you thought. She has quite obviously said nothing to his
detriment in Combe St James.'

'Not yet, Mama. Long may it continue so. What she
told me condemned him unequivocally—I could not
possibly have misunderstood her.'

'Perhaps she has seen how popular he is in the neighbourhood and doesn't wish to discredit him?'

'I sincerely hope so,' said Eleanor soberly. 'Or that
she has decided to be more discreet down here than she
was in London. But the temptation to indulge herself
with a new audience of sympathetic listeners will be
very strong—especially as most of them will press her
to confide in them. You have only to read Cousin
Lousia's letter to see how eager they are to know.' She
picked the note up and read it again. 'I wonder what has
happened to her daughter? Cousin Louisa doesn't
mention her.'

'Why should she?'

'If you had seen Marianne Anstey, Mama, you
wouldn't have to ask. She is the loveliest creature I have
seen in years.'

'We must respond to Cousin Louisa's note immediately! I am consumed with curiosity about the
whole affair!'

Two days later Eleanor and her mother were sitting in
Cousin Louisa's overcrowded parlour. Mrs Southeran
had been placed in a large armchair with a footstool at
her feet and a rug over her knees. She protested in vain
that the day was warm and that she was not at all fatigued.
Cousin Louisa knew that she was merely being brave, so

poor Mrs Southeran sat in discomfort for the rest of the afternoon, unwilling to disabuse her kind hostess.

'I am glad you have arrived so promptly,' Cousin Louisa began, after taking elaborate precautions to see that they were not overheard. 'I must consult you on a most delicate matter before Mrs Anstey comes. Indeed, it is most distressing.'

Mrs Southeran carefully avoided Eleanor's eye and said, 'Dear me, this sounds very ominous. What can it be?'

'Well, it has come to my ears that Mr Guthrie is not all he might appear to be!' She paused dramatically.

'In what way?'

Somewhat disappointed by Mrs Southeran's calm response, Cousin Louisa went on, 'His benevolence appears to be of very recent date—in fact, since he got hold of Stanyards!'

'What are you saying, Louisa? Mr Guthrie did not "get hold of" Stanyards—he bought it in a thoroughly proper manner. More than that, he has been generous throughout.'

'But have you never asked yourself where the money to buy Stanyards came from?'

'I did not consider it my business,' said Mrs Southeran in a warning tone. Cousin Louisa ignored it.

'From what I have heard, he left England nearly twenty years ago with nothing to his name. Where did all this wealth of his come from?'

'Louisa, I have told you, I do not know, nor do I care very much. It is quite simply not our affair. I know he is to be trusted.'

Cousin Louisa looked at her pityingly. 'But then, you have never been very worldly, have you, Anthea?

What if I were to tell you that, according to some, Jonas Guthrie has behaved disgracefully?'

'I would say that it is time you stopped shilly-shallying, and told us exactly what is being said and, even more to the point, who is saying it.'

At first Cousin Louisa refused to be specific, but gradually, under Mrs Southeran's relentless questioning, the same story, but with more detail than had been generally current in London, emerged about Jonas Guthrie. Mrs Anstey, it appeared, had been less discreet in Somerset than she had in London—perhaps because Marianne was now safely engaged to be married to her Irish viscount and was spending the summer with his parents in Oxfordshire.

'The whole neighbourhood is buzzing with it, as you can imagine. There are even one or two who remember the Verekers from the old days, though Thomas and his wife have long been gone, of course, and the estate sold. They are very shocked at Guthrie's behaviour.'

'If they remember Amelia Vereker so well, then they will not accept the unsupported word of such a ninny-hammer!' said Mrs Southeran roundly. 'Really, I might well lose my patience with you, Louisa, if you carry on slandering a good man in this way. Has he not been a good landlord since he came? Has he not been thought an asset to our country society?'

'Yes, but that was before— Ah! Here is Mrs Anstey now—perhaps we can persuade her to tell us herself.'

For the first half-hour the tea party promised to be a success. The two elder lady visitors exchanged happy reminiscences of their youth, with a good many references to people of whom Eleanor had never heard. Neither lady mentioned the name of Jonas Guthrie. Mrs

Anstey complimented Mrs Southeran on having such a charmingly lovely daughter, and Mrs Southeran responded by saying that she had heard much about Marianne Anstey's beauty.

'And now I hear that she is to be Viscountess Morrissey, no less. But why is she not with you?'

'Lord Morrissey and his parents were so kind as to invite both Marianne and me for a visit to their estates in Oxfordshire. I spent some time there with Marianne, but then when Lady Dorothy Rushton and a number of other guests arrived I came down here.'

'Leaving Marianne?'

Mrs Anstey looked nervous, and said, 'I…I wanted to see my old home again. Marianne is in very good hands. Her future parents-in-law are delighted with her, and she is a great favourite with Lady Dorothy, too. I find it difficult to be in company for very long—my husband's death…' Her voice trailed away pathetically and she dabbed her eyes with a tiny handkerchief.

There was a short silence. Then Mrs Southeran said, 'So you came down here. The Vereker lands have been sold, of course. There isn't much of the old place left.'

'No, but that did not surprise me. Sir Thomas always said that he would be the last of the Somerset Verekers.'

'I suppose he was right—though Jonas Guthrie now owns Stanyards, and he is a Vereker on his mother's side.'

There was another silence. Then Mrs Anstey said with some agitation, 'I cannot discuss…that man.'

'Why not, Amelia? You were so close in the old days.'

Cousin Louisa made a gesture of protest. Anthea was being a little too outspoken for her taste. Mrs Southeran ignored it and went on, 'Why not, Amelia? And why do you say you cannot discuss him? Who has been telling all these stories I hear about Jonas?'

'They are not stories!' cried Mrs Anstey. 'I wish they were! You of all people should know that, Anthea! You know how much I loved him!'

'And how much he loved you,' said Mrs Southeran firmly. 'I don't believe he would ever do anything to harm you. Jonas is a good man and a good landlord. Why are you doing your best to destroy his credit in the neighbourhood? Why do you wish to ruin him?'

'Because he ruined—' Mrs Anstey caught her lip and hesitated.

'Go on!'

'Because he ruined my husband and my daughter!'

'From what I have heard, he saw to it that you and your daughters were safe and well provided for.'

Mrs Anstey threw Eleanor a speaking glance.

'I have not betrayed your confidence, Mrs Anstey. My mother is basing what she says on what she has heard in the neighbourhood. Have you perhaps confided in others?' Eleanor's voice was cool. She had decided that she still did not much like this woman.

Cousin Louisa intervened. 'I am sure it would be very natural for Mrs Anstey to seek comfort from her new friends.'

'At the expense of old ones?'

At this Mrs Anstey stood up. 'You will have to excuse me—I do not feel very well.' She turned to Mrs Southeran, and said with a semblance of dignity, 'You are wrong to think so harshly of me, Anthea. I did not abandon my old regard for Jonas without a great deal of distress. But I cannot account for the sudden reversal of our fortunes, and the unhappy situation of my daughter Evadne, in any other way.' She had been getting increasingly agitated during this speech, and could hardly pronounce her final words. 'When you eventually come to see that I was right I hope you will apologise to me for your unkindness this afternoon.' With this she hurried out of the room, followed by Cousin Louisa.

The two Southerans eyed one another ruefully. 'Was I so hard? I had forgotten how irritating Amelia Vereker could be. She used to cry a lot as a child. Jonas was always fighting people who had upset her.'

'But she is a very convincing victim, Mama.'

'Yes. But not of Jonas, Eleanor. Never of Jonas—I must talk to him.'

When Mr Guthrie next visited them, Mrs Southeran wasted no time in telling him of her conversation with Amelia Anstey. She finished, 'But you may rest easy, Jonas. I shall not let Amelia get away with what she is saying of you. When she has had time to calm down I shall talk to her again. She was always very biddable.'

His reaction was unexpected. He had listened to her impassively, but now he said, 'I wish you had not done this, Mrs Southeran. Your kindness was…misplaced.'

Eleanor and her mother gazed at him in astonishment. Mrs Southeran found her voice and said, 'Am I to understand that you do not care what people are saying of you? If someone does not stop her, Jonas, the rumours will soon become accepted fact. You will be an outcast—as I understand you were in London. Is that what you wish?'

'It probably concerns me less than it would you,' he said with a slight smile. 'But no, it is not what I would have wanted. Indeed I wish to heaven Amelia Vereker had not chosen to re-visit the scenes of her childhood. I thought I was safe down here.'

'Safe?' echoed Eleanor, startled.

He turned to her. 'Safe from her accusations,' he said smoothly. Then he went on, 'But since she is here, and has already…told her story, then I'm afraid there is nothing I can do.'

'Nothing! Of course there is—'

'I should have said nothing I wish to do. Nor anything I wish anyone else to do.'

'But Jonas—'

'You will please me best by making no attempt to persuade Amelia to change her mind. Believe me, it is better so.'

'In other words,' said Eleanor, unable to stop herself, 'you are saying what you said to me in the park that morning—that it is none of our concern.'

He hesitated, then said carefully, 'No, I am sorry to say that that is no longer true. I had hoped—' He turned away and stared out of the window. Suddenly he said violently, 'Oh, confound all the Ansteys, and the whole damnable business! Why couldn't Amelia have left me in peace down here? I had hoped it would all eventually be forgotten, that she would go back to Boston once Marianne was safely married, and I would be free to live my own life again.'

He turned back to the room. 'Forgive me, Mrs Southeran, I am not fit for company in my present mood. But remember what I have said. I do not wish you to pursue the question of Amelia Anstey's stories.'

'Very well, if that is your wish, Jonas,' said Mrs Southeran quietly. 'I will not mention the matter to Amelia again.'

With a regretful look at Eleanor, he went out, leaving two very puzzled ladies behind him. After a while Mrs Southeran said thoughtfully, 'I wonder if we still have the address of your father's Boston correspondent—the gentleman who visited him here that last winter before he died? I think his name was Bitteridge. I must look for it.'

'You're going to write to him about the Ansteys? If you only could, Mama! But you promised not to pursue the matter!'

'You should listen to what I say more carefully, Eleanor. I said I would not mention the matter to Amelia Anstey again. That is not quite the same thing, wouldn't you agree?'

That evening Mrs Southeran and Eleanor spent some time composing a carefully phrased letter to Mr Edmund Bitteridge in Tremont Street, Boston. Mrs Anthea Southeran, widow of the late Charles Southeran, presented her compliments to Mr Bitteridge, and asked if he could help her to find information on a former friend of hers, a certain Amelia Vereker, who had married Henry Anstey of Boston, Massachusetts. The matter was not one of idle curiosity, but might serve to throw light on a difficult situation here in England. Any details he might send would be treated with the utmost confidence.

'That will be enough, Eleanor,' said Mrs Southeran, laying down her pen at last. 'He was a most thorough man, with a keen interest in his fellow human beings—most unusual in bibliophiles! Your father hardly noticed the existence of the rest of the world!'

The effect of Mrs Anstey's stories was curious. In general they reversed the situation of Mr Guthrie's first appearance in Stanyards. With the exception of Eleanor's mother, those who had been his keenest advocates now regarded him with disfavour. The Southerans, who had sold their home to him and were forced to live as his neighbours, became objects of sympathy. There were some who regarded Mrs Southeran's staunch support for Mr Guthrie as a brave attempt to put a good face on a bad situation. Others, less charitably, saw it as an unworldly widow's foolishness. Evadne Anstey's story soon became common knowledge, and many whispered their concern lest Eleanor Southeran should go the same way.

But the farmers, who had at first seen Mr Guthrie as an ogre and a tyrant, were now firmly behind him. One or two, Threlfall among them, still resented his high-handed ways, but most of them saw how the estate was improving and had become his keen allies. Mr Guthrie himself was apparently as little affected as he had ever been by either. Perhaps he spent slightly more time with the Southerans. He seemed to enjoy their company, especially as the number of invitations to the other large houses in the neighbourhood had dramatically declined—a fact which did not seem to concern him in the slightest.

The most curious effect of all was on Eleanor. It might have been supposed that the reminder of Mr Guthrie's sins, and his subsequent refusal to permit anyone to attempt to refute Mrs Anstey's tale, would cause her to doubt him even more. But the opposite was the case. Eleanor found herself seeking his company, delighting in his trenchant views and forthright statements, and becoming ever more convinced of his integrity. More than that, she gradually came to the conclusion that his harsh appearance and uncompromising manner concealed a man of feeling.

'Balderdash!' was his instant response when she said something to this effect to him. 'Don't accuse me of anything so mawkish!'

'You may deny it as much as you please, but you will not dissuade me. If nothing else, you have feeling for the land here—'

'Pride of possession—a very different matter.'

'Your expression showed more than pride of possession when you were contemplating this valley a moment ago. Besides, you may well claim pride in possessing the rest of the estate—the farms and fields, the house and its park. But how can anyone claim to possess something as savagely natural as this?' She swept her arm in an arc embracing the bridge on which they had stopped and the steep combe below them. It was the wildest part of the Stanyards estate—the sides of the valley were almost like miniature cliffs, the stream at their foot filled with boulders. Even as she spoke the horses shifted nervously on the wooden planks of the bridge.

'Beautiful and dangerous, I agree. Let's move on to the other side. Captain is not at all sure the bridge is safe.'

'I assure you it is,' said Eleanor as they made their way to the bank. 'This was one of my father's favourite places—wild, lonely and quiet. I expect you would call him a romantic. He didn't bother much with the farms, but he loved this place and made sure he could get to it even when he became infirm. The bridge was built to take a small carriage, let alone two horses! And it is one of the few things which is still in good repair.'

'I know it is. I've had it checked.' He smiled at her

look of surprise. 'I like it, too—not, Miss Southeran, *not* that you could call me a romantic!'

'Heaven forfend!' she laughed. 'And if I am honest I will tell you that I know your liking for this spot, especially in the mornings. Whenever I wish to find you I always look for you first here! Did you never find it surprising how often I seemed to come across you?'

'I was too busy being delighted that you had,' he said, smiling down at her.

She went on a little breathlessly, 'But I still think you are not as hard as you would wish me to believe. And I know that you must have some feeling for people as well as the land.'

'Humanity doesn't rate very high in my esteem, Miss Southeran. I've seen too much of it. Oh, I like some individuals—your mother, for one. Indeed, I have great affection for her. And I suppose I have felt something for others in the past.'

'Your fiancée, for example?' This slipped out before Eleanor could stop herself.

'Who?' he asked, with a frown.

She stared at him. 'Upon my word, sir, I find you an enigma! This is the second time you have forgotten that you were ever engaged. Did you really feel so little for her?'

'Ah, yes! You mean Miss Anstey. I suppose I must have felt something, but I really no longer remember. She was very beautiful.' The indifference with which he said this stung Eleanor into further indiscretion.

'Your effect on her was more far-reaching, I believe!'

'What the devil are you talking about?'

'Evadne Anstey—or Oliver, as she is now called.'

He looked at her blankly, then said, 'You seem to be

misinformed, Miss Southeran. I was never engaged to
Evadne Oliver.'

'Not…? But…I don't understand,' said Eleanor in
confusion.

'No, indeed. Why should you?' he said coolly. 'And
I am not about to enlighten you—not on the subject of
Evadne Oliver, at least. But the Anstey girl I was
engaged to was Phoebe, the eldest. You have seen
Marianne Anstey—Phoebe is even lovelier.'

Eleanor was still reeling from the shock of finding
out that there was yet another Anstey sister, but she
rallied at this. 'That is impossible,' she said firmly.

'Believe me, it is true. She is Marianne's equal in
beauty in every way, and in addition she has more animation. A very handsome creature.'

'But you were clearly not devastated at her loss. Or
is that a brave front?'

'You know very well that I refuse to dissemble, Miss
Southeran. Phoebe and I agreed to part because she
found someone more suited to her taste. I was surprised,
but not unduly put out.' He took a look at the expression of outrage on her face and gave a laugh. 'Come, it
was a long time ago and, whatever it might have meant
at the time, it means less than nothing now, as you saw.
For God's sake, let us forget her.'

Eleanor returned to her former theme. 'But there are
people for whom you do feel—quite strongly?'

'Fishing, Eleanor?'

'Of course not! You know that is not what I meant at
all! I…' She hesitated, then carried on, 'I was thinking
of Mrs Anstey…and Evadne. But you need not say
anything more—I know you wish to keep your own
counsel. As you will undoubtedly say, it is none of my

concern.' She spurred her horse and rode swiftly to the top of the hill.

He did not follow immediately, but sat in thought for a minute. When he rejoined her she was gazing down over Stanyards. 'I'm sorry,' she said. 'I am wrong to mention such matters. You have said that you cannot discuss them.'

'Eleanor, half the county refuses to receive me. The ladies of the neighbourhood are unanimous in condemning me. My position here in Somerset is every bit as uncomfortable as it was in London. Yet I believe I am right in saying that you and your mother have remained my friends. Why?'

There was a short silence. Then Eleanor said slowly, 'In London you said once that you hoped I would regard you more kindly once I knew you better.' She turned towards him. 'You were right. I do now know you better, and I have learnt to trust you. I'm not asking you to explain anything. I simply want you to know that I…that neither my mother nor I believe Mrs Anstey's story. I do not believe that you robbed the Ansteys, and, whatever the nature of your relationship with Evadne Anstey was, I do not believe that you would have abandoned her so heartlessly, not even to marriage with Mr Oliver. I think you might have given him money, but not for…not because you were shuffling off an obligation.' She stole a glance at him but his face was turned away.

'Moreover,' she continued, 'we would not be at all surprised to learn that the support the Verekers gave Mrs Anstey in London was subsidised by you. The mystery in all of this is why you have behaved as you have—but I respect your wish to remain silent on that.'

After a pause Mr Guthrie said in a neutral tone, 'I seem to have more feeling than I thought. Shall we go back?'

The summer wore on. For some weeks it rained every day and the country folk murmured about St Swithin and tried to remember how much it had rained on July the fifteenth. The streams and rivers were unusually full for the time of year and in the combe the water churned darkly through the boulders. The Southeran ladies lived a quiet life. The weather made it difficult for Mrs Southeran to go very far, and in any case the neighbourhood's dislike of Mr Guthrie irritated her. As yet no word had come from Mr Bitteridge—another source of dissatisfaction.

Eleanor continued to ride out on the estate. She learned from one of the farmers' wives that Mrs Anstey was in daily expectation of receiving her daughter at last. Eleanor wondered what Marianne Anstey's effect on the neighbourhood would be. Her fragile beauty was sure to arouse admiration, and would no doubt give extra fuel to the antipathy towards Mr Guthrie.

She decided she would make sure he had heard the news, but when she went up to the house she found he was out riding. This didn't deter her. She knew where she would find him—when he was riding for pleasure he nearly always went in the direction of the combe. Without bothering to disturb her mother, she changed and set off in search of him. Before too long she was approaching the bridge—yes, she had been right. He was standing on top of the hill overlooking the valley, and as soon as he saw her he waved. She made for the bridge, and he started hurrying down the slope, waving all the while. He seemed excited, though she was unable to see him very clearly—the sun was in her eyes. No doubt he would tell her what it was when they met.

She urged her horse on over the bridge—the water below was running swiftly between its ugly-looking boulders, and the animal was uneasy. Mr Guthrie had stopped. He seemed to be waiting. Suddenly there was a loud crack followed by a groaning sound. To her horror, she saw the bridge tilt drunkenly downwards. Her horse reared in terror, throwing her as he did so, and the last thing Eleanor remembered was seeing him leap to the bank. Then she felt herself sliding into oblivion...

Chapter Eight

Eleanor grew conscious of a buzzing sound near her right ear. She opened her eyes slowly, then shut them again as the light dazzled her. Her head was aching, and she felt stiff and cramped. She shifted cautiously, but something seemed to be holding her down. 'Please,' she murmured. 'Please—I feel sick. Let me up!'

There was no reply. She opened her eyes again, turning her head away from the light. Scarlet berries, a hazy suspicion of yellow, and green—bright, glossy green. Christmas! No, that was nonsense—that wasn't holly. The leaves were long and smooth, falling in a graceful curve…hart's tongue, then.

As she watched, a bee flew up out of the centre of the leaves and disappeared from her restricted vision. What were the berries? She twisted round slightly and examined them, screwing her eyes up in an effort to get them into focus. They were still slightly blurred, but she could see that it was the sturdily vivid head of cuckoo-pint. Where on earth was she? And why was she being held down? She closed her eyes again. Memory slowly returned. Mr Guthrie had been on the hill… She had been crossing the bridge to meet him… There was something she had to tell him…

When Eleanor opened her eyes again she felt less sick and her head was feeling better. Where was Mr Guthrie? Why hadn't he come to help her? She struggled to sit up, but it was awkward—she couldn't move her legs. She used her elbows to prop herself up and gasped with dismay at the scene of devastation which met her eye. The bridge had collapsed at one end, though some of the structure was still intact, including the part on which she was lying. The planks which had been the roadway now formed a sloping platform just clear of the waters, which were rushing angrily past underneath. Indeed, she would have been lying actually in the stream but for the small outcrop of rock which diverted it round behind her and which was home to the plants she had observed. What was worse, some of the supports for the bridge, which had broken away after the main platform had fallen, had landed across her legs, and one heavy beam was pinning her down.

In a panic at the restraint, she struggled to release herself, but a sudden, sharp pain caused her to cry out. Something must have damaged her ankle. She lay back again, panting and feeling very dizzy. Mr Guthrie must have gone for help. But why hadn't he stayed to tell her first what he was doing? She wished he were here—it was odd being so alone and so helpless… Frightening… This must stop! She must pull herself together. He would be back soon…

In the Dower House some time later, Mrs Southeran was expressing surprise at seeing Mr Guthrie. 'I thought

Eleanor would be with you, Jonas,' she said. 'She went to the house some time ago to look for you. She had something to tell you.'

'I was up at Badgers' Farm. One of the workers has had an accident. She might have stayed to work in the library—she knows I need some help in cataloguing the books. What was it, do you know?'

'Mrs Anstey's daughter is said to be joining her soon. I have to say that I can hardly wait to see this beauty— Marianne, is it not?'

Mr Guthrie's face had clouded over at the news. 'I hope that it is indeed Marianne who is about to stay with her mother, but I doubt it,' he said. 'My information is that she is very happily established with the Morrisseys, and is unlikely to leave them much before her wedding.'

'But the other girl is in America!'

'The other *girls*. Amelia had three daughters. But yes, you're right. The other two stayed behind in America. And I had hoped that they would remain there.'

'One of the two is Evadne Oliver, if you will forgive my mentioning the name. But who is the other?'

'Did Eleanor not tell you about Phoebe? I had thought she would.'

'Eleanor doesn't tell you everything,' said Mrs Southeran with a small smile. 'Would I be shocked if she did?'

'Not as far as her personal well-being is concerned,' Mr Guthrie replied swiftly. 'But, as you know, there are episodes in my life which are of doubtful merit, to say the least. I was certain that she would tell you that I was once engaged to Phoebe Anstey.'

'Some day I hope you will find your way to telling us about your various relationships with the Anstey family, Jonas. They do seem to be a little confused. But

I know that day is still in the future—I am not about to tease you.'

'The matter of my engagement is perfectly straightforward. It was a mistake. I came from India to Boston with money enough to establish myself and a desire to settle. It all seemed to fit very well. Phoebe Anstey was not only Amelia's daughter—she was just seventeen years old and the loveliest thing I had seen in many a long year. I was completely dazzled by her.' He paused, smiling at the picture in his mind.

'What happened?'

'What? Oh, it was the usual story. I should have had more sense—I was, after all, nearly thirty! It didn't take long for me to find out that we were totally unsuited, and for a while I was in a real dilemma. But Phoebe met a young sprig—a member of what you might call the Boston aristocracy—'

'I wouldn't be surprised to hear that you had arranged that meeting, Jonas.'

He smiled, but went on without comment. 'He was mad for her, and the upshot was that she asked me to release her. So I did—with great relief. I don't think I can ever have been really in love with her. But, by God, she was a stunner.'

'Are you in love with Eleanor?'

If Eleanor's mother had hoped to surprise an answer out of him with the suddenness of her question she was disappointed. He stood in thought for a moment, then looked at her, still without saying anything.

'I have my responsibilities as Eleanor's mother, Jonas, and you spend a great deal of time with her,' said Mrs Southeran, for once absolutely serious. 'You have assured me that she will come to no harm in your company, and I believe you. But there are dangers other than physical ones in any relationship. Eleanor is still a child in matters of the heart, and I think I am justified in asking you what might seem otherwise an impertinent question.'

'I don't deny your right to ask. You have been more than kind in allowing me to share Eleanor's company, and I…I have been grateful for the trust this showed you have in me. I want to be honest with you, even if what I say sounds unworthy of a sensible man. The fact is, I don't know. The feeling I have for her is totally unlike any I have ever experienced before.'

'Not love?'

'I don't think it can be. It's certainly not what I have understood to be love before. I enjoy her company enormously; I enjoy talking to her, seeing things through her eyes, hearing what she has to say. In some ways she's like the best friend a man could have—certainly better than any I have known.'

'Friendship, then?'

'That's not quite it either! There's more to it than that… She has this strange effect on me. There have been times when her obstinacy, her impetuosity have infuriated me to such an extent that I've believed I want never to see her again, then I find myself missing her, and I have to seek her out. And sometimes I suddenly find her completely bewitching. It's a damnable way to be.'

'Poor Jonas!' said Mrs Southeran, beginning to smile.

'You may find it amusing, but I certainly do not. A man doesn't reach my age without having met some women—Phoebe Anstey was one of them—whom he thinks he might marry. But there was never any ambiguity about my feelings for them—no half-tones, no indecision. That's not my way. And after the initial attraction had worn off I knew pretty soon that I didn't want any of them—they bored me beyond measure. But Eleanor... Eleanor doesn't fit! Can you understand that? Can you make sense of it? I wish I could.'

Mrs Southeran said again, 'Poor Jonas! But I'm afraid I can't help you—you'll have to work it out for yourself. Meanwhile I should like you to make certain that you do not hurt Eleanor. She's...vulnerable, whether she realises it or not.' She turned as the maid came into the room.

'If you please, ma'am, Daniel would like a word with Mr Guthrie. He's outside.'

'Bring him in, Betty.'

'I...I can't do that, ma'am. He's in the stables with one of the horses.'

Mr Guthrie rose and, with a word of apology, strode out of the room. Daniel was in the yard, attempting to soothe a bay mare.

'What is it, man?'

'Miss Nell's horse, sir—'er come into the yard just a moment ago. In a rare old state, 'er is. Look at them reins. I asked Bet to get you to come out 'ere. I didn't want to upset the mistress.'

'You did right. Go up to the house and tell them to saddle Captain. Tell the lad to get one or two of the men from the home farm to join me at the house in five minutes. Off you go, Daniel—I must have a word with Mrs Southeran.'

As Mr Guthrie came into the room again Mrs Southeran stood up. 'It's Eleanor, isn't it? I knew there was something wrong. She's not in your library, she's missing.'

'What makes you think that?'

'Don't treat me like a fool, Jonas! Why else would Daniel wish to see you outside? He was probably trying to protect me, as you are.'

Mr Guthrie took her hands in a firm grasp. 'She apparently went riding this afternoon. I've asked Daniel to get some of the men, and we're going to look for her. She won't be far—the Stanyards estate is not that vast, and she seldom goes anywhere else. We'll find her.'

He left the room again without another look, and Mrs Southeran sank back on to her sofa, covering her face with her hands. But after a few moments she stood up and calmly went to call Betty.

'Miss Eleanor will perhaps want some attention when she returns, Betty. Make sure her room is ready for her.' Then she went back to stand by the window.

It was getting cold. The sun didn't reach this part of the combe and the spray from the churning water had made her clothes damp. She must have been here for hours! Where was Mr Guthrie? Eleanor began to get worried. She had tried several times to move her legs, or to shift the block of wood which lay on them. But every attempt had ended in failure and an attack of dizziness. What if no one came…? That was nonsense! Mr Guthrie had seen her—he had been there on the hill when the bridge collapsed; he had even waved.

She lay back again. She would count to a hundred— perhaps that would calm her. One, two, three… The yellow among the hart's tongue ferns was tormentil. A pretty little flower. Four, five, six, seven… How could anyone feel as sick as she felt and yet be hungry? It must be getting quite late. Surely her mother would be worried by now? Eight, nine, ten… This was ridiculous—she wasn't feeling any calmer, in fact, quite the reverse. In a moment she might do something foolish, like screaming or shouting. How Aunt Hetty would scold if she heard—

Wait! Was that the sound of men's voices? She *would* scream and shout. Lifting herself as upright as possible, she called with all her strength. Her voice sounded pathetically feeble, and the effort caused her to feel dizzy again, but she forced herself to try once more.

'Oh, my God! The bridge! What in the name—? She's here! She's down here! Daniel! Silas! Over here!' Mr Guthrie came sliding down the slope on the far side of the combe. Heedless of rocks and water, he leapt over to the outcrop of rock near her, taking care not to touch the precariously balanced platform on which she lay. 'Eleanor!'

'I thought you'd never come back!' Shivering and trembling, she could hardly get the words out. 'I'm trapped.'

'So I see. No, don't touch that beam, you fool!' This was to Silas, who was trying to lift one of the pieces of wood on top of her legs. 'Can't you see that'll bring the other lot down? Get a block from the pile over there and wedge the others up. Hurry!'

Gingerly he stepped on to the platform and crouched down by Eleanor. He touched her face and Eleanor noticed with surprise that his hand was trembling. 'Are you in pain?'

'My ankle hurts—I think the beam struck it when it fell. But I'm all right otherwise, I think. It's just that I'm trapped…'

'I know, I know,' he said. 'It's a devilish feeling. A few minutes—that's all we need. You'll soon be out, my poor girl.' He held Eleanor firmly, and gave directions to the men, but in the end he grew impatient with their struggles to place the block. 'Here, Daniel. You hold Miss Nell! Careful now!' He gave Eleanor's shoulder a slight squeeze, smiling down at her. 'Don't worry. It'll soon be over, my love. Hold her carefully, Daniel, and when I say "Go!" you pull her gently out. Gently, mind!'

He rejected the blocks the men had taken, choosing instead smaller ones. He gradually placed one upon another until the weight was off the beam which was holding Eleanor down. Then he took hold of it. 'Are you ready, Daniel?' Daniel nodded. 'Very gently, remember! Silas, you keep an eye on those blocks! Go!'

With a Herculean effort Mr Guthrie lifted the beam a fraction. Daniel edged Eleanor out, but, though he was as gentle as anyone could have desired, the movement was too much. Eleanor could not hold back a cry of anguish as her foot was dragged free. The platform rocked dangerously as Mr Guthrie swore at Daniel, let the beam down again and came back to crouch at Eleanor's side. 'Steady, my love! We're nearly there. I'll have to lift you in a moment, but I want to feel if there are any broken bones first. Understood?' She nodded, and gentle hands ran over her body. 'I think you're all right, apart from your ankle. Can you sit up?'

Slowly, carefully, Eleanor was carried on to the bank. Here she was set down again, and the men were dispatched to fetch the horses. Because of the loss of the bridge they would have to make a detour to bring them over a causeway further downstream. Soon, Mr Guthrie and Eleanor were alone. He looked with concern at her pale cheeks. 'How can I make you comfortable? Here, I'll put my coat round you. That might stop some of the shivering.'

'But you'll be cold,' protested Eleanor through chattering teeth.

'Nonsense, put it on! May I look at that ankle? I could bind it up so that it can't move so freely. It might save some of the pain.' Though he removed her boot with utmost care, she had to bite her lip to stop herself from crying out again. He worked steadily, keeping his eyes on what he was doing, and when the foot was clear he took off his cravat and wound it carefully round the damaged ankle. Only then did he look up at her face, which was chalk-white. 'Good girl!' he said softly. 'Now we have to wait—and I shall make sure you are warm.'

So saying, he picked her up and settled them both against a boulder, holding her close to him. Cradled in his arms, wrapped in his coat, Eleanor gradually forgot her aching head and throbbing ankle. A feeling of warm contentment overtook her. For the moment she wanted nothing more than to stay there in a half-sleep, listening to the steady beat of his heart. Her eyes closed…

'You should have stayed with me,' she murmured.

'I have stayed with you. The horses are being fetched by the men. They won't be long.'

'No, I meant before. You were looking at me when I fell.'

'Where was I?'

She chuckled sleepily. 'On the hill, of course. You waved. I suppose you were in a hurry to fetch help—but I wish you had told me. And it seemed a very long time before you came back.' Her voice faded and she closed her eyes again. 'I'm glad you're here now,' she murmured.

'So am I. Try to rest till the men return.' His voice was calm and deep, and Eleanor gave a little sigh of contentment. But there was a frown on Mr Guthrie's face as he gazed into the growing darkness.

When Mr Guthrie visited Eleanor the next morning he found her on her mother's sofa, her foot in a large bandage, but looking very much her normal self. 'I wish to heaven Daniel would hurry with that crutch, Mama. Can you not find him and tell him so?'

'I am glad to see you, Jonas. This daughter of mine is driving me frantic. Have you seen Daniel on your way here? He is supposed to be fetching a crutch for Eleanor from Dr Smithson, and madam here cannot wait. Not that I shall allow her to use it for a least another day.'

Mr Guthrie smiled at Eleanor's wail of protest. 'How is she? None the worse for her escapade if the strength of her voice is anything to go by.'

'Dr Smithson said that I had had a lucky escape. The ankle is merely sprained—my riding boot protected the foot from worse damage. I shall be perfectly fit to walk with a crutch today, Mama.'

'And what about the rest? He said that one or two of the smaller bones might possibly be cracked. Eleanor should rest that foot for at least a week, Jonas. But I know she won't, the silly girl.'

'This is a rare situation! I find myself acting the role of peacemaker. If you will lend me your daughter, ma'am, I could do with more help in the library at Stanyards. I haven't time myself to work indoors at the moment—it's a busy time on the estate, as you know. But I'd like someone I can trust to list some books properly before I send them off to London. Wilkes hasn't yet finished with the first lot, but I have now found more which are in need of attention. The listing could easily be done by someone with one foot on a stool, and I could get Silas or one of the others to pack them up. After that is done there's still the cataloguing. What do you think?'

Neither lady was perfectly happy with the arrangement, but it was finally agreed upon as a suitable compromise. It was decided that Eleanor should be conveyed to the library the following afternoon, unless her crutch proved to be more difficult to manage than she thought. For a while it looked as if the whole arrangement would founder on the question of the stairs, but luckily Mrs Southeran recalled that all of Eleanor's needs could be met on the first floor of Stanyards, and if she was carried up at the beginning and down at the end of each session with the books she could manage otherwise with her crutch. Mr Guthrie promised to supply a bell for her to ring for help. The housekeeper or one of the maids would always be on hand.

Eleanor had some questions for Mr Guthrie, but she had to wait. The last thing she wanted to do was to cause her mother any anxiety, and there was a mystery about the accident in the combe which was disquieting. She did manage to say, 'I must thank you, sir, for rescuing me last night. I think you were just in time. I was about to give way to most unheroic tears! Why were you so long?'

'Eleanor! Jonas hurried out and set off to rescue you as soon as Daniel showed him your horse. If it seemed a long time before you were found, then I suppose I am to blame. I told Jonas you were probably in the library, so we didn't at first miss you. How can you be so ungrateful?'

Mr Guthrie was frowning, and Eleanor decided to hold her tongue. She would tackle him later.

The next day at two Eleanor was ceremoniously driven to Stanyards' front door, where the master of the house was waiting to receive her. He lifted her out and set her carefully down, holding her steady until she was handed her crutch by a grinning Daniel. Then he said; 'Let me see you walk.'

'Here?' asked Eleanor, startled.

'It's flat, and relatively smooth. I want to see that you can manage before you go near the first floor.'

'Otherwise?'

'I will send you back to practise some more. Come on, my girl. Off you go!'

On her mettle, Eleanor made her way over the hall to the foot of the stairs, then turned and looked challengingly at him. 'Well?' she said.

'Very good! I'll let you stay.' He swung her into his arms again, and carried her up the stairs, ignoring her protests.

'You shouldn't be doing this! I thought you'd get Silas or one of the others to take me upstairs. Daniel would help.'

'I wanted to make sure it could be done. Now do be quiet. I can't carry you and talk at the same time… How do you like your throne?' He had rigged up a makeshift desk which extended over an armchair and footstool. It stood in one of the window embrasures, so there was plenty of light, and chair and footstool were covered in cushions and shawls. Eleanor laughed when she saw it.

'No maharanee could ask for a better one,' she said gaily.

'Right, then I will leave you. I believe everything is to hand—books, paper, pen and ink, sand, bell. Yes, it's all there. In any case, you can send for anything you need. Work well!'

'Wait!' she cried as he turned to go. 'We must talk about what happened in the combe.'

He came back to her chair, looking almost reluctant. 'I thought you would rather forget it.'

'What nonsense! How could anyone ignore what happened? I think I was lucky to escape with a damaged ankle. I think… I think I could have been killed, Jonas.'

He drew in a deep breath. 'Yes,' he said. 'Yes, I realise that. It…it was a shock. It made me realise…' He turned away from her. After a pause he said, 'I should have made more certain that that bridge was safe.'

There was a significant silence. 'That may be a suitable tale for my mother, Mr Guthrie, but it isn't enough for me. And it isn't worthy of you. You know that the wood in that bridge was sound and the bridge itself perfectly safe—until its supports were sawn through.'

'What rubb—' Mr Guthrie began, but he stopped when he saw Eleanor's expression. He went on, 'I hoped you hadn't noticed—you were injured and only half conscious most of the time. I suppose I should have known better. You don't usually miss much.'

'I may have been out of sorts but my wits were still sound! I know the difference between rotten wood and sawn wood!'

'A most unusual attribute in a lady,' he said with a smile.

'I don't want compliments, Mr Guthrie. I want to know why someone wanted to kill me.' She looked at him and realisation dawned. She said slowly, 'I wasn't the one it was meant for. It was for you!'

'What nonsense!' he said, but Eleanor was not to be put off.

'Someone is trying to kill you,' she said slowly.

'Some gypsy with a grudge—'

'No! The same thing happened in London—that wire. You said at the time that there had been a man...watching.' She held his gaze. 'It wasn't you on that hill, was it?'

'I wasn't there, no. Are you sure you saw someone?'

'Of course I am,' she said impatiently. 'But I couldn't say what he looked like. The sun was in my eyes, and I thought it was you. I suppose he must have been fairly tall. He...'

'Yes?'

'I have the impression that he favoured one leg slightly. I remember thinking that you must have hurt yourself running down the hill.'

'I see.' A quiet statement, but Eleanor was convinced that her description had meant something to him. He gave a deep sigh, then said, 'I think you'll be safe enough here. Mrs Cartwright is near by and she'll make sure that either Dora or Annie is within call. Silas won't be far away—nor will Daniel if I know him!'

'Surrounded by an army,' she said. 'But what about you?'

'I can't stay. There's a deal of work to be done. That's why you're doing this for me.'

'That isn't what I meant. What about your safety?'

He got up and crouched down beside her chair.

'I can take care of myself—especially as I now know...'

'Know what?'

'Never mind. But I will be careful.' He bent forward and lightly touched her lips with his. 'Since the day before yesterday I know what I wish to live for.'

She held him when he would have moved away. 'Take care! Please take care.'

He looked down at her troubled face, then put his hands round it and suddenly kissed her again, with more feeling. Eleanor clung to his arms, murmuring his name. Passion suddenly flared up between them, a danger-ously exciting whirlwind, as, still holding her face in trembling hands, he kissed her again and again. Eleanor had never before been in the grip of such a strong emotion, and afterwards she was to remember with shame that she had not been the first to call a halt. He pulled away and stood looking at her flushed cheeks and trembling lips. 'I...I'm sorry, Eleanor,' he said. 'I forgot myself. I shouldn't have done that. Please forgive me. Try not to let it make a difference to our friendship, I beg you. That...is all I can offer you at the moment. Can you forgive me? Forget it, even?'

Eleanor nodded. She could not have spoken if her life had depended on it. He waited a little longer, then gave her a wry smile and went. She heard him calling to Annie to make sure that Miss Southeran had everything she needed.

Eleanor sat for some minutes waiting for the wild beating of her heart to slow down. Then she shook her head and tried to get on with her work. But Mr Guthrie's face kept coming between her eyes and the books, and when she found herself making the same mistake for the fourth time in succession she put down her pen and sat back to think.

She rather thought she had just tasted 'uncontrol-lable passion'. Mr Guthrie had been right that day in the drive—it was certainly not something to make jokes about. The loss of all thought, all self-control ... She hid her face in her hands. After a while she grew calmer and sat staring out at the view. Had Evadne Anstey experi-

enced the same uncontrollable passion…? It would
explain a lot. But what had happened after the passion
was spent? Why had the affair ended the way it had?

Eleanor uttered an impatient exclamation and took
herself to task. She would not allow herself to speculate, or become jealous. Friendship was what he offered,
in spite of that moment of madness. She must be content
with that. 'All I can offer you at the moment', he had
said. Did that mean…? No, she would not speculate!
She bent over her work again.

But it was no use. She had put one problem to the
back of her mind only to have another take its place.
She was full of apprehension. There was no doubt that
Jonas Guthrie's life was in danger, and she was certain he knew who was threatening it. He had known
as soon as she had told him about the limp. He had
not been surprised—it was as if he had been waiting
for confirmation, hoping even for something different.
The information had not been welcome—there had
been anger behind that quiet acceptance. She tried to
comfort herself with the thought that he would stand
a better chance of protecting himself now that he knew
where the threat lay.

At four o'clock she gave up trying to work and sent
for Silas. She hopped downstairs with his help and
waited in the sunshine while he fetched the little
carriage her father had used about the estate. She was
glad not to have to face Mr Guthrie again that day—she
was sure she could show him a calm demeanour,
suitable for friends, when they next met, but an extra day
would make it more secure.

Her mother was delighted to see her back so soon,
and attributed Eleanor's wan looks and subdued manner

to her experiences on the bridge. 'You will spend the rest of the evening on the sofa, my love.'

'But I do not wish to usurp your sofa, Mama! You need it more than I.'

'Do you know, Eleanor, I feel so much better now that we live here? I think I must have been suffering from the damp of Stanyards for years without realising it. No, my dear, your need is greater than mine. I knew you were over-eager to be on your feet again. Come, I shall get Betty to arrange the sofa near my desk and we can share the lamplight. Would you like to hear what I have written today?'

The peaceful atmosphere of her mother's sitting-room, the soft cadence of her mother's voice and the comforting light of the lamp did much to calm Eleanor's agitated mind. The violent emotion which had flared between herself and Mr Guthrie that afternoon had taken its toll, but it now seemed to belong to another world, insubstantial, like a dream. It was even more difficult to imagine that threats of danger and death could be real.

Chapter Nine

When Mr Guthrie called on them quite early the next day Eleanor discovered that she was not yet capable of facing him as calmly as she would have wished. She found him gazing at her with a smile in his eyes which raised a faint staining of colour in her pale cheeks. But when he then announced that he was paying a visit to London, she was startled into protest. 'What about all the work on the estate? You said it could not wait.'

'I know, Miss Southeran, it is very awkward. But it can't be helped. The matter is urgent. You, of course, will be able to continue with your work in the library—at least, I hope you will?'

'Not for a day or two, Jonas,' said Mrs Southeran in a voice which admitted no opposition. 'Eleanor was quite knocked up when she came back yesterday. She must rest a little longer. The work surely isn't that urgent?'

'Of course not, ma'am.' He turned back to Eleanor, his face full of concern. 'I'm sorry to hear you are not well. Even sorrier if I was to blame in any way. That is the last thing I would wish, I assure you. You must rest as long as you need, Miss Southeran, but when you do return I think I can promise you a comparatively peaceful time. Then when matters are clearer we can sort things out a little more. Are you content with that?'

'I think so,' replied Eleanor, managing a smile. 'Are you…are you planning to stay in London for long?'

'I hope not. But I will remain there until the matter is settled, and I'm not sure how long that will take.' He turned to Mrs Southeran. 'I shall let you know if I can. Now I shall have to leave you. Er…I have taken the liberty of telling my household that you are nominally in charge of the house and estate while I am away. Do you mind? The men know what to do, and there shouldn't be any difficulties.'

Mrs Southeran assured him that she was perfectly ready to step in, adding with a twinkle in her eye, 'And Eleanor, as you know, is always ready to take charge of Stanyards estate. I dare swear she will wish you to prolong your stay in London till Christmas.'

'Mama! That is not so!'

'Your mother knows that—she is teasing you. But I will call her bluff, Miss Southeran, and tell you that you are free to take charge whenever you wish. We have worked together long enough for me to have absolute confidence in your judgement.'

Mr Guthrie could not have paid Eleanor a compliment which pleased her more. It did a little to leaven the shock of his departure.

There was no opportunity for them to talk in private—nor would Eleanor have sought one. But she spent some time after he had gone touching her hand where had kissed it in farewell. Had he taken just a little longer than was conventional on such occasions? Or was she deceiving herself?

* ***

Mr Guthrie had taken no pains to conceal the fact that he was leaving for London. The whole county seemed to know—or so it seemed to Eleanor. She didn't know which she disliked more—the commiserations from those who thought she would miss him, or the congratulations from those who believed that the ladies in the Dower House would be happier without him. Of course there were others who ascribed Mr Guthrie's sudden removal to London to the arrival in Somerset of not one but two of Mrs Anstey's daughters.

The neighbourhood had been agog to see for itself the much famed beauty of Marianne Anstey. After all, though practically penniless herself, she had captured the heart of one of London's most eligible bachelors. And when, the day after Mr Guthrie's departure, a handsome chaise drew up outside Church Cottage, those who were fortunate enough to be near by were not disappointed. Out stepped an exquisite vision dressed all in white—from her French silk bonnet with its flourish of ostrich plumes, down to the white leather slippers on her tiny feet. Face and hair were hidden by the bonnet, but the lady's figure was gracefully elegant, and her voice musical. She was accompanied by two grooms, her maidservant, and another lady, dressed more soberly in grey. It was a long time since Combe St James had seen such an elegant equipage, such an impressive retinue, and there was some speculation as to whether Miss Marianne had already married her viscount. But in that case where was her husband?

Quiet Mrs Anstey was showered with invitations, many of which she had to refuse. The newcomers were not seen in public for some days—it was said that they had found the exertions of the journey too much, and were resting. Confused reports began to circulate, centring on the identity of the lady in grey. At first she was generally thought to be a companion for Marianne. Then it was said that Mrs Phoebe Gardiner, Mrs Anstey's eldest daughter, who had recently been widowed, had travelled with her sister. Then Mrs Desmond told Cousin Louisa she had it on the best authority that Evadne Oliver had come to see her mother. Which sister was the lady who had travelled with Marianne Anstey? Combe St James had to possess its soul in patience and wait for the ladies—and the truth—to emerge.

Eleanor had been surprised to find how much she missed Mr Guthrie, and it took some determination to ignore the ache in her heart, to put a swift end to occasional bouts of daydreaming, and to concentrate on the work in the library. Her foot had now nearly recovered, but Dr Smithson had advised her to continue to rest it, so even the solace of riding round the estate was denied her. Mrs Southeran was immersed in her writing. She was absorbed in an assignment for a prestigious literary review, and had little time for neighbourhood gossip.

So the two Southerans, living as they did some way from the village, were spared most of Combe St James' excitement about Mrs Anstey's visitors. In any case, their known support for Mr Guthrie made their position uncertain. But when Eleanor heard the debate about the second visitor, she was consumed with curiosity. Evadne or Phoebe—she would find either of them interesting and wished she could meet whichever one it was. In the event, she was one of the first to find out.

About ten days after Mr Guthrie's departure Eleanor was working as usual on the catalogue when a movement behind her caused her to turn round. At first sight she thought Marianne Anstey was standing in the doorway, but she quickly decided that she was mistaken. There was a self-possession, an awareness of her own charms about the figure in the doorway which was alien to Marianne's modest, slightly hesitant demeanour. This was no girl, this was a mature, self-confident young woman.

Eleanor started to get up, but the desk hampered her movements. 'Please don't!' said the woman in the doorway, and she came into the room. 'Don't let me interrupt you—it's unusual to see a female doing the work of a secretary. Are you a relation of Jonas's?'

'My name is Southeran. Eleanor Southeran.'

The Southeran name clearly meant nothing to the visitor. 'Are you his housekeeper? Though it's unusual work for… Oh, forgive me. You are perhaps—er—his guest? A dear friend, perhaps?'

This time Eleanor succeeded in standing. She said with all the dignity she could muster, 'My family owned the Stanyards estate, including a library of rare books, before Mr Guthrie bought it earlier this year. I have offered to catalogue the books for him.'

One finely arched eyebrow was raised in surprise. 'That seems very obliging of you. I'm afraid I would find such work terribly dull. But you must excuse my remark of a moment ago. I was trying to place you, and I'm afraid that I made a…a *faux pas*. One never knows, does one?'

Eleanor ignored the slightly ambiguous remark and said politely, 'You must in turn forgive me. I am afraid I don't know your name, though I think you must be Marianne Anstey's sister—you are very like her in looks. I am surprised that the housekeeper didn't announce you—she is normally the soul of propriety.'

'I am Phoebe Gardiner, and you are right—I am one of Marianne's sisters. And I'm afraid I didn't see anyone when I came in. The door downstairs was open, so I simply walked up. I knew Jonas wouldn't mind, and I wanted to see him.'

'I'm afraid he isn't here.'

'So I observe. Will he be long? Or don't you know?'

'He is in London.'

A small frown, quickly erased, wrinkled the perfection of Phoebe's brow. 'How tiresome.' She came in and wandered round the room, lifting her skirt and stepping delicately, like a cat. 'How dusty it is in here!'

'Libraries often are!' said Eleanor drily.

Phoebe came to a halt by the window at the end of the room. 'Where do you live?'

'I am surprised that it should interest you, Mrs Gardiner. But I live in the Dower House on the estate. You can see it from that window.' Phoebe looked out at the handsome building a little distance away. She came towards Eleanor, who was standing stiffly by her chair.

'I've made you angry,' she said, charmingly rueful. 'I'd forgotten my manners—in America we tend to be less formal, you see. Forgive me, Miss Southeran. Please?' This was accompanied by a delightful smile, a smile which Eleanor found impossible to resist.

She said in a warmer tone, 'Would you like to sit, Mrs Gardiner? The chair next to mine is reasonably free of dust, I think. Or would you prefer to—?'

'No, I'd like to sit next to you.' She took one of her gloves off and dusted the seat of the chair, then sat down carefully, arranging her dress as she did so. 'You have no idea what a nuisance it is always to have to wear white, Miss Southeran. The slightest speck of dirt shows so! Some days I change five or six times—seven, even!'

'I'll send for some tea,' said Eleanor, picking up her bell. 'Or would you prefer some lemonade?'

'Lemonade would be perfectly lovely—I never drink tea; it's bad for the complexion. Thank you.'

'Why must you always wear white?' asked Eleanor, settling herself in her chair again once the refreshments had been served.

Phoebe opened her eyes wide and said, 'Why, Miss Southeran, because I'm in mourning, of course. I lost my dearest husband not a year ago. And no one could expect me to wear black all the time—or even at all. It simply washes me out. No, I prefer to mourn Gilbert in purest white. He always liked me in white—or blue. Perhaps I could wear blue sometimes? What do you think?'

Eleanor began to enjoy herself. She was not really sure whether her extraordinary visitor meant what she said, or was asking her to share in a huge joke. One thing was certain: Phoebe did not seem to be unduly saddened by her husband's demise.

'If you don't think me impertinent, Mrs Gardiner, I would say that you would look ravishing in whatever colour you chose to wear.' Her visitor flushed with delight at this perfectly genuine compliment, but she shuddered when Eleanor added, 'Black or possibly purple or grey are more usually considered to be mourning colours in England.'

'It is quite out of the question,' Phoebe said with determination, 'that I should ever be seen in purple or grey. No one who knows me could possibly ask it. No, I shall have to stay with white. Does Jonas help you when you are working here?'

'Mr Guthrie is seldom in the house. He spends most of his time out of doors—there's a great deal to do.'

'And he enjoys doing it. He hasn't changed,' said Phoebe. 'Do you know, Miss Southeran, Jonas Guthrie was one of the richest men in Boston, but he was never content to behave like a gentleman?'

'Whatever do you mean?' asked Eleanor, startled into disapproval.

'Oh, goodness, gracious, I've upset you again! Please don't misunderstand me! He was always perfectly proper. I only meant that he was never content to sit back and enjoy himself. He always had to be busy, always having ideas. Quite exhausting. We were engaged once, Jonas and I, you know.'

'Really?' murmured Eleanor.

'Yes.' Mrs Gardiner smiled reminiscently. 'I was just seventeen, a mere child. He said he was dazzled by me. That was his very word, Miss Southeran. "Dazzled".'

'That is hardly surprising, Mrs Gardiner.'

'You are kind to say so. Marianne is generally held to be the family beauty now. What a match she has made! If only…'

The tiny frown returned and disappeared again. 'But there! She deserves it—she is a gem.' There was a short silence.

'You were talking of your engagement to Mr Guthrie?' said Eleanor, trying hard not to sound as if the matter was of any personal interest.

'Oh, yes! I was painfully young, of course. Far too young to appreciate Jonas's real worth. When I met Gilbert—Mr Gardiner—he seemed to be so much gentler, so much easier to talk to. He liked me as I was, too, whereas Jonas was always trying to make me into something different. So I asked to be released from our engagement. It was a big mistake.'

'The engagement?'

'No! Asking Jonas to release me. He was so very gallant about it, too. He must have suffered, Miss Southeran, but I was too young to notice. It would be different now.'

'But what about your husband, Mr Gardiner? Were you not, after all, happy with him?'

'I was *very* happy with him,' said Mrs Gardiner, opening gentian-blue eyes wide again. 'But he was in a stupid street accident and died before we had any children.'

'How…how sad,' said Eleanor, feeling the response to be inadequate, but at a loss to think of anything more suitable.

'Yes, it was. If he had lived a little longer, or if we had had an heir to the Gardiner fortune, I shouldn't be forced to live on a widow's jointure—the merest pittance, Miss Southeran. Gilbert never had any money of his own, you see. His father made us an allowance.'

Eleanor looked at the Parisian bonnet, the fashionable dress and the fine white kid of Phoebe's shoes and concluded that the pittance couldn't be all that meagre. But she decided to say nothing. Her visitor seemed to feel that Eleanor's silence expressed disapproval.

'I hope you don't think me disloyal to my darling Gilbert's memory—I was truly very upset by his death.' She took out a minute lace handkerchief and dabbed at her eyes. Eleanor had a sudden picture of Mrs Anstey making much the same gesture at their first meeting. She was thinking that perhaps Phoebe Gardiner was not so very different from her mother when, with a lightning change of mood, Phoebe said briskly, 'But you should not allow me to run on in this fashion, Miss

Southeran. I have decided that the future is what I must think of now—I must put the sad past behind me.' She smiled bravely and went on, 'When will Jonas return from London, do you know?' thus making it quite clear where she thought her future might lie.

'I'm afraid I have no idea,' said Eleanor politely.

'It's very vexing. I could have stayed on with my cousins and seen Jonas at the same time. London is sadly empty of people of consequence, but there were one or two…' She sat in thought for a moment and then said with decision, 'I shall stay a little longer in Somerset in case he returns, and then I shall go back to Berkeley Square.' She gave Eleanor another of her enchanting smiles. 'May I call on you at your home?'

'I am sure that my mother would be delighted to make your acquaintance.' This was no less than the truth. Eleanor was quite certain that her mother would never forgive her if she was deprived of meeting this fascinating creature. 'Er…would Mrs Anstey like to accompany you? Or is there someone else—your companion, perhaps?'

'My companion? Oh, you mean Mrs Oliver, my sister? I shall ask them, of course, but I doubt they will come. To tell truth, I am really quite concerned about them, Miss Southeran. My mother is fast becoming a recluse, and Evadne is little better.'

A certain delicacy prevented Eleanor from suggesting a reason for Evadne Oliver's desire for seclusion. But the thought that the key to the whole mystery of Mr Guthrie's involvement with the Anstey family might be residing in Church Cottage, Combe St James was irresistibly intriguing. However, since it was impossible to ask Phoebe to be as frank about her sister's situation as she had been about her own, Eleanor decided to let matters take their course.

'Then do try to persuade them to come,' was all she replied.

They decided on a date and a time and Phoebe then shook out her skirts energetically, looked with distaste at the marks on her gloves, and left.

Once again Eleanor abandoned her work in order to think of Jonas Guthrie. What would these arrivals mean to him? Phoebe made no secret of the fact that she intended to rectify the mistake she had made in her youth. Would Jonas be dazzled once again? On the whole, Eleanor thought it unlikely. She felt she knew the man sufficiently well to doubt that such a shallow, self-centred nature would attract him, any more than it had in the past.

But who could say? Phoebe Gardiner's beauty, her enchanting smile, might charm anyone into forgetting her shortcomings. She would certainly make a fitting jewel in a rich man's crown. Was that what Jonas might decide? Eleanor grew cold at the thought. But what right had she, Eleanor, to expect anything? Jonas Guthrie had never given her any unequivocal reason to hope, only hints. Friendship was what he had offered her—'for the moment'. What *had* he meant by that?

In London the subject of Eleanor's thoughts attacked the business on hand with his usual brisk energy. Some of what he did was what might have been expected of a prosperous man of affairs. He sought out acquaintances at the Foreign Office, he consulted lawyers and visited his bank, he sent off detailed messages to Boston—all this he did quite openly, with the air of a man who knew exactly what he was doing and why.

But some of his other activities were distinctly strange. He seemed to be conscious of this fact, for he took some pains to keep them out of the public eye. One could not blame him for this, for it was hardly the thing for a respectable man of business to spend time in the less salubrious quarters of London, making enquiries in disreputable inns and taverns, and talking to some very questionable characters—obviously seafaring men— on the wharves and docksides of London. Moreover his constant companion on these expeditions was a man whose appearance and accomplishments would clearly be more suited to a dockside fight than to a soirée or a rout party.

Mr Guthrie eventually seemed satisfied with his labours and returned to his cousins' house in Berkeley Square to await results. Meanwhile he was visited here by agents and architects—he was clearly intending to buy a house in London, and the few members of society left in the capital in September started to speculate on the name of the lady he was intending to invite to share it.

He also seemed to have developed a taste for gambling, winning and losing considerable sums at Brooks, Whites and other, less reputable gambling hells in Pall Mall. It was interesting that though, of course, his erstwhile companion in the darker quarters of London was not to be seen in such elevated company, he was never very far away when Mr Guthrie finally emerged from these pleasure spots.

Eventually Mr Guthrie's patience was rewarded.

'Oliver, my dear fellow!' he said one evening to one of his fellow gamblers, clapping him on the back.

Nathaniel Oliver, a handsome, dark-haired man of middle height, turned swiftly round. 'Oh—er—it's you, Guthrie. Good evening to you.'

'What a fortunate chance that we've met! Come and join me in a glass of wine, Oliver, and you can give me all your news. Come, I insist.' Mr Guthrie took Mr Oliver's arm and led him firmly to a small table in one of the alcoves. Here he ordered a bottle of Burgundy and poured a generously filled glass for his guest and himself.

Mr Oliver seemed to gain some comfort from the wine. 'I didn't expect to see you in London, Guthrie,' he said, sitting back in a more relaxed attitude.

'Didn't you, my dear chap?' said Mr Guthrie genially. 'A pleasant surprise for both of us, then. I quite thought you were in Somerset.'

'Somerset? Why?' said Mr Oliver sharply.

'To be with your wife. What else? From what I hear, she's visiting Amelia in Combe St James. Am I right?'

'Yes, of course. I shall be joining her in a few days.'

'And meanwhile you're enjoying the fleshpots before returning to the bosom of your family. I quite understand. How are they?'

'Who?'

'Why, your wife and the little fellow.'

'They're well,' said Mr Oliver shortly. 'But we've left the boy behind in Boston with his nurse. It's too far to bring him to England, and he isn't strong.'

'So I had heard.'

'You've heard? How?'

'I keep in touch. After all, it's natural I should take an interest in the child, wouldn't you say? But you're not drinking, my dear fellow.' He poured another generous glass. 'You seem on edge, Oliver. Are you waiting for someone? Christopher Digby, perhaps?'

'Christopher?'

Mr Guthrie leant forward, his voice full of concern.

'That's the third or fourth time you've repeated what I've said, Oliver. Are you suffering a little in your hearing? You should get it seen to—before it is too late.'

'There's nothing wrong with my hearing,' said Mr Oliver coldly. 'Or with my memory, either, so don't try threatening me. I believe we made a bargain in Boston.'

'We did indeed. Recently I've been wondering whether you remember the terms.'

Mr Oliver leaned back and said, 'I don't know what you mean, Guthrie. What the devil are you talking about? I've kept my side of it. I married Evadne, and I've kept silent on…certain matters. That hasn't changed.'

Mr Guthrie was nodding. 'And in return I paid you a sum of money—quite a large sum. And more was settled on Evadne and the child. Do you remember what I said at the time?'

'No, I don't. But I dare swear you are about to tell me.'

Mr Guthrie leaned forward till his face was close to Mr Oliver's. 'I said that I wasn't a man who submitted easily to blackmail; that on this occasion you had me in a cleft stick where I was forced to go along with it, but that didn't make me like it.'

Mr Oliver said, with a mocking smile, 'My dear fellow, do forgive me! But where is all this leading? I wasn't interested in your feelings at the time, and am even less so now.'

'I said, Oliver, that if you did anything more, if that wasn't the end of the matter, one payment, one agreement, then the bargain was null and void.'

'I still don't see…?'

'I was willing to give you my reputation along with the money. I am not willing to give you my life.'

'Your life? You must be mad! What would I want

with your life?' Mr Oliver had gone slightly pale, but he was still apparently at ease. 'We have never liked each other, Guthrie, but this is going beyond what is tolerable. What are you accusing me of?'

'Greed. Folly.'

'Folly?'

'It was foolish to persuade Christopher to come down to Somerset. It must have been against his better judgement. Did he tell you that I warned him after the first attempt on my life here in London what would happen if he tried again?'

'I don't know what you're talking about.'

'Then I am sorry for you. The game is over, Oliver. Take Evadne back to Boston and patch up what you can.'

Mr Oliver got up and walked away, giving Mr Guthrie a malevolent look as he went. At the door he was met by a tall, young-looking man, handsome and well-built, whose only physical flaw seemed to be a very slight limp… Mr Oliver took his arm and they hurried away, deep in conversation.

In the early hours of the morning there was a slight disturbance outside the small inn where Mr Oliver was staying—not enough to disturb the guests, certainly not Mr Oliver. Some seafaring gentlemen seemed to have drunk a trifle too much—indeed one of their band could hardly walk. They were making their way back to their ship—an East Indiaman, bound for Madras.

His work in London done, Mr Guthrie came back to Stanyards on a golden day early in September. The chestnut trees in the drive were heavy with fruit and their leaves were starting to turn. Gaps in their ranks reminded him that there was still a deal to do here at Stanyards. He breathed a deep sigh of satisfaction—a challenge was what he had asked for, and so far his work at Stanyards had been richly rewarding. There were glimpses through the trees of fields of pale gold corn, some already harvested. It had been a good year for the farms, and next year and the one after that would be even better, he was sure.

A flight of swallows swooped and wheeled over-head—they would soon make their long journey south. He was sorry to see them go, but they would be back next spring. He himself had no desire to leave Somerset again for any length of time. Occasional visits to London, perhaps—it was as well to keep one's hand in, so to speak. But voyages further afield, to America or India—those belonged to the past.

His lawyers and bankers in London had reminded him what a very rich man he was. His friends at the Foreign Office had made it clear that he could, if he wished, be a man of consequence, a friend of princes, could own a mansion in London and an imposing country seat, complete with an army of servants and hangers-on. A title was not out of the question.

But that was not what he wanted. Apart from a rela-tively small house near Grosvenor Square for occa-sional visits to London, the simple life he lived here at Stanyards would suit him very well. He would engage more servants—he had neglected the household side of affairs in favour of the estate—but his wife would be able to advise him on what was needed. His wife. That had a good sound to it. And if things went as planned he would be able to start acquiring a wife very soon.

He drew up at the front steps of Stanyards, where

Silas was waiting to take the horses and Mrs Cartwright was ready to welcome him back. There was none of the impassive, well-trained servant about Silas. His weatherbeaten face was covered in a huge smile of welcome. Even Mrs Cartwright, a woman of superior education and training, was permitting herself a discreet smile.

'Good day to you, Mrs Cartwright. How do you go on? And Silas—you're looking well. Give the horses a good watering and feed. I was so anxious to be home that I've driven them a little hard. Now, Mrs Cartwright, how are things at Stanyards?'

'Pretty fair, sir. The men have been doing the rooms upstairs. I'm afraid there's a bit of a mess. Would you like something to eat after your journey?'

'No, I ate on the way. Is Miss Southeran still at work in the library?'

'She has been, sir. But yesterday and today she has been out riding round the estate again. Dr Smithson says her foot is cured.'

'That's good news! Tell Silas I'd like Captain brought round in half an hour, would you?' said Mr Guthrie. 'And I'd like a can of hot water in my room as soon as possible—I need to tidy up. I suppose the room is free?'

'The men finished in there yesterday, sir. But you're surely not going out again after your journey?'

'I cannot wait to see what's been happening in my absence, Mrs Cartwright. Hurry up with that water!'

Chapter Ten

$\mathcal{E}$leanor had finished her tour of the estate and was at the combe. This was her second visit back to the scene of the accident. She had ridden over the day before, but her horse had balked every time she had attempted to cross the bridge. She should have insisted, and, failing that, she should have led Shanty across. But she had felt the same reluctance as the horse to set foot on the structure, even though she had been assured by the estate carpenters that it was completely safe again. So, ashamed of her fears of the day before, she was here to try again.

'Come, Shanty, we shall go together. That's right, straight on now…'

But the horse, sensing Eleanor's own feelings perhaps, stopped short where the plank roadway began. 'Shanty!' Eleanor dismounted and started to soothe the animal, to coax it on to the bridge. She was still engaged in doing this when Mr Guthrie rode up. He stopped and dismounted some distance away when he saw what was going on. Slowly, calmly, Eleanor urged Shanty forward. But, sensing Captain's presence, Shanty turned to see the newcomers. Eleanor gave an exasperated sigh and looked to see who had interrupted her efforts.

'Jonas!' Her frown instantly changed into an expression of joy and, heedless of all the rules of proper behaviour for a young lady, she dropped Shanty's rein and ran towards him. She was caught in his outstretched arms. 'You're back!' she said. 'Oh, what a stupid thing to say— of course you are; you wouldn't be here otherwise.'

When he raised an eyebrow and smiled down at her she grinned and said, 'You needn't look at me like that, Jonas; I know I'm babbling. It's the shock. We didn't expect you so soon.'

'I know I said I would let your mother know—but it seemed simpler to come myself. How are you? I see the ankle is better.'

Eleanor suddenly became aware that she was still clasped tightly in Mr Guthrie's arms and made to free herself. 'My ankle is perfectly cured. But you must let me go, Jonas,' she said nervously. 'It won't do!'

'Well, there's ingratitude! I catch you to prevent us both from being knocked over, hold you merely till you get your balance, and now you accuse me of… what, Eleanor?'

'Both of us suffer from lack of any sense of what is proper! I ought to be ashamed of myself… You took me by surprise, that is all.'

'I must surprise you more often,' he said, again with his particular, quizzical smile. 'But since you mention propriety…' He let her go. 'What were you doing with Shanty? Is she refusing the bridge?'

Eleanor explained her problem to him, including the fact that she was sure the horse could sense her own fear.

'Come, we shall walk across together first, and then

we shall lead both horses over. Give me your hand—if that won't offend your belated sense of propriety.'

Holding her hand in his warm, firm grip, he took her confidently across to the other side. Here he stopped and said, 'Well?'

'No shivers at all. Thank you.'

'Now for the horses. I'll go first with Captain. The lady will follow, don't you think?'

'In these circumstances, perhaps. I would not always agree, Mr Guthrie!'

'Concentrate on your horse, Eleanor. We shall fight other battles elsewhere.'

On the other side they let the horses loose to graze, and he stood for a moment looking at her. 'Hmm—a touch pale, now that the shock of seeing me has worn off. Have you been cooped up in the library for too long?'

'I suppose that is it. The records are almost finished.'

'Come, sit down here. I want to talk to you.' They settled themselves on a huge boulder near by. 'Do you remember when we were last here? This is the very rock I leant against, I believe. I have never admired you more than that night. You were wet, cold, and in pain. But you were so brave.'

'I don't remember being brave,' said Eleanor with a shudder. 'Towards the end, before you came, I remember being distinctly frightened. I thought it was you on the hillside, you see, and expected you to come to the rescue almost at once. It seemed like eternity before you did come. Jonas, you know who the man on the hillside was, don't you?'

'Yes,' he said grimly. 'Yes, I do. But you needn't be afraid he'll come back. I've dealt with him.'

A cold shiver went down Eleanor's spine at the tone

of Mr Guthrie's voice. She asked hesitantly, 'Why did he want to kill you?'

'It's a long story, Eleanor, and not a pleasant one. I might tell you some other time, but not here and now. Not when I've just come back to you and Stanyards.'

Eleanor gave a little nod. She said, 'And then afterwards—after you had found me here—I remember that you made me so comfortable with your coat and…the rest. I'm afraid it was less pleasant for you—this rock is very hard!'

'I was so…immeasurably glad to find you that I would cheerfully have put up with much worse. I shall never forget my first sight of you—lying there with that great beam across you. The only thing that kept me from complete panic was that I had heard you shout just a minute before.'

'You, nearly in a panic? I don't believe it!'

'You may do so. I've never known anything like it.'

They gazed at one another and suddenly they were in each other's arms, holding one another so tightly that Eleanor could hardly breathe. Mr Guthrie was murmuring her name, his voice trembling and hoarse. Then he released her slightly, but only in order to lift her face to his and cover her mouth with kisses. Eleanor thought vaguely, Uncontrollable passion— that's what this is. Now I know, before she was swept into a vortex of emotion in which she would willingly have drowned.

After some minutes he held her away from him and smiled at her again. Then he suddenly frowned and said, 'Your lips are bruised. I'm sorry. Does it hurt?'

'No,' said Eleanor dreamily. 'And I wouldn't mind if it did.'

He laughed delightedly. 'You're completely bewitching!' He caught her in his arms again and hugged her to him. Then he said firmly, 'But I mustn't hurt you any more. We must go back while we are still able to be sensible. I promised your mother…'

She looked up at him with a little question in her eyes. He groaned and said, 'Eleanor, I cannot say what I want to say to you until I have removed the shadows from my name and my life. Our lives. It shouldn't be long now. Will you wait?'

'I'll try,' said Eleanor with a sigh. 'If I must. But it's very hard.'

'I know,' he said. 'Believe me, Eleanor, I know very well. But it is essential.' He got up and began to walk towards the horses, which had wandered a little distance away. 'We must concentrate on other matters. Tell me about Stanyards.'

When Eleanor had caught up with him she said, 'There is something I want to ask you. When I went round the estate yesterday I heard something that I think must be wrong. The farmers are saying that you have given Threlfall notice to quit his farm by Michaelmas. Surely that isn't so?'

'It is. I told him before I left for London. He hasn't been making trouble, has he?'

'But his family has been on that farm for generations!'

'Well, I don't know about his forebears, but Threlfall is a poor farmer and a bad tenant. The estate will be well shot of him.'

'You can't throw him out! He has a wife and children.'

'From what I hear they'd be better off without him, too. He's a drunkard and a bully.'

'Jonas, I can't believe I'm hearing what my ears tell

me. Everyone now says what a good landlord you are. Why are you acting so ruthlessly?'

'Firstly because I am a good landlord, and cannot stand by while a good farm is neglected and unproductive. The whole estate suffers when one of its farms lies covered in weeds. And secondly, because I *am* ruthless. I've told you that before. When I see something that needs to be done, I do it.'

'You play to win. You said so in London soon after we met. But I thought… Please don't do this, Jonas! Not here at Stanyards.'

'Threlfall has had more warnings than I have ever given anyone before. Don't look at me like that, Eleanor! I am not altogether without a heart. Threlfall won't be completely homeless; I have set aside a cottage near the village for him and his family. He can do as he wishes—stay there, or if he chooses he can seek work elsewhere. I would be glad to see the back of him, and so, I suspect, would his wife.' He looked at Eleanor's downcast face. 'Don't let your heart rule your judgement, Eleanor. I thought you had outgrown that.'

'And I thought…' she said miserably.

'What? That, because of my feeling for you and your family, you could persuade me to do something that I know is wrong? No, that is not my way. I have fallen into that trap once before, and I won't let it happen again. Threlfall will go.'

Eleanor had been pale, but now she flushed in anger. She said sharply, 'Then since you have clearly made up your mind there is nothing more to be said. Forgive me for interfering. And now I have things to do—I must go back.'

She waited in silence while he helped her mount, rode off over the bridge without even noticing she was doing so, and galloped off. Mr Guthrie followed her with a face of thunder.

Eleanor now had Dr Smithson's permission to ride as much as she chose. She used her new freedom to go about the estate and learn more of the Threlfall affair. To her surprise, the farmers, even those who had been Threlfall's friends, were solidly in favour of his dismissal. In the days when everyone had done much as they pleased on their farms, Threlfall had been a leader. He had persuaded them that an easy life was better than a rich one, that to do the minimum required to keep the land marginally productive was better than to slave away—his words—to enrich the landlords.

But now his day was over. Mr Guthrie's coming had changed the spirit of the place and the farmers on Stanyards lands had come alive, were eager to work to profit both the landlord and themselves. Threlfall had failed to change with the others. He had always been ready to bluster, quick to feel aggrieved. Now he had made himself unpopular with everyone, including his long-suffering wife.

All this did not at first reconcile Eleanor to Mr Guthrie's action. Her crusading spirit, dormant under the happy time she had recently enjoyed on Stanyards, now came to life. She went to see Threlfall, and listened to his ramblings. She rode about his farm and saw the state it was in for herself. She discussed with him what could be done about it—without success, it might be said. In the end she found she had merely encouraged Threlfall to feel even more aggrieved at the high-handed action of the new landlord. He was now even more convinced that things would have turned out very differently under the old regime. Eleanor had to admit failure. The general view was that the master had acted very properly, generously even, in providing the Threlfall family with a home—and she was forced to agree.

She was now faced with the difficulty of conveying this change of heart to Mr Guthrie. She had not seen him since their quarrel at the combe—she had avoided meeting him. That quarrel. Such a short time before it they had been lost to the world in each other's arms— why had she even mentioned the name of Threlfall? They had been so close, and were now so far apart— and she knew that the bitterness between them when they parted had been caused by her lack of understanding, her lack of faith.

How could she best put things right between them? The memory of previous apologies kept intruding as she wrestled with the problem. But surely things were different now? Then she had merely been the daughter of an old friend. But now... Mr Guthrie might not have said in so many words that he was in love with her, but it had been implicit in all he had said and done. Yes, it would be different. She would just have to find the right occasion.

Meanwhile Combe St James was once again excited by the arrival of yet another visitor at Mrs Anstey's house. Another elegant chaise had brought a visitor to Church Cottage—this time a handsome, polished man of fashion, and in a very short time it had been established that this was Mrs Oliver's husband.

Unlike his wife and mother-in-law, Mr Oliver positively revelled in meeting people. Though one or two sticklers at first looked askance at a man who had agreed to such a curious start to his marriage, they were soon disarmed by Mr Oliver's obvious devotion to his wife, and his impeccable manners to everyone. What a contrast he was to Mr Guthrie, who, even at the height of his popularity, had occasionally offended with his blunt way of speaking and his lack of ceremony!

Yes, it was soon decided that, in spite of being an American, Mr Oliver was a true gentleman, a distinct asset to the neighbourhood, and he was welcomed wherever he went.

The ladies in the Dower House were kept informed of these developments by Cousin Louisa, who was among Mr Oliver's greatest admirers.

'Such distinguished manners! He has put many a lady's heart in a flutter, in spite of being married! But, though he talks to us all charmingly, he has no eyes for anyone but that dowdy wife of his. We cannot really understand it. Especially as his sister-in-law is so absolutely beautiful. One would have thought… But there's no accounting for taste.'

'I cannot wait to meet him, Louisa,' said Mrs Southeran. 'And the Anstey sisters, too. But am I wrong? Wasn't there a child in all this unhappy story?'

'Oh, it is so sad! The little boy is not strong. His parents thought it better to leave him at home in Boston with his nurse. I am sure Mrs Oliver must miss him.'

'Then why did they leave him? Why are they here?'

Mrs Southeran's voice was mild, but there was a slight element of censure in it that Cousin Louisa hastened to dispel.

'Mr Oliver says that he had to come over to Europe on business this year, and his wife decided that she would like to see her mother and sister Marianne. They had heard what a great success Marianne was in London. It wasn't until they got here that they learned she was actually engaged to be married. I expect they will stay for the wedding. As will Mrs Gardiner.'

'I have invited Mrs Gardiner to visit us here the day after tomorrow. Perhaps I will include Mr and Mrs Oliver in the invitation. Would your man take a note round to Church Cottage for me, Louisa?'

'Certainly. I am sure you will not be disappointed, Anthea. Such a handsome man. So charming!'

'I already find Mr Oliver a fascinating character, Louisa. I am quite sure I shall not be disappointed.'

The note was duly written and handed to Cousin Louisa for delivery to the Ansteys. As a matter of form Mrs Anstey was included, though neither Eleanor nor her mother expected to see the lady.

Eleanor was still trying to find an opportunity to make her apology to Mr Guthrie, but he had been busy with a backlog of work after his absence in London, and had not been seen in the Dower House. Then she heard that he had been to Exeter to see Mr Lucombe, the tree nurseryman, and it was difficult to suppress a feeling of hurt that he had not told her he was going. She was feeling altogether low, and the prospect of some interesting visitors was welcome—they might take her mind off her troubles for a while. She made one last attempt to see Mr Guthrie before they came. She rode over to the combe, hoping she might find him there.

Mr Guthrie was nowhere to be seen but somebody else was there—a well-dressed man of medium height, dark and quite handsome. He was standing on the bank by the bridge, gazing down into the water below. Eleanor pulled up her horse a little distance away from him. The man was a complete stranger.

'Good morning!' he called.

'Good morning. I don't think I know you, do I?' said Eleanor warily. She didn't enjoy meeting strangers in this particular spot.

He made no attempt to come nearer, but said, 'You must be Miss Southeran. I'm Nathaniel Oliver. I'm staying at present with a friend of yours—my mother-in-law, Mrs Anstey.'

'You are a long way from Combe St James, Mr Oliver.'

'I know. I came to see Jonas, but they couldn't find him. They said he might be here.'

'How did you find your way? It's quite a distance from the house.'

'Indeed it is,' he replied with a charming smile. 'And even further when you lose your way as often as I did! Don't be afraid, Miss Southeran. I'm perfectly respectable. I'm a friend of your cousin Louisa.'

Eleanor was reassured. She dismounted and led Shanty down to the riverbank. 'How do you do?' she said. 'Have you seen Jo—Mr Guthrie?'

'No. I thought I would wait a little longer, then I shall give up for today. My wife will be wondering where I have got to. I am delighted to meet you at last, Miss Southeran. I have heard a great deal about you.'

'Really, sir?' said Eleanor, with a cool smile. 'Well, I will not ask you from whom or to what effect, in case your reply is not what I would wish to hear.'

He looked gallant, and said that her anxieties were quite out of place. 'But I was sorry to hear of your accident, Miss Southeran.'

'Who told you of my accident?' asked Eleanor sharply, her suspicions returning.

'Why, your cousin Louisa has told everyone in

Combe St James about your narrow escape. You don't appear to have suffered any lasting damage, if I may say so. It was here, wasn't it?'

Eleanor admitted stiffly that this was so. She was not quite sure why this man was so interested in the matter, and was reluctant to discuss it with him.

He disarmed her suspicions almost immediately by saying sympathetically, 'But I can see that the memory is not a pleasant one, so we won't talk about it. Shall we ride back together, Miss Southeran? I would be glad to have a guide.'

On the way back he talked amusingly of his experiences in Combe St James. He kept Eleanor entertained, for, though his stories were witty, they were never unkind, and they revealed a surprising insight into the ways of a small country village. By the time they had reached the Dower House Eleanor was in perfect charity with him.

'Goodbye, Mr Oliver—for the moment. I believe you are paying us a visit tomorrow with your wife and sister-in-law.'

'*Au revoir*, Miss Southeran. I am looking forward to it.'

He rode off, and Eleanor watched him go. So that was the famous Mr Oliver, who had married for money. Or had he? He had certainly talked of his wife with great affection. What would she be like?

When the two Anstey sisters walked into Mrs Southeran's sitting-room, no greater contrast could have been imagined. Phoebe was dazzling in a bonnet of white crape, and a white mull muslin dress which was delicately tucked and frilled. Eleanor gave a fleeting thought to the poor maidservant who had to iron such confections—six of them a day! But she was amused to see that, perhaps in deference to public opinion, Phoebe had a floating lavender-grey scarf draped round her shoulders. She greeted Eleanor warmly and expressed delight at seeing her again.

Evadne was soberly dressed in a dun-coloured round gown with few trimmings. Her bonnet was of black straw, with a small feather to one side. Though her features were not unattractive, they lacked her sister's colour and animation. Her eyes were greenish-grey, and her cheeks pale and slightly sallow. Her expression was composed, guarded even, and she waited quietly in the background until Mrs Southeran invited her to come over and be introduced. Phoebe was already sitting next to her hostess, her white dress making a striking contrast with the blue velvet of the sofa.

Mr Oliver's manners were indeed charming. He waited till Mrs Southeran had finished greeting his wife and sister-in-law, then stepped forward and bowed over her hand. He complimented her on her roses, which could be seen through the open windows, and waited till she had finished her short conversation with him before moving to Eleanor and saying with a twinkle in his eye, 'Now, Miss Southeran, may I claim to have been officially introduced to you? Or shall I ask your mother to perform that office?'

Eleanor smiled and said, 'I think we may dispense with that last touch of formality, sir. But I have yet to meet your wife. Would you present me to her?'

They went over to the sofa and Eleanor at last found herself face to face with the woman who had caused so much trouble for Jonas. At first sight this was not a face to 'launch a thousand ships'—Evadne's sister was much more likely to start a conflict for her favours. But Mr

Oliver seemed devoted. He was very protective of her and hovered over her after he had performed the introduction, looking on while she responded to Eleanor's conversation, encouraging her to say more. Evadne's voice was a surprise. It was deep and low, and had a distinctive, attractively husky note. She seemed reticent, but after a while Eleanor became convinced that this was not the result of shyness, but rather a deliberate withholding of personality. A most intriguing woman, in spite of her colourless manner.

Meanwhile Phoebe was enchanting Mrs Southeran. 'Do you really think this shawl suits me? I have never worn grey before, Mrs Southeran. Grey is not a colour that suits me. Mr Gardiner would not have liked it, I am sure, but he is no longer with us, and I wouldn't like people to think that I lacked respect for his memory. When one is in mourning one must not think of one's looks, don't you agree? Do I look hideous?'

'Mrs Gardiner, I assure you, you look delightful. The lilac shadows in that scarf deserve a poem all to themselves.'

'Oh,' said Phoebe, growing pink. 'How kind of you! When will you write it—the poem, I mean? I should dearly love to have a poem about me! Several of my admirers have said they wished to write one, but they never have.'

Mrs Southeran was fortunately saved from reply by the entry of Mr Guthrie. As Betty explained afterwards, she was so used to seeing him that she never thought for one moment that her mistress would not wish to receive him, and he, as was his custom, strode in without ceremony. He stopped short when he saw who the visitors were.

Mrs Southeran, who was an accomplished hostess, would not have chosen to mix such an unfortunate selection of people, but she faced the inevitable with grace. In fact, the situation appealed to her puckish sense of humour and, as a keen observer of the human race, she was more than somewhat intrigued to see how they would all behave.

'Jonas! How kind of you to call! I…I believe you already know my visitors.'

'Good afternoon, Mrs Southeran. Yes, I believe I do. Very well, in fact.' He bowed to each in turn. 'Phoebe… Evadne… Oliver…' His face was still unsmiling as he turned to greet Eleanor, and she felt her heart sink. She had hoped he would have softened towards her—it would have made things so much easier. But perhaps he might grow kinder during the course of the afternoon— and, in any case, this was clearly not the occasion to attempt to say anything at all about their differences.

Phoebe rose from the sofa in one swift, graceful movement and took Mr Guthrie's arm. She said gaily, 'You must all excuse me. I have so much to say to Jonas, and have been waiting an age to see him.' She led him over to the window-seat and sat down, patting the seat beside her with a smile of invitation. 'When did you return from London, Jonas? Did you hurry back when you heard I was here?'

'Not…not exactly,' he replied, and Eleanor suffered a pang as she saw him give Phoebe his special, quizzical smile as he joined her on the seat.

'Oh, Jonas, I have missed you so. Poor Gilbert is dead, you know…'

The rest of the party were forgotten by at least one of the two on the window-seat as Phoebe proceeded to entrance Mr Guthrie—or so it seemed to Eleanor. Mrs Southeran, unperturbed by Phoebe's ruthless lack of manners, which she quite rightly thought was totally characteristic, turned to her other guests. They were soon immersed in a discussion about Marianne Anstey's wedding, which was due to take place in a very short time.

'Will your mama be able to travel so far? I have heard she is not very well,' said Mrs Southeran to Evadne.

'Mama will certainly wish to be present. She is very proud of Marianne. As we all are,' she added, but her voice was devoid of feeling.

There was a pause. Mr Oliver's eyes had been fixed on Phoebe and Mr Guthrie, but he now suddenly recollected himself and said, 'Forgive me, my thoughts were wandering. Of course Mrs Anstey will be well enough. We might all go—what do you think, my love?'

'I am not sure Mama would wish for that,' replied his wife.

'Of course she would! And you shall have a pretty dress and a new bonnet.' Mr Oliver turned with a smile to Mrs Southeran. 'You may find it hard to believe, Mrs Southeran, but I have great difficulty in persuading my wife to buy pretty clothes. I think it must be her only fault.'

'If that is Mrs Oliver's only shortcoming, then you are a fortunate man. Not many husbands would complain of such a fault, sir! But tell me, how long will your business keep you in England, Mr Oliver?' said Mrs Southeran. 'I can imagine that you must also be quite anxious to return to Boston.' The Olivers looked blank. She went on, 'Your little son. I am sure you must both be missing him.'

In the circumstances this was an unfortunate remark, but Eleanor was never quite sure afterwards whether her mother had made it deliberately or not. Evadne went paler than ever, and Mr Oliver looked embarrassed. He said finally, 'We miss him, of course. But he is well cared for in Boston. I am hoping to return quite soon, Mrs Southeran, but I am not quite sure when. We may yet see Marianne married.' His eye rested on Mr Guthrie, still deep in conversation with Phoebe, and he smiled at Evadne. 'Quite soon,' he repeated, as if to reassure her.

Mr Guthrie rose and came over to the little group round Mrs Southeran's sofa. 'Forgive me. I have been catching up on Phoebe's news. It is sad about Gilbert Gardiner. How are you, Evadne?'

There was no sign of consciousness in either face. 'Well, thank you,' was the brief reply. The group lapsed into silence until Mrs Southeran made some remark about the glorious weather Somerset was enjoying, and how fortunate the visitors were. Mr Oliver took up the conversational gambit and went on to amuse his hostess with a description of the scenery he had admired as he had wandered, lost, the day before.

'Then I met your lovely daughter, ma'am, and was rescued. A reversal of roles, wouldn't you say? The Beast saved by Beauty?'

'Where was this, Oliver?' asked Mr Guthrie abruptly.

'Some valley or other. I believe it was where Miss Southeran had her accident.'

Phoebe Gardiner said, 'You've had an accident, Miss Southeran? So that was why your foot was bandaged up when I saw you in the library? I was quite worried about it, but I didn't like to ask what was wrong. Gilbert had an uncle who suffered dreadfully with gout, but he used to get ridiculously angry if anyone mentioned it.'

'I think my daughter is safe from gout, Mrs Gardiner,' said Mrs Southeran solemnly. 'We have never had any in the family, and Eleanor is very abstemious.'

Mr Guthrie gave a curious choking sound, which he turned into a cough, and Eleanor said hastily, 'It was kind of you to worry, but, as you see, it is perfectly cured now. Tell me, are you planning to make any excursions while you are here? Lyme Regis is very pretty.'

Chapter Eleven

Thinking it over afterwards, Eleanor realised that apart from that one question the only exchange between the two men had taken place shortly before Mr Guthrie left.

'Guthrie, I need a word with you. When may I call?'

'There are workmen all over my house at the moment, but I should think the library would be free. How about tomorrow at noon? You are not working at the moment, are you, Miss Southeran?'

Eleanor had shaken her head, cleared her throat and said, 'No. Indeed, I have almost finished, Mr Guthrie. A day or two longer, and then I will not trouble you any more. Tomorrow's work can easily be left to another time.'

She had done her best to keep her voice calm, but a slight tremble at the end had betrayed her anxiety, at least to Mr Guthrie. His expression had softened and he'd said, 'I am sorry not to have seen you these past days. I think we, too, have things to discuss. May I see you tomorrow afternoon?' He'd turned to Mr Oliver. 'I don't think our talk will take very long, do you?'

Mr Oliver had not replied immediately. He'd looked

first at Eleanor, then at Phoebe, then back at Eleanor again. There had been a look of speculation in his eye, as if he was making an assessment. Eleanor had suddenly no longer liked him quite so much. She'd turned her head away and looked instead at Mr Guthrie.

'What? Oh, no!' said Mr Oliver. 'It won't take long at all, but it is urgent. I should prefer to see you today if that is possible. I want to ask you about some property of mine.' Something in Mr Oliver's voice caused Eleanor to hold her breath. She saw that Mr Guthrie was smiling. But it was a very different smile from the one he had employed to Phoebe Gardiner.

'Tonight, then. At eight. I shall forward to it. Mrs Southeran, I must thank you for inviting me in to such an…interesting occasion.' His voice was solemn but there was an undercurrent of laughter in it, which made Mrs Southeran smile.

'You are, as always, welcome, Jonas.'

This provoked another sharp look from Mr Oliver.

'Jonas, you cannot be going! I haven't talked to you nearly long enough.' Phoebe Gardiner followed Mr Guthrie to the door and put her hand on his arm. She gave him a look from her gentian eyes and pouted prettily. 'Don't go yet. Please?'

'You are an outrageous minx, Phoebe,' he said, looking at her indulgently. 'I am sorry to observe that time has not taught you how to behave.'

'I always like it when you tease me, Jonas. But you know that I never stand on ceremony with you. And I am sure Mrs Southeran understands—' this was said with a brilliant smile at her hostess '—what it is like to meet an old friend—a very old friend—in a strange country. Now I wish you to be serious. If you cannot stay now, we must meet another time. When are you going to call on me? Soon, I hope?'

'Will the day after tomorrow suit? I should like to see your mother again, too.'

It was evident that this did not suit Mrs Gardiner at all—she had clearly had something more intimate in mind—but Mr Guthrie overrode her protests and took his leave of them all.

After the other visitors had departed a few minutes later, Mrs Southeran collapsed into her sofa and gave way to her amusement. 'You warned me about Phoebe Gardiner, Nell, though you really didn't do her justice. But you were right in one thing—there is something very taking about her, in spite of her total self-absorption. There's no malice in Phoebe Gardiner. I am not at all sure I could say the same of her sister. There's a deep one. I wonder what the Olivers are up to?'

Eleanor did not ask her mother what she meant. She, too, had been aware of the undertones. And what was the exact relationship betwen Mr Guthrie and Mr Oliver? Not a friendly one. The smile Jonas had given Mr Oliver just before he left had made her blood run cold…

The same smile was on Mr Guthrie's face that evening when the two men were left alone. Mr Oliver had walked in behind the housekeeper to find his host sitting at a table, on which stood a handsome colza lamp. The pool of light was directed on to some papers which were spread out before him, and the upper half of Mr Guthrie's face was in shadow. After seeing that the tray with wine and biscuits was to hand, Mrs Cartwright left the room, closing the heavy door quietly behind her.

The ladies of Combe St James would not have recognised their charming favourite in the man who now
stood facing Jonas Guthrie. His face was hard and
watchful and his hands clenched and unclenched as he
waited impatiently for the housekeeper to leave. His
manners had lost some of their charm, too.

'Where is he?' he asked as soon as they were alone.

'No, no. Let me offer you a glass of wine first, Oliver.
And do sit down.'

'Damn you, what have you done with him?'

'Sit down, Oliver! And take this glass of wine. You
might need it.'

Mr Oliver sat down and drained the glass in one long
draught. 'Damn you, now will you tell me where he is?'

'I take it you mean Christopher Digby? You would
scarcely show this degree of concern for anyone else—
not even Evadne. But I see you have finished your wine.
Allow me.' Mr Guthrie poured another glass.

Mr Oliver sat staring at his host. 'You're playing a
dangerous game, Guthrie. I hope you haven't forgotten
what I could do if I chose.'

'No, I haven't forgotten.'

'I'll do it, too, if you don't tell me what you've done
with Christopher. Or do you think to hold me to ransom?'

'No,' said Mr Guthrie, his lip curling, but his voice
still calm. 'I don't deal in ransoms, any more than I deal
in blackmail. I leave that to people of your kidney.'

Mr Oliver got up and leaned over the desk. 'In that
case, my high-minded friend, you'd better do as I ask.
Perhaps you don't believe I'll do what I say?'

'Sit down, Oliver! I do believe that you would make
public the facts about Henry Anstey's misdeeds, in spite
of the bargain we made at the time in Boston. But I also

think that you might find the impact of your tales would not be as great as you once thought. Henry Anstey has been dead these two years now. There's a new generation of politicians and businessmen in Boston. They're not going to make a fuss about a dead man's peccadilloes.' He smiled cynically. 'They're too busy covering up their own!'

'What about Amelia? You were so devoted to her—how will she feel? And Marianne?'

'I'm sorry about Amelia. I would have preferred her not to know the truth about Henry, but I have now come to believe that she will recover in time. Marianne? I think Marianne's position is sufficiently secure to survive any slight scandal you might cause. It's a long way from London to Boston, and there's an even greater divide between her future world and yours. She is already part of the Morrissey's circle and they will protect their own. No, I don't think you can blight her young life now.' Mr Guthrie got up. 'So. I am no longer as ready as I once was to jump to your whip, Oliver.'

'Henry Anstey was still a criminal. He embezzled the state and he borrowed money he had no right to from his clients. I still think I could create enough of a scandal to make you all rue the day.'

'God's teeth, man, what do you think I've been doing for the last two years? The money Henry stole—you observe that I am not afraid to use the correct word—has been repaid, the contracts he sold have been destroyed! Did you imagine that I would be content to live my life under the heel of a blackmailer forever? No, Oliver, believe me, there's not much evidence to uphold any accusations you choose to make.'

It was clear that Mr Oliver had suffered a shock. 'You cunning devil, Guthrie,' he said slowly. 'You never intended from the beginning to keep to our bargain!'

'Oh, indeed I did! I have! I kept silent when people whispered that I was a villain and a rake. I paid and paid, but allowed the world to think that I had ruined the Ansteys with my own greed. I had other sources of wealth with which to survive the disaster, and I flattered myself that I could eventually outlive the gossip. Indeed, I was on the way to doing it, at least with people whose opinion I most value.

'Yes, Oliver, I was prepared to let you and Evadne get away with your tricks. It was the price you forced me to pay for Amelia's peace of mind, and Marianne's future. But I would have been a fool not to use the time since then to ensure that I could be free of you when I wished.' He gazed sombrely into his glass.

'But then you decided that you wanted more,' he went on. 'God knows how, but you found out that Amelia would inherit what was left of my fortune if I died. So you decided that I would be better dead. Was Evadne in on that, too? You surely cannot have supposed that I would suffer Christopher's attempts to murder me and do nothing about it? My willingness to do anything to save Amelia and Marianne two years ago gave you a false impression. You must have thought me a mindless idiot!'

'What have you done with Christopher?'

'I warned Christopher. I don't usually give people a second chance.'

'You've killed him!' said Oliver, his voice rising.

'I would have, if it had been necessary. Though he wouldn't have deserved it—he's a poor thing. Your tool, as well as your catamite.'

'*What* have you *done* with him?'

'I'm afraid you've lost him, Oliver, perhaps forever. I've shipped him out to Madras—that should keep him out of the way for a while. I shouldn't be surprised if he stays. A handsome lad like Christopher, with Christopher's propensities, could well find a rich patron out there.'

Mr Oliver thrust his chair back and leapt up. 'You…you fiend, Guthrie!' he shouted. 'I'll kill you for this!'

He drew a wicked-looking stiletto out of his pocket and launched himself at his enemy without thought, without caution. Mr Guthrie caught Oliver's arm with ease and twisted it back till the knife was wrested from him. Then he forced Oliver to his knees, and, still holding him in an iron grip, he said softly, 'Go back to America, Oliver, and take Evadne with you. For Amelia's sake, I won't pursue this, but I don't want to see either of you any more. Now leave me, you scum.' He flung Oliver away from him, and the man lay abjectly on the floor, moaning Christopher's name.

'Get up!'

Oliver pulled himself together and got up.

'There's just one more thing, my friend,' said Mr Guthrie, with a grim smile. 'In case you still have any lingering ambition, I should tell you that I've changed my lawyers and my will. You won't gain by my death, Oliver.'

'I know why you're doing this, Guthrie.' Oliver's voice was low, but it shook with the intensity of his feelings. 'You're planning to marry. I've heard the rumours in London. That's why you're so eager to clear your name, and that's why you've changed your will. And why…' He stopped as his feelings overcame him. 'And why you've taken Christopher from me. But I swear, Guthrie, by God I swear, I will make you sorry for it.' His voice rose, and his face, usually so pale, was suffused with blood. 'You will suffer as you are making me suffer. Take what care you like of your wife-to-be, Guthrie. Once I am certain who she is, I shall see that you never marry her!'

He tore out of the room and down the stairs. Mr Guthrie listened as Oliver's horse galloped away as if chased by the hounds of hell. He stood for some time, lost in his thoughts, and, from the look on his face, they were disquieting. Then he cursed, flung himself into the chair by the table, and poured himself a generous glass of brandy.

The knowledge that she was to see Jonas the next day, that she would have her chance to explain how far she had changed her mind, kept Eleanor awake half the night. She tossed and turned, planning what she would say, rearranging this, rejecting that, until she eventually fell into an uneasy sleep. But when she woke again it was still early. She decided to get up—a walk might clear her mind. The early morning mist was still lying on the fields, but the sun would soon disperse it. It was going to be a beautiful day.

Her heart lifted and she was suddenly quite certain that it would be all right. Jonas would forgive her, and then they would carry on as before until such time as he could, in his own words, say what he really wanted to say. She was practically certain she knew what that would be. She had had little experience of such things, it was true, but surely he couldn't have held her as he had, kissed her as he had, spoken as he had, without loving her!

She wandered down the covered path towards the

main house. This was where he had first kissed her. Their argument that day, too, had started when she had tried to defend Threlfall. That had been a mistake, as well. Jonas had been angry, and she had been so unhappy when all her work on Stanyards estate had seemed to be worth nothing. He had tried to comfort her, but his own honesty had got in the way.

She smiled at the thought. It was so very Jonas-like, that inability to fudge, to lie, even when it was to his advantage to do so. And then he had kissed her... What a stormy relationship theirs had been! Almost immediately after that, when everything had seemed to be going so well, she had accused him of trying to sell her father's books. Well, at least all that was over. Whatever happened when she met Jonas, she was sure now that she could trust him.

Eleanor turned back towards the Dower House. It was too early to call on Jonas, and yet the afternoon seemed an eternity away. But just as she came into the courtyard he appeared round the corner, much as he had done the first time she had seen him here at Stanyards. He even had Becky with him. There was a frown on his face, and he was so preoccupied that he did not at first see her.

'Jonas! Down, Becky! Jonas, I'm so glad you're here. It seemed an age till this afternoon.'

'Eleanor—I...I... What are you doing up so early? I didn't expect to see you.'

'What are you doing here? You look as if you are inspecting the Dower House. You are not thinking of altering it, are you? My mother likes it just as it is.'

'No, I...I was wondering how safe it was.'

'*Safe*? Of course it is safe!'

'Yes, of course. But I think I'll have the men look at it, all the same.' Eleanor decided not to pursue the matter. She didn't want to start her apology with a disagreement. He went on, 'How can I help you?' His voice, which till now had been perfectly normal, had suddenly become cool. He was clearly remembering their quarrel. Eleanor hastened to put things right.

'I want to apologise, to ask you to forgive me yet again, Jonas. I was wrong about Threlfall.'

'Yes, he's a nasty piece of work. But I suppose it was natural you should want to see things for yourself.' He still sounded distant. She had hurt him more than she had thought by her lack of confidence.

'No, I should have known that you would not take such a drastic decision without very good cause.' Eleanor smiled ruefully at him. 'I never seem to learn, do I?'

Jonas looked at her almost as if she were a stranger. His mind seemed to be elsewhere and it was a minute before he spoke. 'No,' he said finally. 'No, you don't seem to learn. It's a pity. I'm sorry, you'll have to excuse me—I have things to do. I must get back.' He took a few steps, the stopped and turned. 'I forgot. I have to go to Badgers Farm this afternoon, so I shan't be in. Did you wish to see me about anything else?'

'No,' said Eleanor numbly.

'Right. Come, Becky!' He gave her a nod and strode up the path to Stanyards without looking at her again.

Eleanor was stunned. What had happened to the man she thought she knew? This behaviour was ungenerous, to say the least, and to stride away like that, without giving her any chance to respond, to protest… Was what she had done so awful that he couldn't face her? But he hadn't seemed to feel that the day before at her mother's gathering. He had been cool at first, but towards the end she had been quite optimistic.

She swallowed hard—in a moment she would disgrace herself by bursting into tears. She must get back to her room.

'Marnin', Miss Nell! It's going ter be a fine old day again.'

'Oh, good morning, Daniel,' said Eleanor with commendable self-discipline. 'Yes, it will…it will be lovely, I think.'

'I saw Mrs Gardiner yesterday. The others had told me 'bout 'er, but my, 'er's a beauty!'

'She's lovely,' Eleanor agreed.

Something in her voice must have warned Daniel that his Miss Nell wasn't feeling very happy. He came closer and said kindly, 'Not a patch on you, though. Why, there bain't a soul on the estate that don't think you're the prettiest girl in Somerset.'

Eleanor laughed tremulously and said, 'Thank you! It isn't true, but it's kind of you to say so, and I'm flattered.'

Daniel was still anxious to comfort. 'And folks like working for you. They do say that Mrs Gardiner is fearsome hard on that poor maid of hers.'

'Come, Daniel, you know we mustn't gossip about Mrs Gardiner.'

'Oh, I'm not one for gossip, Miss Nell. I leave that to the wimmin!' He grinned and went off to the stables.

Eleanor was left with her own thoughts again. Phoebe Gardiner was not only lovely, she was also determined to win Jonas Guthrie again. And, from what she had observed yesterday, Jonas still had a great deal of affection for her. Was that why he had been so cool this morning? No, she would not believe that to be the case. Jonas was not so fickle that he would turn to a newcomer after being so close to Eleanor. But she isn't a newcomer, her private devil whispered. He was once engaged to her, remember?

She shook her head impatiently in an effort to clear her thoughts. Jonas Guthrie was a man of honour. She must hold on to that fact. He would not have all but declared himself to her, Eleanor, if he had had any doubts or reservations. She had hurt him—worse than she had thought—and it was going to take time for him to recover. Meanwhile she must act as naturally as possible until he did.

It was easy to come to a sensible conclusion. It was much harder to act accordingly, especially for one of Eleanor's impetuous temper. Several times during the course of the day she decided that the situation was absurd, that she must seek Jonas out, tell him how much his good opinion meant to her, plead with him for under-standing and sympathy. But his manner that morning had been so brusque, so forbidding, that she was afraid of another rebuff.

She would have confided in her mother, but Mrs Southeran was finishing the project for her literary review, and Eleanor did not want to distract her. Things would come right eventually, she was sure. She must just have patience and trust to her instinct that time would cure the rift between herself and Jonas.

She confined herself to tasks about the Dower House, thus avoiding the risk of meeting him either on the estate or in his library. But after a day or two of this she decided that she could reasonably set about finishing the catalogue, and went up to Stanyards.

Eleanor had found a number of problems in cataloguing the books, and these she had till now put aside. She decided that she would sort them out today before going any further. In order to do this she would have to search through her father's archives, many of which were still stored in his safe-room at Stanyards. Not many non-family members knew of this room, and she was certain that no one had discovered it, even during the recent renovations.

During the middle ages Stanyards had been a fortified manor. Later generations had added to the house, but when religious and political loyalties had come to be a source of trouble, part of the original defensive wall had been turned into a hiding place for people in danger—priests, soldiers, even rebellious members of the family. This little room now served as a strong-room. It lay at the far end of the library, and was reached through what appeared to be part of the window embrasure. This gave access to a long stone screen passage which opened out into a tiny room in the thickness of the corner wall. The room itself was entirely of stone, lit and ventilated by a narrow slit which was so arranged as to be invisible from the ground outside.

After extracting the documents she wanted out of the chest in which they were stored, Eleanor spread them out and studied them. She was so completely absorbed in the papers that she was at first only dimly aware of voices. One curious feature of this room was that, unless the door to it was firmly shut, conversations taking place in the library were clearly audible there. Eleanor listened for a moment—a woman's voice. Annie or Dora? They must be cleaning the library, and she tried to remember whether she had left anything on the table.

No, she had come straight into the safe-room before starting anything else. That was good—she could stay here until they left. The older servants might suspect the existence of a secret room, but none of them knew exactly where its entrance was, and Eleanor didn't wish to reveal it.

She had been very careless. Not only had she forgotten to follow her usual practice of locking the library door before using the safe-room, she had even left the door in the window embrasure slightly ajar. She would just have to hope that the servants didn't notice it. She went back to her papers, but something about the timbre of the voice in the library caught her attention. It wasn't Annie, or Dora. That voice belonged to Evadne Oliver!

There was a short silence, then Eleanor heard Jonas say, 'All the same, Evadne, I think it neither wise nor even desirable that you should come here. Hasn't your husband yet given you an account of our conversation the other night?'

'Nathaniel doesn't tell me everything, Jonas.'

'My impression is, however, that you are usually in his confidence. You were certainly both in league when you blackmailed me into giving you a handsome sum of money. Why did you do it, Evadne?'

Eleanor was in a dilemma. This was clearly an intensely private conversation, and she should not be listening to it, however involuntarily. But what was she to do? To reveal herself now would betray the secret of this room, not only to Stanyards' new owner, who might reasonably expect to be told, but also to this woman, a stranger. Besides, it was already too late to avoid embarrassment on all sides. She would have to keep silent. Evadne was speaking.

'You know why. I was desperate. Father was dead, and none of us had any money—except you.'

'But had you no compunction about what you were threatening? No concern for your mother's feelings? Or Marianne's?'

The beautiful voice was now full of scorn. 'You never really understood, did you, Jonas? I had—indeed I *have* no compunction about any of it. I despised all of them. My father was a cheat and a liar, my mother a silly woman afraid of everything—even life itself—and my sisters…ah, my sisters! They were beautiful.' The manner in which Evadne pronounced this last word made it sound obscene.

There was distaste in Jonas's voice as he said, 'You were cleverer than any of them. Was that not enough?'

'Enough? No, it wasn't anything like enough. You are a man, Jonas. It is not demanded of men that they should be beautiful. Clever? Yes. Strong? Yes. Well-mannered? Perhaps. But a woman—she is nothing if she is not beautiful.

'As a child I would always behave better than Phoebe, but Phoebe was the one who was taken before the guests, and petted, and made much of. I knew my tables long before she mastered them, but it was Phoebe of whom everyone spoke with pride. And then there was Marianne. A beautiful, amiable doll, the image of my elder sister, but so good! All the world loved Marianne! Why should I feel sorry for them?'

'This jealousy wasn't necessary, Evadne. You were witty, amusing, clever… I always enjoyed your company.'

'It was Phoebe you asked to marry you, Jonas! It was Marianne's fate you were concerned with, not mine!'

There was a silence in the room. Eleanor held her breath. She was learning at last about the Ansteys and their relationship with Jonas Guthrie, and, though it was not in a manner she would have wished, she could not now have stopped listening if her life had depended on it.

'What about Oliver?' said Jonas slowly. 'What part did he play in all this?'

'I thought Nathaniel Oliver was offering me what no one else had offered before. To come first in his attentions. To be important to him. I couldn't resist it.'

'You didn't know about Christopher?'

Eleanor heard a rustle of movement. When Evadne spoke again her voice was clearer—she must be standing next to the window.

'I thought Chistopher was simply the son of an old friend. It…it was a shock when I found out what the relationship really was. Nathaniel had never given me any reason to suppose that he was interested in men as well as women.'

Jonas drew in his breath through his teeth, and his voice was, for the first time, more sympathetic. 'I'm sorry. It must have been very hard.'

There was sudden passion in Evadne's voice. 'Don't pity me, Jonas Guthrie! I need no one's pity, least of all yours! It turned out much better than one might have expected. We have a delightful *ménage à trois*. Nathaniel admires me enormously—I am so much cleverer than he. It's one way of being needed.'

'But you don't have a *ménage à quatre*.'

'What do you mean?'

'The baby, Evadne. What about the baby?'

There was another silence. When Evadne spoke it was once again in her normal manner, devoid of feeling. 'I think you know about the baby. Don't you, Jonas?'

'Yes.'

'I thought so. It was never strong, and it didn't survive the first winter. We decided not to tell you—instead we used the money you settled on it for ourselves. We needed it more than you. Are you angry, Jonas?'

'No; why should I be angry? It's no more than I would have expected. What does make me angry is the way you speak of the child. "It" wasn't strong, "it" didn't survive—did the baby mean so little to you? "It" was a human being. A boy.'

'From the moment it was born we knew it wouldn't live for long. I wouldn't let myself be fond of it. And Nathaniel wasn't interested in it at all,' she said indifferently. 'But this isn't leading us anywhere, Jonas. I've come today for a purpose.'

'Which is?'

'To warn you.'

'Warn me? Why would you wish to do that?'

'I don't know what passed between you and Nathaniel the other night. I do know that he intends you no good.'

'I told him that I had put a stop to Christopher's attempts to kill me by shipping him off to India.'

'So that's why he was in such a rage! Jonas, he will kill you himself for this!'

'I doubt it. Nathaniel Oliver hasn't the stomach to do anything so risky himself. But you've come here to warn me. How very kind of you, Evadne!'

'I still have some feeling for you—'

'Spare me that, my dear. You've never felt anything for anyone except yourself. In your own way you are every bit as ruthlessly self-absorbed as Phoebe. You are here for your own purposes—whatever they are.'

'If you will pay no heed for yourself, then I want you to warn Eleanor Southeran.'

Eleanor almost dropped the papers she was holding. What on earth did Evadne mean?

'Miss Southeran? What about?'

'I think you love her—and Nathaniel will try to hurt you through her.'

'That would be his way,' said Jonas contemptuously. 'Having failed twice to have me killed, he might just get up enough courage to attack a woman. But why should he think it would hurt me particularly? Miss Southeran is a charming girl—young woman, I suppose I should say, for she's past the age of being a girl. But, apart from being the daughter of an old friend, she means nothing to me.'

Chapter Twelve

Eleanor had to put a hand to her mouth to stifle a protest when she heard these words. She stood, unable to believe them, sure it was a mistake. She must have misheard. She must! But Evadne was speaking. Eleanor strained to listen.

'He has heard that you are planning to marry, and he believes you mean to marry Miss Southeran.'

'You mean he's been picking up gossip where he can and has put two and two together to make seventeen!' said Jonas with scorn. 'It's true that when I was in London I looked at houses there with a view to acquiring one, and that gave rise to rumours that I intended to marry. But I assure you—and him—that, if I did marry, I would look for someone who would suit the life I intend to lead, not a pretty little country girl!

'I'll be frank with you, Evadne—there's no reason you shouldn't know; it'll be public knowledge shortly— I've been offered a title. And now that I'm free of your family's affairs there's no reason why I shouldn't accept it. I've a fancy to become a great lord. Can you imagine Miss Southeran as a great lady? I can't.'

'People say that you've been seen in her company a great deal…'

'Well, where's the harm in that? A man seeks his amusement where he can, and, believe me, there aren't many alternatives down here. She has helped me to while away the odd hour. Besides, it was very useful—I learned a lot about the estate from her. Has Eleanor Southeran been claiming that there's more to it than that? I'm sorry for her if she has, but I've never given her the slightest reason to suppose I was serious.'

'I see… What about Phoebe? You were serious about her once.'

'Ah, Phoebe! She's more the thing. I can imagine her in society, can't you? And she and Marianne would make as lovely a pair of viscountesses as you could wish to see. But there again, as you reminded me just before, Phoebe hasn't a great deal to offer a man other than her beauty. No, if I were to marry—I say, *if*—I think I would look for someone suitable in next year's crop of débutantes. I may be a little old, and my looks won't win me a bride, but my wealth will. Oliver may threaten, but we both know he wants to return to Boston. He'll give up in time. I don't mind waiting—I have no special candidate in mind.' He chuckled. 'I'll enjoy inspecting the field.'

Eleanor sat like a stone in the room. It seemed to have become icy. The hateful voice went on, 'What's the matter? I know what it is—you are wishing you were free. It's a pity you're not, Evadne. I'm beginning to think I picked the wrong sister all those years ago. But you never gave any sign…'

'If I were free…?'

'No.' Jonas's voice was full of regret. 'It wouldn't

do, my dear. Much as I'm intrigued at the thought of having you, I'm not going to jeopardise my future by marrying a divorced woman—nor a widow. But I won't deny that I'd like Oliver out of the way—in Boston. If you could persuade him to return, there might be something in it for you…'

Evadne's voice was colourless again. 'I'll see what I can do. Goodbye, Jonas.'

Eleanor heard Evadne's footsteps fade and then the sound of a door closing. There was a sudden release of breath from Jonas Guthrie and she heard him slump into a chair. She could hardly bear the thought of being so close to him. She wanted to get away, right away, never see him again. But she sat there like a statue, not thinking, trying not to feel, waiting for him to leave the library.

Eventually he got up. She heard him opening and shutting some drawers and then the door to the library slammed again. He was gone. Like a mechanical doll Eleanor put her papers away—she did not know when she would be back to deal with them, perhaps not ever… Then she edged her way along the passage and cautiously peered out. The library was, as she had expected, empty. When she heard the sound of a horse outside she looked out of the window—he was riding away along the lane towards Badgers. Swiftly Eleanor walked out of the library, out of Stanyards, and out of Jonas Guthrie's life. When Eleanor had learned that Stanyards was lost to her she had roamed the estate all day in an effort to rid herself of the pain. This course was not possible now—there was the danger that she might inadvertently come across its owner, and that thought made her feel physically ill. Instead she went to earth. She walked as unseeing, as heedless as that first time, but with the clear purpose of seeking the refuge of the Dower House. No one saw her, no one stopped her and once she reached her bedchamber there she sat huddled in a chair for hours.

Towards evening Betty came into the room and stopped short when she saw her. 'Miss Nell! Whatever are you doing there? I thought you were out!'

Eleanor turned her head away to the window. 'I… I didn't feel well…'

'Indeed you don't! You're cold as ice!' exclaimed Betty, feeling Eleanor's hands. 'Come, Miss Nell, let me get you into bed.' She bustled about, calling on one of the maids to warm the sheets, and sending another to make a hot drink. By this time reaction was causing Eleanor to shiver, and Betty was convinced that she had caught a feverish cold. 'You shouldn't have done all that visiting on the farms, Miss Nell. There's a lot of sickness about down there. Let's hope it is a cold, and not something worse!'

By this time Mrs Southeran had been told, and, ignoring Betty's protests about the risk, she came hurrying into Eleanor's room.

'What nonsense! As if I should not wish to see for myself what is wrong! Eleanor, my dear child!'

While Betty scolded and Mrs Southeran talked of sending someone for Dr Smithson, Eleanor lay passive and silent in her bed, wishing they would go away. Eventually the two women decided that Eleanor should be made as comfortable as possible for the present and that Dr Smithson should be summoned if she grew worse the next day. Betty fussed about for a minute or two longer, then left Mrs Southeran in charge. There was silence in the little room.

After a while Mrs Southeran said tentatively, 'Nell? Are you awake?' Eleanor slowly turned her head towards her mother, who was sitting in a chair by the bed with a shaded lamp on the table next to her. 'Does it hurt? Does your head ache?'

Eleanor looked at her mother's anxious face and whispered, 'No. Not my head. Try not to worry, Mama. I'm not ill, truly. I'll…I'll be all right tomorrow.'

'Something has happened, hasn't it? No, don't turn your head away again. I won't pry.'

'Perhaps I'll tell you tomorrow. I can't just now. I think I'd like to sleep.' Mrs Southeran nodded, and got up and kissed her.

'Call me if you need me, my darling. I'll see you in the morning.' They both knew that Eleanor was not likely to sleep, but rather that she wanted to be alone. 'Do you wish me to leave the lamp?'

'No—you take it.'

Mrs Southeran went out quietly, leaving the door open a crack lest her daughter should call, and the room was in darkness.

Eleanor lay dry-eyed, staring at the shaft of moonlight which came through the curtains. If asked she would have said afterwards that her mind had been empty throughout the night—she was certainly not conscious of thought. But the next morning she found she had made a decision. Mrs Southeran was seated at the breakfast table when Eleanor walked in. 'Good morning, Mama,' she said, kissing her mother. 'I hope you slept well? As you see, your anxieties were unnecessary last night. I am perfectly well again this morning. No fever, no aches and pains!'

Mrs Southeran looked at her daughter's hollow eyes

and pale cheeks, at the evidence of the control she was exercising in her trembling hands and set mouth, and said gently, 'I'm glad. Will you have some breakfast?'

'Of course!' Smiling brightly, Eleanor sat down. 'I would like to talk to you, Mama.' Mrs Southeran looked up sharply, but it was clear that Eleanor was not about to say anything about her distress of the night before. She went on, 'You remember Aunt Hetty wrote the other day to say that she and my uncle were back in London? I think I should like to visit them again. Would you object? I am sure Cousin Louisa would be ready to stay with you here.'

The fleeting expression of dismay on Mrs Southeran's face was quickly replaced with a smile. 'I think that is an excellent idea! I expect Hetty is missing Bella still, and would like your company. She probably wishes to carry on improving you, Nell, or die in the attempt! And as for me, I really do not need Louisa. I am so much better now that I think I should prefer to be on my own. How long would you wish to be in London?'

Eleanor caught the wistful note in her mother's voice, and came over to kneel down beside her. 'Not very long. Two weeks? Three at the most. I…' Her voice showed signs of strain. 'I must get away, Mama.'

'It's Jonas, isn't it, Nell?'

'Yes,' said Eleanor briefly. 'But I cannot talk about it. And you must not worry, Mama—no lasting damage has been done. But I need some time to come to terms with it.'

'Well, then, you must go as soon as possible! I have a little money saved. You shall travel in comfort!'

A letter to Lady Walcot was dispatched immediately, but, having seen her daughter's impatience to be away, Mrs Southeran decided that it was unnecessary to wait for a reply—they both knew what it would be. Within three days of the scene in the library Eleanor was on her way to London. Mrs Southeran had a word with Betty, and soon it became known about the neighbourhood that Miss Southeran had gone to London on an errand of mercy. When she had heard that her aunt was confined to her bed, and that Bella, Lady Walcot's daughter, was still away, Miss Southeran had volunteered to look after her. In this way, any possible curiosity about Eleanor's sudden departure was satisfied. But Mrs Southeran did not leave it at that. Jonas Guthrie was invited to the Dower House the day after Eleanor had left.

'I am glad you've come, Jonas,' said Mrs Southeran as her visitor came in. 'I wondered a little whether you would.'

'Of course I would come, when you send such an intriguing invitation. I am not used to such formality from you. How are you? And…and how is Eleanor?'

'You know she has gone to London?'

'Yes, I had heard. Lady Walcot is ill, I hear. I'm sorry.'

'Sorry that my sister-in-law is ill, or sorry that Eleanor is not here?'

His face closed up. 'That is a strange question, Mrs Southeran.'

'And I want an honest answer, Jonas.' There was a pause during which Jonas Guthrie stared moodily at his hostess. 'Well?'

'I have to admit that I am glad Eleanor is not here for the moment.'

'Why?'

'I'm not sure I am prepared to tell you.'

'If you value my friendship, if you wish to retain the confidence I have always shown in you, you will tell me,

Jonas,' said Mrs Southeran steadily. 'You have made my daughter unhappier than she has ever been in her life, and I wish to know why.'

'We…we had a disagreement—a trivial one, you would say.'

'About something on the estate? Threlfall, perhaps?'

'What else would we quarrel about?' he said, with an involuntary laugh. 'It's the only thing we differ on. And you cannot say it hasn't happened before.'

'Exactly! But in this case it is more than that. What have you said to her?'

'I?' he asked, startled. 'Why, nothing.'

'Jonas, stop playing with me. I am deadly serious.'

'And so am I, by God,' he said with feeling.

'Then you will tell me why you have made Eleanor so unhappy, when you once promised me that you would not. And I trusted you.'

Jonas looked at his hostess doubtfully, then seemed to come to some conclusion. 'I have always confided in you. May I confide in you this time with an assurance that you will tell no one—no one at all, not even Eleanor—what I say?'

'If it is important to Eleanor's happiness, then yes, you have my word. I will tell no one.'

'It may be important to Eleanor's…safety. What would you say if I told you that any interest I show in her puts her at risk?'

Mrs Southeran stared at him. 'I'd say you were moonstruck! What on earth are you talking about?'

'Nathaniel Oliver. I think he is mad, but I dare not ignore what he said. He thinks he can best punish me for something I have done to him by…hurting anyone I hold dear.'

'Nathaniel Oliver said this?' asked Mrs Southeran incredulously. 'I could imagine it of his wife, perhaps, but not of that milksop!'

'Believe me, I think it is wise to take him seriously for the moment. I am hoping he will eventually give up and go back to Boston, and I have done my best to see that he does, but until then I dare not provoke his malice. And consequently I have used the excuse of our quarrel to avoid Eleanor's company.'

'And do you hold Eleanor dear? I know I have asked you this before, but things have advanced since then, have they not?'

He turned round and said fiercely, 'Not even to you will I say anything of my feelings! When the time comes I shall make them clear to the world, including the person they most affect, but until Oliver is safely out of the country the only course is for them to remain unknown. Eleanor is safe in London. Let her stay there for a while.'

'Very well. But I still do not understand, Jonas. When she left she was…not just unhappy. She was devastated. Are you sure there has been nothing more than a certain coolness between you?'

'Quite certain.'

'Then someone else must have said something to her. I wonder who it was…?'

'Mrs Southeran, I beg of you, do nothing to make my interest in Eleanor apparent. Or hers in me.'

'No, I see that I mustn't. But I must write to her—oh, don't worry! I shall not tell her of Oliver's threats.'

'Can I ask you not even to mention my name? Oliver is like a cat—he scents things out. I would trust no one to conceal things from him.'

'May I not even tell her that you are not as indifferent as she apparently thinks?'

'For God's sake, do not! I cannot over-emphasise the danger.'

Mrs Southeran looked at him wide-eyed. 'You really *are* afraid of him, aren't you, Jonas? Then I will do as you say.'

He went to the door, but stopped there and said with uncharacteristic hesitation, 'If you hear from Eleanor, could you…will you let me know—in confidence—how she is?'

'Yes, I will. Now go and get rid of Mr Oliver as quickly as you can.'

But after a while it seemed that Mr Oliver had decided to abandon his vendetta for the time being. Mrs Anstey and Phoebe were to travel to Oxfordshire for Marianne's wedding, and Mr and Mrs Oliver decided to accompany them. When Jonas gave this news to Mrs Southeran she thought for a moment, then said, 'But I cannot see that this changes the situation as far as you and Mr Oliver are concerned—unless he returns to Boston direct from the wedding?'

'No, he will not do that. I keep a very careful check on the gentleman's actions, and the Olivers have left a good number of their possessions at Church Cottage. They will be back. But at least they will be occupied for a while, enjoying themsleves in Oxfordshire—the wedding might have been held in London!'

'That would have been worrying, I agree. I do not like to think of Mr Oliver near Eleanor. Thank God he isn't! But, tell me, is it true that Phoebe Gardiner is also going with her mother? That is surely a sudden decision—the last time I spoke to her she seemed set on

staying in Somerset.' When Jonas looked slightly uncomfortable, she went on, 'Am I to take it she is aban-
doning her pursuit of you, Jonas?'

'Let us say, rather, that when I mentioned one or two
very eligible gentlemen who were certain to be at
Marianne's wedding she decided her duty lay with her
family. I do not think she will return to Combe St James.
But I am glad to say that we parted friends.'

'I must make sure I see her before she leaves. I have
written a little poem for her—knowing her has given me
so much pleasure, I could do no less!'

Mrs Anstey, Mrs Gardiner and the Olivers set off in state
with the good wishes and admiration of the neighbourhood, and after they had gone life in and around Combe
St James resumed its normal, uneventful course.
However, in picturing the Olivers safe in Oxfordshire,
Mrs Southeran and Jonas were deceiving themselves. It
was true that this was what the Olivers had originally
intended, but there was a change of plan after the first day
of their journey. It resulted from a conversation between
man and wife in the Woolpack Inn at Trowbridge, where
they spent the night.

'Phoebe is quite cast down, Nathaniel.'

'Really, my dear? Why?'

'It has become clear to her that she will not entice
Jonas into her net again. She did not say so in so many
words, but it is evident that he is no longer attracted to
her—if he ever was.'

'Are you sure, Evadne? Perhaps he is feigning indifference to put us off?'

'No, I do not think so. There must be someone else. Yet
I thought he was convincing about the Southeran girl.'

'Then perhaps what he told you was true—he intends to catch one of next year's fillies?'

'It's possible. Though…'

'What?'

'Well, why did Miss Southeran disappear so quickly to London?'

'Her aunt is ill.'

'Do you believe it? Might Jonas not have seen to it that she was sent out of the way? It is a possibility.'

There was a silence. Then Nathaniel Oliver said, 'My love, I think I may not, after all, come with you to Marianne's wedding. Weddings do not, as you know, interest me a great deal. Would you mind if I left the party when we reach the Bath Road, and take the stage instead to London? You have the two grooms to protect you.'

'Do not do anything rash, Nathaniel.'

'I would just like to see for myself if Lady Walcot is ill. If not…perhaps we could test Mr Jonas Damned Guthrie's feelings. Do you think you could let someone in Combe St James know of our change of plan?'

'Let me see… I could arrange for one of the men here to fetch something for me…something I had forgotten. I could write a note to Mrs Desmond. Now, what could it be…?'

Lady Walcot expressed surprised delight at seeing her niece so soon after her last visit, and her husband came in several times to interrupt Eleanor's conversation with her aunt just to say how pleased he was that she was back in London again.

'I've laid on a horse and groom for you, Eleanor, my dear. Don't let your aunt dissuade you from your early morning rides. Best time of the day.'

But, in the privacy of Lady Walcot's bedroom that night, the Walcots gave voice to their shock at the change in their niece's appearance. 'Anthea didn't say what was wrong. She merely asked me to take care of Eleanor until she was herself again. What can it be, Charles?'

'Has she been ill?'

'I don't think so.'

'Perhaps she's been crossed in love? That's often the case with females when there isn't any other explanation.'

'That's it, Charles! That is it! It's that man Guthrie! Oh, I know everyone hints now that he has been misjudged—though how that can be I don't know—but I *knew* no good would come of Eleanor's association with him. How could Anthea have sold Stanyards to him? It was simply asking for trouble.'

'Er…better not say anything to Eleanor, Hetty. If it isn't Guthrie, you'll have wasted your breath, and if it is…'

'Do you take me for a fool? We must distract her mind from it all until she forgets him. Once I am certain she is strong enough, I intend to show her a great deal more of London than she had time for in the spring. When are you free in the next few days, Charles?'

So after a day or two's rest Eleanor was taken on what was to prove a relentless round of pleasure. She welcomed the fact that she never stopped meeting people, visiting exhibitions, seeing the sights, that she never, ever seemed to have time to think—during the day.

It was different at night. Then, however exhausted she was, sleep eluded her till the early hours of the morning, and her mind turned and turned on a treadmill of despair. She despised Jonas Guthrie for the creature he was, but, worse, she despised herself for falling victim to his lies. She had thought him honest. He was a liar and a cheat. She had thought him an idealist. He was a shabby trickster, filling her mind with his visions for the future, while all the time he had merely been making use of her. How could she live with the thought of her idiocy? She, who had taken such pride in the quickness of her wits, had congratulated herself on the independence of her opinions!

But, gradually, her aunt's care and her uncle's obvious pride in his niece had their effect. Her bruised spirit slowly began to heal, and Eleanor at last started to recover her self-respect.

She had been in London for two weeks, and was reluctantly beginning to think of returning to Somerset. If she had had only herself to think of, she would have stayed in London much longer, although, she thought bitterly, Guthrie had been right—she was a country girl at heart. After a while, life in the capital seemed too confined; there were too many streets and not enough greenery, too much smoke and not enough air. Her reluctance to go back was not so much a desire to stay in London, but more a dislike of returning to Stanyards.

But her mother was on her conscience. She really should not be left alone for too long. Perhaps she might persuade her to think of moving elsewhere? There was nothing to keep them at Stanyards now, and, as far as Eleanor was concerned, every reason why they should leave. There must be other places in Somerset which were as attractive—or nearly. She must talk to her mother when she got back.

Of course the Walcots were disappointed that she was planning to leave them so soon. They had made plans for the next month at least, and were already talking of Christmas for everyone on their estate in

Kent. But Eleanor was adamant—for the moment she must return.

'Well, if you must, you must, Eleanor. And I have to say that you are looking a great deal more the thing than when you arrived. London has done you good.' Lady Walcot hesitated, then added, 'I have not enquired what was wrong, though I have my own ideas on the subject. But I should like to congratulate you, Eleanor, on the way you have refused to give in to your unhappiness. I have been full of admiration for the breeding and discipline you have shown—it has almost caused me to change my mind about this independence of yours.'

Eleanor was so touched at her aunt's tribute that she almost ruined the occasion by bursting into tears! But not quite. The hard days and even harder nights had taught her a great deal. She might have experienced uncontrollable passion, and, for a short while, paid for it with uncontrollable pain. But feelings of any kind were now firmly in her control again, and that was how they would stay.

Lady Walcot went on, 'I think you should choose what you wish to do before going back. Is there something that we still have not shown you?'

'You have shown me so much, I don't think there can be…unless…'

'Yes?'

'I should dearly love to see Vauxhall Gardens, Aunt Hetty. I've heard they are very pretty.'

'My dear, I think they have closed till next year—or are they open till the end of September? Let us hope so.'

It was soon established that the gardens were still open, and Lady Walcot set about arranging a party there with enthusiasm. In the end, a group of twelve people

of varying ages set off a few nights later across the
Thames to the famous pleasure gardens. The river was
busy, and it was not surprising that the party failed to
notice one of the other boats which was taking passen-
gers to Vauxhall. It might have given rise to comment
if they had, for one of the three men in it looked
strangely out of keeping with the other two. The first
was undoubtedly a gentleman. His two companions
were quite as obviously not...

Chapter Thirteen

Lord Walcot had taken two of the best boxes for the evening, and Eleanor was so delighted with the lights and the music which wafted through the night air that she forgot for a little the stony feeling in her heart. There was a certain coolness in the air—it was, after all, September—and the ladies kept their wraps on. In company with the younger members of the party Eleanor wandered along the colonnades lit by hundreds of lamps, stood before the orchestra and watched the musicians, and took some refreshment in the rotunda. But when her companions went in search of other, more lively amusements she decided to return to her seat in the box to watch the world parade by.

By this time she was feeling a little tired and, truth to tell, weary in spirit as well as in body. When the rest of the party went in search of supper Eleanor was relieved to hear that Lord Walcot was staying where he was and she elected to stay with him.

'Does it live up to your expectations?' he asked when they were alone.

'Oh, yes, Uncle Charles!' she replied, rousing herself. 'It's like a fairyland! The lights, the music…'

'You don't have to pretend with me, you know. You have been splendid during your stay with us, but you don't have to keep it up before me. Has your aunt told you how proud we both are of you?'

'Don't!' she whispered. 'Please! I…'

'Yes, well, that's enough of that. I've told you and we can now forget it. Are you sure you don't want supper— a glass of wine, even? It would be warmer there, and I would take you if you wished.'

Eleanor looked at the noisy crowds streaming in and out of the rotunda. 'If you don't mind, Uncle Charles, I would rather stay here. The supper-rooms are a little hot and…airless. Would you object if we just sat quietly for a while? I have a touch of the headache—and the megrims. To tell truth, I am not looking forward to going back to Somerset.'

'Then stay in London,' he said promptly.

'You mustn't tempt me,' Eleanor replied with a smile. 'I must face it like a man! Besides, Mama looks to see me before too long. Perhaps we shall come to Kent, both of us together.'

'That would be delightful.' They sat in companionable silence for a while, and Eleanor felt some of her stretched nerves easing. The crowds were thinning now—the night air was cool enough to tempt them inside. Even Eleanor started to feel the cold. She gave a little shiver.

'Right, that's it, Eleanor! It's time we went. I wonder where your aunt can have got to? If you'll wait here for a moment—you'll be perfectly safe if you stay well back in the box—I'll fetch her. Don't leave the box, mind!'

His tall figure disappeared in the direction of the rotunda and Eleanor closed her eyes...

'Please!' The voice broke in on her thoughts and she sat up and leaned forward to see who or what it was. A young woman was standing in front of the box. 'Are you Miss Southeran?'

When Eleanor said she was, the girl, for she wasn't much more than that, went on, 'It's your aunt, Miss Southeran. She's hurt her foot on the way back from supper. She can't walk. Is Lord Walcot with you?'

'No,' said Eleanor, standing up, alarmed. 'He thought she was still having supper, and has gone to fetch her. Where is my aunt?'

The girl pointed towards the avenue of trees leading away from the central walk. 'She's sitting under that tree—can you see her?'

Peering, Eleanor could just make out a muffled figure on the grass under the first of the trees. 'Lord Walcot is probably in the rotunda—could you please let him know? I'll see if I can help her.'

Quite forgetting her uncle's admonition, Eleanor left the box and ran over to the tree, only to stop with a cry when a ruffianly-looking man stepped out from behind it, and advanced towards her. She looked down—a second man lay there laughing at her. She turned and made to run back, but they caught her with ease.

'Here's a little beauty! I didn't know we were going to catch such a queen, did you, Jack? Look at this!' Between them the two men had dragged her further down the path to a more secluded spot, and had now paused in their endeavours.

'It's a real shame to spoil this,' said the one called

Jack, examining Eleanor while the first man held her, his huge hand over her mouth.

Eleanor had been paralysed by fright and the unexpected attack, but she now suddenly recovered. She bit the hand over her mouth, and as the man swore and pulled it away she screamed as loudly as she could. The scream was broken off abruptly as Jack clamped his hand roughly over her mouth, and snatched her into a rough embrace. 'You should've watched out for that, Bart—she's a girl of spirit, this one. I like her!' He grinned evilly down into her face, his breath stale and reeking of brandy. 'I think we could have a bit of sport with her, don't you? There's no hurry, is there?'

'Yes, there is—they'll be lookin' for her soon,' said Bart sullenly, sucking his hand. 'Come on, let's finish it, then we can get our money and be off.'

Suddenly the man holding her was torn away and hurled to the ground. Eleanor stood in shock as she heard Mr Guthrie's voice say, 'Miss Southeran! Are you all right? Here, lean against this tree.'

She held on to the tree for dear life while her rescuer turned on the second man, who was rushing up to attack. Mr Guthrie met him head-on and Eleanor watched, horrified, as the man doubled up in pain, then was jerked up and lifted bodily by a blow to his jaw. He fell heavily some feet away and lay motionless. The first man started to get up, but fell back as Mr Guthrie turned to stand over him, his fists clenched and an expression of raw fury on his dark face. Eleanor had never before seen anyone look so dangerous.

'Have you…have you killed him?' she whispered, looking at the unconscious form of her attacker.

He turned, his face still grim. 'Not even half,' he

assured her. 'He'll wake up with a headache, that's all. What do you wish me to do with them?'

Eleanor thought, half hysterically, that he might be offering to murder them if that was what she wanted! 'I… What did they want with me?'

Mr Guthrie gave the man on the ground at his feet a none too gentle nudge, and hauled him up by the collar. 'Tell her!'

'We was…we was hired.'

'To do what?'

'Not to kill 'er, I swear! Just frighten her for a bit. He said you'd come.'

There was a sudden significant silence. Then Mr Guthrie rapped out, 'Who?'

'He didn't say who he was—no, don't hit me, I swear that's true! Bart would tell you the same…if he was conscious. He said we 'ad to frighten her, mebbe knock her about a bit. Aaggh! You're choking me!'

'You scum!'

'No, we didn't like the idea a bit, guv'nor! But he paid us a good bit on account, and said there was more… And he said you'd come before any real damage was done to her. If you didn't, we was to leave 'er here.' He added resentfully, 'But he didn't say you was a prize fighter!'

Guthrie turned to Eleanor. 'I think I know what happened and why.'

'Then tell me!'

'I will, but not here and now. Do you want me to give these two some more of their own medicine?'

Eleanor shuddered again. 'No! Leave them where they are. I'd rather forget them.'

'They ought to be handed over…'

'No! I don't want the fuss! I want to go…to go…
back. Leave them!'

'Very well.' He poked the first man with his foot. 'Have
you had enough? Or would you like another round?' His
teeth gleamed in a ferocious smile, and the man cringed
back, shaking his head. 'Then make yourself scarce—and
take the other piece of vermin with you.'

The man on the ground nodded vigorously, and Mr
Guthrie turned away to Eleanor. 'Come, let me help
you, Miss Southeran.'

'No,' said Eleanor, nervously backing away.

He gazed at her in astonishment. 'But you are very
shaken, I can see you are! You must allow me to help you!'

'You will help me best by leaving me alone!' said
Eleanor, her voice rising slightly. 'I am obliged to you—
very obliged to you—for rescuing me from those men,
but I do not wish for anything more.'

'This is absurd! Eleanor—'

'And I would be obliged if you would not make free
with my name, sir.'

'God damn it…' At a snort of derision from the man
behind him, Mr Guthrie swung round dangerously.

'Just going, guv'nor,' Jack said hastily, and hurried off.

But Eleanor had seized her chance and was now
some distance away, running to meet the Walcots. The
incident which had seemed to last an eternity to her
had, in fact, lasted the same length of time it had taken
her uncle to find his wife and return with her.

They were horrified when she began to tell them
what had happened, and their first reaction was to put
it down to the general lack of supervision in the Gardens
which accompanied the end of the season, and the con-
sequent increase in crime. But when Mr Guthrie arrived,

incidentally much to their surprise, he put the affair in a different light, and it began to acquire more sinister overtones. Lord Walcot was seriously concerned.

'We cannot let this pass, and I should like to discuss it further with you, Guthrie. But this is clearly neither the place nor the time. May I suggest that you come round to South Audley Street tomorrow—at ten?'

Eleanor went to bed exhausted, but found sleep once again impossible. Shivering in her bed, she relived her terrifying experience over and over, and whenever she dozed off she would wake up with a start, and it would all begin again. That there was some kind of unpleasant mystery behind it she did not doubt. Those men had known who she was, had enticed her deliberately into the avenue.

And how had Mr Guthrie turned up so fortuitously? She would rather have been rescued by almost any other man in London. She was haunted, too, by the violence of his attack on the two men, and the expression on his face as he'd looked at them afterwards. The memory of that dark, violent face kept her awake, and when she did sleep she was back with her nightmare.

Eleanor was not present during most of Lord Walcot's discussion with Mr Guthrie, but was invited to join them towards the end. She had spent the time alternately fuming at not being included in a matter which concerned her so closely, and feeling relieved at not having to be in the same room as Mr Guthrie for longer than was necessary. This was not because she might be distressed or feel regret for what was lost, but rather because she felt such distaste for his company. Even the night before, in her vulnerable state after being attacked, her only desire afterwards had been to escape from him.

So when she entered her uncle's study she was composed, but in no mood to suffer any attempt to treat her as if she were a defenceless woman needing male support.

'Eleanor, come in and sit down.' She went over to the chair her uncle indicated, giving a cool nod to Mr Guthrie on the way, but without actually meeting his eye. 'What Mr Guthrie has been telling me has astonished me beyond belief. May I ask you a few questions, my dear? Or would you rather not talk about last night?'

'Of course I will, Uncle Charles. What do you wish to know?'

'Your uncle wishes to know how the men enticed you to come over to them, Miss Southeran. Can you recall the woman's exact words?'

Eleanor thought for a moment, then, looking at Lord Walcot, she said, 'I cannot remember the order exactly, but she told me that Aunt Hetty had hurt herself, and was lying under the tree. She asked if you were there, Uncle Charles.'

'How did she describe your uncle?'

Eleanor looked at Mr Guthrie and said dismissively, 'I don't know what you mean. She didn't describe him at all.'

'I think Mr Guthrie meant, did she mention my name? Or simply call me "your uncle"?'

'She called you Lord Walcot.'

'And you?' her uncle went on. 'Did she call you by name, too?'

'Yes. She called me Miss Southeran.'

Mr Guthrie, who had been sitting forward in his

chair, now sat back with the air of a man who had just proved a point.

Lord Walcot looked very grave. 'You were right, Guthrie. The plot was specifically against Eleanor. It is a pity you did not wait till the men could be apprehended and questioned.'

'I've told you, Lord Walcot. I know who the real villain is. And it isn't either of those two men.' He turned to Eleanor. 'Before I came, did they say anything about waiting for me, or expecting me?'

She turned to her uncle. 'Do you wish to know that, Uncle Charles?'

'Good God, Eleanor, we're not going to get very far if you persist in treating me as if I don't exist!'

'I know you exist, sir.' Her tone implied that she found this regrettable. 'And I have no desire to get anywhere as far as you are concerned.'

Lord Walcot had listened to this exchange with some amusement, but he now said, 'Mr Guthrie is right, Eleanor, my dear. The affair is too serious to play with. Did the men mention Mr Guthrie—or anyone else?'

Eleanor thought again. 'I think so. They…one of them said that he would…would like to h-have some sport.' In spite of herself her voice trembled, and Mr Guthrie got up and went over to the window, swearing under his breath. He came back.

'I should have killed them,' he said baldly.

'Sit down, Guthrie!' said Lord Walcot. 'I agree with the sentiment, but it would not have solved anything, only complicated things even more. Go on,' he said gently to Eleanor.

'Can't you see she's on the edge? At least give her some time to recover herself!' Mr Guthrie exclaimed.

'I am perfectly ready to continue now. The other one said, "they'll be looking for her soon"—I thought that meant you, Uncle Charles. He wanted to get his money and go.'

'Where?'

Eleanor looked blankly at Mr Guthrie. 'Where they were to go? I don't know.'

'The money, the money. Where were they going to collect the money?'

When Eleanor repeated that she didn't know, Mr Guthrie gave a snort of impatience. This roused Eleanor to say coldly, 'Do forgive me—I suppose I should have asked, but I forgot. I had other things on my mind.'

Lord Walcot shook his head with a smile, but then grew very serious. 'I apologise, Guthrie, for not believing you. I think you are right. Eleanor is under threat while she stays in London.'

'She is under threat wherever she is, until Oliver is caught. As yet, there isn't any real proof, and he appears to have gone underground. He is now certain which is his quarry, of course. I'm afraid I revealed my hand by following him to London to protect Eleanor.'

'What are you talking about?' asked Eleanor. 'Threats, proof, protection—what is it all about?'

'Mr Guthrie is certain that a man called Oliver intends to hurt him by hurting you, Eleanor. It seems incredible, but, I must say, the evidence of last night seems to confirm that. Mr Guthrie advises that we send you back to Somerset in his care, where he feels he can give you better protection. London is too full of villains for hire of all kinds. You'd be safer in the country, where strangers would stand out.'

Eleanor rose with dignity. 'I am not,' she said clearly, 'going anywhere with Mr Guthrie. Not now. Not ever.'

'Eleanor—'

'I have asked you not to be so free with my name, Mr Guthrie.'

Lord Walcot intervened. 'I think,' he said carefully, 'that I am going to leave you two alone for a few minutes. It seems to me,' he continued, overriding his niece's cry of protest, 'that, before we can get very far with this question of protection, other matters must be resolved first. No, Eleanor, I insist that you stay. I should like you both to remember that nothing—nothing at all—should be allowed to endanger Eleanor's life.'

He went out, leaving Mr Guthrie standing by the window and Eleanor glaring at the door.

'Eleanor, why are you so very angry with me?'

She turned to find him gazing at her with that same quizzical gleam in his eye which had disarmed her so often before. 'I am not angry with you, Mr Guthrie, although I wish you would do me the courtesy of listening when I ask you not to call me by my given name.'

'I thought I had been given that privilege?'

'It is withdrawn. If I appear angry, it is because I deeply resent my uncle's insistence that I stay in this room with you.'

Mr Guthrie came towards her. 'He loves you and wishes you to be protected.'

'The only protection I need at the moment is from you!'

'Isn't that what I said? I can protect you far better than anyone else.'

'That is not what I meant, and you know it! But why? Why are you doing this? What have you told my uncle to persuade him that you should be responsible for my safety? I find that intolerable.'

'I told him I loved you.'

There was a sudden silence. Then Eleanor said harshly, 'And he believed you? I must tell you that I do not.' He started to say something, but she went on, 'And if you try to say any more on that topic I will risk my uncle's displeasure and leave this room immediately.'

'But I do, God damn it— No! Don't go! I won't mention it again if you'll only stay. It's important that you listen to the rest. Please, El—Miss Southeran, come away from the door!'

Eleanor took her hand away from the door-handle and turned round slowly.

'Would you…would you sit down? This may take some time.' He had the sense to walk right away from her, after offering her a small upright chair not far from the door.

'I am waiting, Mr Guthrie.'

'I know, I know. It's just…'

Eleanor realised with surprise that he was nervous, and she wondered why. What lies was he preparing now?

Finally Mr Guthrie began, 'Rumour has it that I seduced Evadne Anstey. That is not true. When she came to me after Henry Anstey died and told me that she was having a child, she told me then that Oliver was the father. She said that he was prepared to marry her if she could find some money—a dowry, so to speak. I knew Oliver, and I advised Evadne to have nothing more to do with him. I offered to help her to go away until the child was born and could be adopted. She could then come back afterwards to resume her life in Boston. I wish now I had insisted.'

He walked about the room. 'Instead I gave her the

dowry Oliver demanded.' He came to a halt in front of Eleanor. 'I had the money, and it was what she wanted,' he said, as if to explain.

Eleanor remained silent, though the words she had overheard in the library were echoing in her mind. Evadne Anstey had *blackmailed* Mr Guthrie into giving her the money. It hadn't been the voluntary, charitable gift he was claiming. What had been Evadne's hold over him, if not the fact that he had seduced her? And what about the settlement on the child once it had been born?

Mr Guthrie gave up waiting for a response and went on, 'Oliver was—is—a strange man. Evadne found that he already had a young man, Christopher Digby, living with him, of whom he was…very fond. In fact, he was devoted to him. Christopher is that curious phenomenon, a person without any moral sense whatsoever—not immoral so much as amoral. When Oliver learned that Amelia Anstey, his wife's mother, stood to inherit my estate if I should die before marrying, he decided to have me killed off. Christopher was his intended instrument—fortunately an incompetent one. You yourself witnessed one attempt in Hyde Park. There were others, including the last, disastrous attempt which might have cost you your life.'

Eleanor made a sudden movement. 'The man on the hill,' she said. 'It was Christopher?'

'Yes. I had hoped that they would give up when I moved to Somerset. I kept my destination a secret from all but a few people in London. But then Amelia came to Combe St James and my efforts were wasted. I had to act—so I decided to deprive Oliver of his tool. I abducted Christopher Digby, and sent him willy-nilly to Madras. I have friends there, and they will keep an eye on him.' He added with a slight grin, 'One way or another.'

Mr Guthrie had so far been talking almost dispassionately, as if the events he had been recounting did not concern him closely. But now the atmosphere changed, and he said very gravely, 'Oliver has taken the loss of Christopher very hard. He won't risk attacking me himself—but the accident on the bridge has given him the idea of making me suffer through you. He has sworn to damage, maim, even to kill any woman I love, anyone I intend to marry.'

Eleanor rose from her chair. She was paler than ever. 'And that was the reason for the attack on me last night? The man is a madman!'

'He is all the more dangerous if he is. It is fast becoming an obsession with him.'

'But you must tell him that you do not love me!' she cried.

'He will not believe me—especially as I raced to London the minute I heard you and he were both here. I see now that that was what he intended. It gave the confirmation he was seeking. I must take you back to Somerset, Eleanor—Miss Southeran.'

'Tell him that I do not love you!'

He was pale. 'Is that true?'

'Yes, it is! How can you ask? I would not, could not, think of loving you ever again.'

'Why? Because I was unkind to you in the stable yard? Don't you think you are being excessively sensitive about that? I've told you the reason—it was to put Oliver off the scent.'

Eleanor was in a dilemma. She could not bring herself to tell him that she had overheard his conversation with Evadne when he had denied that he loved Eleanor Southeran. Yet the pain she had suffered because of it lay at the heart of her refusal to consider that he might now be sincere. How could she ever trust him unreservedly again? He had been totally convincing in his denials of any interest in her, his claim to have been dallying.

'Tell him!' she said again.

'It would make no difference,' he said grimly. 'As long as he believes you are important to me, you are at risk.' He turned away. 'Is it not ironic? I have as little chance of convincing him that you are not important to me as I apparently have of convincing you that you are—that I love you, and want more than anything in the world to marry you.'

'What about your title?' said Eleanor bitterly. 'I wouldn't be much of a great lady!'

'What do you mean?' His eyes narrowed. 'When did you hear of my title?'

'Never mind. I am not travelling to Somerset in your company, Mr Guthrie!'

'And if your uncle insists?'

'He knows me well enough not to insist.'

'Eleanor— Oh, God damn it, Miss Southeran! This is not a game! Lord Walcot would be risking your life if he does not see that you have adequate protection. I tell you, Oliver is dangerous!'

'I do not think the risk is nearly as great as you fear. But in any case I would take it—and more—rather than suffer your company for two days.'

On this Eleanor would not be moved, not by Mr Guthrie, nor later by her uncle.

'May I suggest, Lord Walcot, that your niece at least has an escort to Hounslow? That might be far enough from London—especially as Oliver can have no suspicion that she is leaving tomorrow instead of later in the week.'

Lord Walcot was not at first at all happy with this compromise, but finally gave in. Eleanor would leave the next day in the Walcot coach, and would change over to a post-chaise at Hounslow. Lord Walcot's coachman would see to the post-boys and horses himself, before he returned.

Eleanor left London the next morning. In contrast to her departure earlier in the year there was little ceremony, for the aim this time was to make it as unobtrusive as possible.

She had said her farewells the night before, and had been touched and relieved when her uncle had returned unusually early from his club to spend some time with her. Lord Walcot had clearly been impressed with Mr Guthrie, and she had been afraid that her obstinate refusal to have anything to do with the man might have offended him. But he had been as affectionate as ever, merely anxious for her safety. He had told her that, though the Walcot coach and driver would return from Hounslow, John, the groom, would stay with her all the way to Somerset.

'I can be sure then that you will travel in comfort and safety, my dear. Please don't refuse this precaution as you did the others!'

'Thank you, Uncle Charles. I confess I shall be relieved to have someone I can trust with me.'

'You could have had Mr Guthrie.'

'I trust John.'

No more was said on that score, and the following morning Eleanor climbed into her uncle's well-sprung coach and set off on the first stage of her journey.

They made good time through Kensington village,

Hammersmith and Brentford and arrived in Hounslow about nine o'clock. Here they stopped, and Eleanor went into the inn to have a light breakfast while John arranged for a post-chaise and horses. There were always plenty to choose from. Hounslow was said to stable over two thousand horses, and was one of the busiest posting centres in England—all the Western Mails stopped here. Travellers could be reasonably certain of finding a comfortable chaise and some good, reliable horses.

She finished her breakfast, was shown one of the bedrooms where she could tidy herself up, and then decided to go in search of John. He would be in the stable yard behind the inn. At the bottom of the stairs she hesitated, uncertain of the way.

'It's to your right, ma'am,' said one of the maids who was flitting past. Eleanor took the doorway on her right and walked up the passage. The morning sun streaming in through the opening at the end dazzled her, and she could hardly see where to put her feet. Suddenly someone grabbed her from behind, put a gloved hand over her mouth and dragged her into a dark store-room to the side of the passage. She struggled and kicked, and once almost escaped, but in the end it was to no avail. Whoever it was had a grip of iron.

'Put the sack on her. You'll have to tie it on—there's no time to waste,' said a hoarse voice. A rough sack was put over Eleanor's head, and tied round her middle. The hand had been removed and she screamed, but the sound was lost in the folds of the sack.

'Scream away, darlin'. They won't hear you through there in the taproom, and there ain't anyone else,' said a second voice.

Eleanor felt completely helpless. The rope which held the sack in place also bound her arms to her sides, making resistance impossible. She tried to kick, but her feet were caught and tied together. Then she was slung up over a man's shoulder like a bundle of rags.

'Where do you want 'er, guv'nor?' said the second voice. There was no reply that Eleanor could hear, but she was carried along the passage and out into the fresh air. 'Hold the door and mind 'er 'ead. We don't want to damage 'er, do we?' said the same man, with a spine-chilling laugh.

Eleanor was deposited on a narrow strip of floor, the door was slammed shut and the coach—for that was what she surmised it was—set off. She strained her ears for any sound, any clue as to what was happening, but she could hear nothing out of the way, only the ordinary noises of the inns and houses lining their route.

She seemed to be alone inside the coach. It travelled sedately till it was on the high road, then it picked up speed. Eleanor was unable to prevent herself from rolling backwards and forwards as they went over the potholes and bumps in the road. She was very uncomfortable, but, more than that, she was very frightened. What were they going to do with her?

If they were travelling over Hounslow Heath, which she rather thought they were, then anything could happen, for it was a long stretch of deserted road, with plenty of bushes and scrub in which to hide a body. Was that what they were going to do—kill her? Or were they going to abandon her, as they would have done the other night, but this time on the Heath, a known haunt of highwaymen and thieves? The sack suddenly seemed unbearably constricting, and she felt choked, panic rising within her.

She must think about something else quickly. What about John? What had happened to him? Perhaps he was now lying injured, or worse, in some dark corner in Hounslow. Oh, how could she have been so pigheaded? Her uncle had been right to be anxious, and she should have paid more attention to him, especially after the attack at Vauxhall. Why had she allowed her dislike of Guthrie to override her common sense? She was about to pay dearly for her stupidity.

Eleanor's spirits were rapidly reaching a low ebb when the coach suddenly turned off the road and stopped. She held her breath and braced herself. The door was opened, two people climbed in, and she was hauled up and placed on the seat. They sat down, one each side of her. Oh, God, what were they going to do? There was a knot of fear in her stomach, and she felt sick.

But then the coach started off again! One of her captors grasped her arms and held her, while the other started to release her bonds. What on earth were these people up to? Unless she was very much mistaken, the person holding her was a woman! Suddenly the sack was removed and she was gazing into the face of the maidservant from the inn!

'You are a formidable woman, Miss Southeran. You fought so fiercely that we had to truss you up like a chicken before we could persuade you to come with us. I'm sorry if you have been uncomfortable.'

Eleanor whirled round. Mr Guthrie sat looking at her with a sardonic smile on his face.

Chapter Fourteen

Eleanor was overcome with a mixture of relief and scorching fury. 'You…you villain!' she shouted. 'You heartless, scheming villain!' She swung her hand to hit him, but he laughed and held her wrists. She snatched her hands away and beat her fists against his chest, out of her mind with anger. Then she burst into tears. Mr Guthrie put his arm around her, but she leapt up, only to lose her balance in the lurching of the coach and fall on to the seat opposite. He leant forward, and she backed away into the corner.

'Don't touch me!'

'I wasn't going to touch you, only to try to speak to you. Pull yourself together, Eleanor.'

'My name is Miss Southeran,' she shouted.

'I shall call you Miss Southeran when you start behaving less like a child and more like a lady.'

Eleanor stopped short. She looked down at her dirty dress, at the inelegant way she had pulled her legs up on to the seat to avoid contact with him, and was shocked. She straightened herself and tried to smooth her hair with hands that still trembled.

'May I help you, Miss Southeran?' It was the maid-servant.

'Not until I know who you are, and what you are doing here.'

Mr Guthrie replied for her. 'Her name is Maggie Carver. When she heard of the danger you were in she agreed to help me. She is an old friend.'

'I'm sure she is,' agreed Eleanor sweetly.

'Er, excuse me, Miss Southeran, but what Mr Guthrie should have said is that my husband, Sam, and I are old friends of his. Both of us,' said Maggie calmly. 'I'm not sure Sam would like your tone, begging your pardon.'

'You can hardly blame me for thinking the worst. Abduction is hardly the work of honest people,' said Eleanor, not giving ground.

'Sam is driving the coach now. I should prefer not to stop again, but if you wish to meet him I will ask him to draw up for a second,' said Mr Guthrie.

'I would prefer not to have met any of you. I can do without meeting Mr Carver—his wife was enough.'

'Eleanor, stop this. Maggie and Sam have done you a favour, possibly even saved your life. Now let Maggie help you to get yourself in order. Your hair needs urgent attention, and your bonnet must be here somewhere. We threw it in after you.' He picked up a sad confection from the floor. 'Er…I think you must have rolled on it.'

'Of course I did,' said Eleanor, her temper rising again. 'I rolled on everything! I couldn't stop myself. I must have bruises everywhere.'

He grew serious. 'We didn't intend to hurt you. That was the last thing I wanted. But you were fighting like a wildcat. Where *did* you pick up some of those tricks? We had seen Oliver arriving in Hounslow, so we had to hide you and get away with speed. That's why you were on the floor of the coach.'

'Oliver?'

'Yes, he's a determined man. God knows how he picked up your trail. Did you make a great fuss when you left? I advised your uncle against it.'

'My uncle— That reminds me! What have you done with John?'

'He has gone back to London to report that all is well.'

'Gone back! To report! You mean that my uncle knew about this?'

'We planned it together last night, after you had been so stupidly determined to let your prejudice against me override all caution. I'm glad we did. You might otherwise be facing Oliver here on the Heath, instead of me.'

'Are you trying to tell me that all this rough treatment of me was with my uncle's consent? I don't believe you!'

'You must, of course, believe what you choose. I don't think he realised quite what an Amazon you are. I certainly never expected to have to fight you, or to tie you up so comprehensively. Nor to have to deposit you on the floor. We released you as soon as we could, but we had to get well clear of Hounslow before stopping. Now, if you stop complaining, and concentrate instead on repairing the damage, Maggie will soon put you to rights. I'll look the other way.'

Maggie opened a small dressing-case which was on the seat beside Eleanor. She took out various toilet articles, and a clean tucker, and set to work.

'Thank you, Mrs Carver,' said Eleanor reluctantly. 'I'm sorry if I insulted you before. I was angry. In fact, I still am.' She glared at Mr Guthrie, who was studying the drear landscape outside.

'It's very natural, miss. You must have suffered a terrible shock. And I didn't like lying to you back there at the inn, but Mr Guthrie said it was vital that we got you away. We all know Mr Oliver.'

'You do? How?'

'We were in Mr Guthrie's service while he was in Boston. Mr Oliver is a wicked man.'

'Well, now, Miss Southeran,' said a voice from the other corner of the carriage. 'May I look round?'

'I am in your power, sir. How can I stop you?' said Eleanor coldly.

'You know that's not true. If you were, I should do a lot more than look round, believe me. Ah! You've worked miracles, Maggie. What about Miss Southeran's bonnet?'

'I'm afraid the bonnet is beyond repair, sir. I'll get another one out of her valise when we arrive at Salisbury.'

'We are staying the night at Salisbury, Miss Southeran,' said Mr Guthrie, turning to Eleanor. 'We should make it easily. Maggie here will look after you at the inn, though it won't be the most comfortable in the town. We shall stay somewhere less conspicuous, somewhere from which we can observe Oliver without being observed ourselves. Then when he sets off tomorrow we can see which road he chooses—Shaftesbury or Blandford—and we shall take the other. It will make for a more relaxed journey.'

'Mr Guthrie, I have been frightened half to death, tossed about like a sack of potatoes, am forced to endure your company to Somerset when you know the thought is anathema to me—how can you say that this journey could in any way be relaxed?' Eleanor's voice rose on these last words. It was obvious that she was not at all reconciled to her circumstances.

Mr Guthrie pulled a face and said to Maggie grimly, 'Would you object to joining Sam on the box for a while, Maggie? I think some matters are best sorted out in private.'

Maggie smiled sympathetically at him and said she would like a breath of fresh air. It would do her good.

When the change had been effected Mr Guthrie turned to Eleanor and said, 'Now you may give free vent to your spleen, Miss Southeran. Let us have it out in the open. Why *do* you dislike me to this extent, when I have given you no real reason?'

'No real reason? What of your treatment of me in Hounslow?'

'That isn't the issue, and you know it. Don't fence with me, Eleanor. It isn't worthy of you! This question is far too important to both of us.'

Eleanor was silent.

'Eleanor?'

'Don't call m—'

'God damn it, girl, stop playing! You know I have a right to call you Eleanor! Or have you forgotten that you once lay in my arms, begging me to kiss you again, lost to all sense of time or place, caught up in a passion over which you had no control? I am not too much of a gentleman to remind you that it wasn't you who called a halt before we reached the point of no return, Eleanor Southeran!'

Eleanor had listened to this impassioned speech with growing horror. She had tried to stop him, but he swept on, disregarding her frantic pleas.

'You love me, Eleanor Southeran, every bit as much as I love you. Don't try to deny it, or claim that you have forgotten any part of the episode by the combe!'

Eleanor, who had taken pride in the way she had

suppressed her feelings, who had refused to let them surface for the past two weeks, was now almost beside herself with pain. The stoic restraint, the iron control she had exercised, at least in public, were shattered, and the storm of tears over Jonas Guthrie's perfidy, which she had never before allowed herself, now broke.

'Stop it, stop it!' she cried. 'Of course I remember! I can't stop remembering! I would to God I could forget! You are not worthy of all this pain. You do not love me— you are a liar and a cheat, and I despise myself for having been deceived into thinking you were ever anything else!'

She huddled into the corner and cried as if her heart was breaking—hard, dry sobs which were not any easy relief from shattered nerves, but deep, bitter grief.

Mr Guthrie looked at her incredulously. 'Eleanor! Don't! Don't, my love, I can't bear it. What is all this for? What have I done? Oh, my God, tell me…' He looked helplessly at her, not daring to approach her, for once in his life at a complete loss.

Finally, when the storm of grief was calming down, he said quietly, 'You must talk to me again. I didn't realise… I thought you were simply being difficult… But this…' He stopped abruptly. Eleanor took her hands from her face and looked up. He was gazing at her uncertainly, with such baffled misery in his eyes that a tiny seed of doubt was planted in her mind.

He went on, 'I honestly don't understand why you think so badly of me. I love you, Eleanor, more than my life. Why can't you believe that? You had such amazing, such incredibly illogical trust in me before—against all reason, all reputation. Why has that gone?'

'You never said that you loved me,' she whispered.

'You only ever offered me friendship. But I thought you did…love me. You…we behaved as if you did. You talked of the future.' The tears came now, rolling down her cheeks unchecked as she went on. 'And then you…then you said that you didn't, that you never had loved me. You were very convincing.' She turned her head away from him. 'I don't know what to think. But I can't quite believe anything you say any more.'

He was frowning. 'When did I say this, Eleanor? That I didn't love you?'

Eleanor was feeling wearier than she had ever felt in her life before. The experiences of the morning, on top of the many sleepless nights preceding them, had overwhelmed her. She was incapable of fencing with him. She yawned and made an effort to respond. 'I…can't remember…'

Her voice trailed away. She heard Jonas get up and sit beside her. He took her into his arms and when she somewhat half-heartedly protested he said soothingly, 'Have a rest, my love. Things will be better when you wake. We can sort all this out another time. Sleep now.' That was the last Eleanor knew.

Jonas sat with Eleanor asleep in his arms for the rest of the way to Salisbury. Occasionally he rested his cheek on her hair, or kissed the top of her head. But for the most part he simply sat there, deep in thought. It was clear now that Eleanor had been told something of his conversation with Evadne Oliver. But who had done this? There had been no witnesses. Had Evadne herself spoken to Eleanor? It was unlikely, but not impossible. Though Eleanor had disappeared to London quite soon after the scene in the library, she hadn't left straight away.

His mind turned to that visit to London. To help Lady Walcot while she was ill, it had been said. This wasn't so, of course—Mrs Southeran had told him her daughter had fled to London 'unhappier than she had ever been in her life', and she had taken him to task for it.

Evadne must have seen Eleanor! And if Eleanor had been told what he had said to Evadne in the library, and had believed it, then he was not surprised at her distress when she had fled to London. His mouth tightened as he thought of what she must have suffered.

It was dark when they reached Salisbury. They found an inn slightly off the beaten track but not too far from the centre. After a short meal Eleanor, still exhausted, went upstairs accompanied by Maggie, who was to sleep on a truckle bed in her room. Sam went out as soon as he had eaten on a tour of the inns and taverns in the town. He came back after an hour or so and gave Mr Guthrie a nod. Oliver had been spotted.

'I hope you don't mind, guv'nor—I've given a couple of lads some of the ready to keep an eye on the gent. He won't go without us knowin' about it.'

Jonas and Sam spent a convivial half-hour in the taproom, and if there were some who looked askance at the oddly assorted pair neither of them minded. They had known each other a long time, and been through a good many fights together.

The next morning the party, having been informed that Mr Oliver was taking the more popular route by way of Blandford and Dorchester, prepared to leave for Shaftesbury and Sherborne.

Eleanor woke up much refreshed after an uninter-rupted night's sleep—the first for some weeks. Maggie was standing by her bed, holding a cup of chocolate. 'I wasn't sure whether you would want this, Miss Southeran,' she said. 'But Mr Guthrie insisted I should bring it up. He was concerned that you had so little to eat last night. Very thoughtful, is Mr Guthrie, ma'am.'

Eleanor lay back on her pillows and smiled at Maggie.

'I can see you're his friend, Maggie—and your husband,' she added, with a twinkle.

'That we are. But *I* can see you're feeling better, ma'am. Wonderful what a night's sleep will do. Would you like me to help you dress? I've ironed your clothes, and laid them out. I think Mr Guthrie would like to leave in half an hour.'

Eleanor finished her chocolate, then leapt out of bed and, with Maggie's help, was downstairs in a surprisingly short time, ready to go.

'My goodness, you look better!' was Mr Guthrie's greeting. He looked admiringly at Eleanor's yellow muslin dress, and grey pelisse. 'And I like this bonnet better than the last!'

Indeed, it was very pretty—a grey silk, lined with white sarsnet, with a small yellow ostrich plume at the side, and it framed the face beneath it delightfully. Eleanor looked at him sideways, uncertain how to respond. She was feeling better than she had done for weeks, but her emotions, now having surfaced, so to speak, were still raw, still easily disturbed—especially by this man.

'Shall we set off?' said Mr Guthrie, not sounding unduly perturbed by her lack of response.

They went out to the yard where Mr Guthrie's coach was already waiting in the morning sunshine, the boxes tied on the back. Here Eleanor met Sam—a fearsome-looking character with a voice she had heard the day before. He looked as if he would be more at home in a dockside fight than driving a coach. But when she greeted him he shifted nervously and said, 'Maggie told me off yesterday, ma'am. She said I'd been too rough. I'm sorry, and I hope as how you will forgive me.'

He thereupon smiled, and Eleanor, who had been wondering how a decent-looking, respectable body like Maggie had brought herself to marry him, could suddenly see why. Sam's smile was like sunshine breaking through storm clouds.

'I am perfectly sound in wind and limb now, Mr Carver. It was good of you to feel you ought to help me. And if there *is* any blame, I know where to apportion it!' She glanced darkly at Mr Guthrie, who laughed, but merely ordered them to stop wasting time.

'I would like to reach Stanyards before dark,' he said.

Maggie climbed up beside Sam, and Mr Guthrie held the door open for Eleanor. She hesitated, then got inside. As soon as Mr Guthrie joined her, Sam wasted no more time, but set the coach in motion. She could see now that, though it had a plain exterior, it was luxuriously appointed inside, with velvet squabs and handsome woodwork.

'I see that you believe in comfort when you travel, Mr Guthrie,' she said nervously.

'It depends on my company. Sometimes I prefer a high-perch phaeton, Miss Southeran,' was his solemn response.

She shot him a glance. He was smiling at her with that familiar quizzical smile in his eyes. 'Don't. Please don't,' she faltered.

'What was I doing?'

'You were smiling at me…in a particular way. I… I

don't want you to.' She paused, then they both started to speak together. 'Mr Guthrie, I—'

'Miss Southeran—'

They stopped, then Mr Guthrie said, 'You first, Eleanor.'

'I only wanted to say that I am sorry.'

'*You* are sorry?'

'For the exhibition I exposed you to yesterday. You were very patient.'

'I'm glad you think so. I didn't know what to do, I confess. Are you feeling better this morning? You look it.'

'Thank you, yes. And I am obliged to you for all the trouble you took to save me from my own foolhardiness. If I seemed ungrateful at the time, you must forgive me.'

She looked at him to see how he would take this. He was smiling as he said, 'Now that really isn't fair. You ask me not to look at you in a particular way, then you immediately offer me provocation!' He hesitated, then added, 'There are a number of things I wish to tell you, Eleanor. The most important, and one that I hope you will not immediately reject, is that I do love you. No, don't say anything. I can see that you are still too vulnerable at the moment, and the last thing I want is to upset you again. All I wish is that you should know it. We shall talk about it when we are back at Stanyards.'

'Thank you. If I have misjudged you yet again, then I am sorry for that, too.'

'Your feeling of betrayal was perfectly justified if Evadne Oliver reported verbatim what I said to her.'

'How did you know it was that…?' asked Eleanor, astonished.

'Something you quoted. It must have been the conversation with her—I haven't talked to anyone else in those terms, and never wish to again. I lied, but not to you, Eleanor. Never to you. I had guessed that Evadne would report everything I said to Oliver, and was fighting to prevent him from knowing the truth. I wasn't very successful, as it turns out. All I did was to cause you unnecessary distress, and now I may have lost you because of it. Damn Evadne and her malice!' He stared moodily at the passing landscape.

There was silence in the coach for a while. Eleanor thought she ought to say something, but what could she say? She didn't know herself what she felt. Mr Guthrie's sudden transformation from complete hero to complete villain and back again was too much for her overburdened emotions. She wanted time to think, to get rid of old scars, before entering into a new relationship with him. But one thing she must clear up.

'Jonas,' she began, using his name deliberately.

He was very still for a moment, then he turned towards her.

'Yes, Eleanor?'

'I ought to tell you. It wasn't Evadne Oliver. She didn't report what you said. I heard your conversation with her for myself.'

She could see him thinking. 'You weren't in the room with us, I'm certain of that. You weren't outside the door, either—in any case, the door is too thick. A concealed passage? A priest hole? Stanyards is old enough to have one. But why have I never been told?'

'You would have been eventually. The Southeran archives are hidden in it. I was consulting them for the catalogue when you and Evadne came into the library that day. I couldn't escape, but because I'd left the door to it slightly open I…I heard everything.'

'Oh, God! You were listening while I was working to convince Evadne… I can't remember everything I said— I was watching her all the time to see how she was taking it, and inventing as I went along. I must have sounded completely heartless.' Eleanor nodded. 'But why didn't you come out and face me with it afterwards?'

'I never wanted to see you or Stanyards again.'

'And you fled to London. I see. I wish to heaven you had let us know you were there, Eleanor.'

'I couldn't! Not without betraying the secret of the room—to Evadne as well as to you. And then I was too…too disturbed.'

He took a deep breath. 'So what is to happen now? I'll look after you while there's any danger, there's no doubt about that. But Oliver must give up some time— he hasn't the funds to stay long in England. What happens then, Eleanor? Will you never wish to see me again after that?'

'No! I mean, I would like to see you, but…we've had such a stormy acquaintance, Jonas. I need time. I don't know what I want, except time to think—and peace…no demands.'

He smiled down at her. 'Undemanding friendship, Eleanor? Is that what you want of me for the time being? You shall have it. It won't be easy, but I'll try—for a short while.'

'That's it, then,' she said contentedly. But if she had seen the expression on his face as she sat back and closed her eyes, she would have wondered how long the friendship would remain undemanding!

The rest of the journey passed without incident, and they arrived at the Dower House in the evening just before dark. Mrs Southeran was not expecting them, of course, and there was a flurry of activity while Daniel and Betty worked to make the rooms ready. It had been decided that Maggie and Sam would stay for a little while in Somerset, and Jonas wanted them near the Dower House, to act as a kind of extra bodyguard for Eleanor. Mrs Southeran was easily persuaded to offer them rooms in the newly refurbished stable block. Daniel eyed Sam somewhat doubtfully at first, but after a few careful exchanges he decided to accept the stranger's presence gracefully. Betty and Maggie were instant friends.

Jonas had a meal with the Southerans and over it Mrs Southeran brought them up to date on the news. It was much the usual, familiar gossip, but there were two items of particular interest.

'Evadne Oliver is alone in Church Cottage. Her mother has decided to stay in Oxfordshire to be near Marianne—I hear she has been offered a small house on the Morrissey estate. The redoubtable Phoebe is staying with her at present. It must be quite sensational to have two such beauties as Phoebe and her sister living so near to each other, wouldn't you say? And quite difficult for the elder sister to have to give precedence to the younger! But I doubt it will be long before Phoebe has a coronet of her own.'

'Have you heard anything of Mr Oliver, Mama?' asked Eleanor. She and Jonas had decided not to frighten Mrs Southeran more than they had to. They would not tell her of the attack in Vauxhall, nor of their journey.

'Nothing! He did not return with Evadne from the wedding. But he must come back soon, if only to help her remove. The cottage will be let to someone else before long.'

Just as Jonas was leaving he said, 'You said there were two items. What was the other?'

Mrs Southeran glanced at Eleanor. 'Threlfall has gone from the farm, but they say he's out of his mind with fury at losing it. I'm afraid he is seldom sober now, and is issuing dire threats against you, Jonas. You'll watch out for him, won't you?'

'I'm not afraid of Threlfall, ma'am. He's a poor thing. It's natural he should rage against me—how could he possibly acknowledge the truth, that he only has himself to blame? But I'll watch. I don't want matters made worse. Goodnight, Mrs Southeran, Eleanor.' But Eleanor followed him to the door.

'You will be careful, Jonas?'

He smiled at her. 'I like it when you are so concerned. But you needn't be. Get some rest—you're looking tired again. I'll see you tomorrow. If you can bear it, I should like you to show me where this famous room of yours is. I don't like the thought that it is there without my knowing where precisely.'

'We should have told you before now. I'll show you tomorrow. Goodnight, Jonas. And…and thank you.'

He bent and kissed her swiftly, then walked away towards the path to Stanyards.

Mr Oliver had arrived home the same evening, but not to the same enthusiastic welcome. Evadne was distinctly jaded over their meal, and though she gave him the gossip of the neighbourhood she was impatient with him even in front of the servant.

After the covers had been removed and the girl had

gone to bed, she asked him how he had fared in London. What he had to say displeased her, and when he would have excused himself, when he talked of waiting for the right moment, she said, 'Nathaniel, you have had several opportunities to get rid of Jonas and now he has changed his will and it is too late! I went to considerable trouble to establish who it was that Jonas really preferred, and what have you done to dispose of Eleanor Southeran? Nothing!'

'Did I not tell you about Vauxhall?'

'Vauxhall!' she said contemptuously. 'It was all there for you and you couldn't bring youself to tell those men to get rid of her. You are a procrastinator and a coward, Nathaniel, no better than poor Threlfall, who raves about what he will do, but does nothing.'

'Perhaps you're sorry you married me,' he sneered.

She looked at him dispassionately. 'Well, yes,' she said. 'I rather think I am.'

He went pale. 'Evadne! You cannot mean it. You love me!'

'Did you think for one moment,' she said cruelly, 'that I would have married you if I had thought Jonas Guthrie would look twice at me? You were mistaken if you did.'

'So I was a poor substitute? When you swore you loved me, when you had my child, it was Guthrie you really wanted?'

'There was never any question of Guthrie wanting me. And you were there, making sheep's eyes at me.'

'I never thought I would marry, Evadne. You know that. But you were so young, so alive... You made me laugh. And when I knew you were having my child I loved you enough to marry you...in spite of Christopher.'

'With suitable recompense, Nathaniel. Guthrie gave me a very good dowry.'

'Gave you! That's rich. The blackmail idea may have been yours, but it was I who had the evidence about your father, don't forget.'

'And what have you done with it? You've allowed Guthrie to destroy it! We can't even get anything more from that! You're a fool as well as all the rest.'

'Evadne…why are you like this? I would have had you without any dowry, you know that. Don't say you regret our marriage—now that Christopher has gone I…I depend on you.'

'I can get more money from Guthrie if you will forget this stupid affair and come back to Boston with me.'

'No! Not yet. I have a score to settle—now more than ever.'

'Then settle it! But I won't wait much longer. And now I am going to bed. I have had my mother's room prepared for you. Goodnight, Nathaniel.'

Evadne swept out, leaving her husband a prey to his fears and fantasies. He sat at the table, drinking, until the candles were guttering and the bottle empty.

So Evadne had wanted Guthrie all along. Damn him! Everywhere he looked Guthrie was in the way, first taking Christopher and now Evadne. Evadne was right—he must brace himself to act.

But how? He was not brave like Christopher; he was afraid. Why was Christopher not here, when he needed him? There was no one else to depend on, no one else who loved him as Christopher had…

Mr Oliver put his head down on the table and wept. Damn Guthrie! Damn him!

But after a few minutes he lifted his head. There was someone he might be able to use… A germ of an idea formed in his mind. God, he was tired—he couldn't think any more tonight and this would need careful planning if he was to remain unsuspected. Tomorrow he would consider it more carefully to see if it could be done. It had a number of merits. If it worked, he could rid himself of his enemy and a lot more besides, with little risk to himself. He would show Evadne!

Chapter Fifteen

As if to compensate for the rain and dull weather in August and early September, Somerset was having an Indian summer over Michaelmas. The sun shone day after day, and, though it was chilly at night and in the early morning, during the day it was hot and dry. It was the season of the Goose Fairs, and the excitement among the farmers and countryfolk ran high as the pedlars and chapmen, gypsies and jugglers started to gather in the small country towns.

For the people who worked hard in the fields for most of the year this was the great holiday. During the three days of the fair they could meet exotic travellers from afar and buy goods and trinkets with their hard-earned pennies before returning home to prepare for the winter. The people of Stanyards were no exception. It was a tradition that the estate and its gentry were left to fend for themselves for one day while everyone else attended the local Goose Fair—farmers, servants, stable hands alike.

Jonas was worried. Though he said nothing to anyone

else, it seemed to him an ideal occasion for Nathaniel Oliver to strike. Time was running out for the man, and he must do something soon or go back to Boston defeated. Well, let him try! At least it would clear the situation once and for all. It infuriated Jonas that, though he knew all about Oliver's crimes and criminal intentions, there was no evidence, nothing with which to charge him before a magistrate. Perhaps, after the Goose Fair, there might be.

If he were to be trapped, however, Oliver must not be put off from making an attempt, so Jonas decided that any precautions he took must not be obvious. He had a word with Sam, but he kept his own counsel otherwise and let the rest carry on with their plans. Daniel and Betty had filled Maggie's head with tales about the fair, and she could hardly wait to see it for herself. Even staid Mrs Cartwright was accompanying Annie and Dora and the other staff from Stanyards and the Dower House— though she managed to convey the impression that she was not going for her own enjoyment but rather to keep an eye on the maids!

Jonas had managed to get himself invited to the Dower House for the day, which suited his plans very well. He would be able to keep a close eye on Eleanor, while Sam watched from his vantage point over the stable for any unwelcome visitors.

The expedition to the fair set off early in the morning with much merriment and noise. Maggie had been somewhat annoyed with her Sam for his refusal to go to the fair, but even she cheered up when he bade her a most affectionate farewell and gave her money to buy herself a trinket or two.

'I'm not the sort to enjoy all that bustle,' he said to

her. 'I'll have a nice easy day here and wait for you to come back and tell me all about it.'

Stanyards seemed very quiet as Jonas walked along the path to the Dower House. The park and fields around it were empty, the house deserted. Jonas was not a fanciful man, but it seemed to him almost as if the place was waiting for something to happen—it was like the silence in a theatre just before the play began.

Mrs Southeran was unaffectedly glad to see him. Her manner to him had always been as direct as his own, and the slight coolness which had appeared when Eleanor had gone to London in such distress had quite gone. It was now clear to anyone who chose to look that Jonas was deeply in love with her daughter—and that Eleanor's spirits visibly improved every time he appeared. She was now certain that the hope she had cherished almost from the moment Jonas had bought Stanyards was about to be realised.

Eleanor herself was very subdued, still struggling to cope with the after-effects of the flood of emotion which had almost swamped her. Until Jonas Guthrie had come into her life she had remained a child, emotionally speaking. Of course she had felt normal family affection, and she had always been devoted to her mother. But, until Jonas Guthrie had appeared, her deeply passionate nature had remained largely dormant, its only outlet her love and care for Stanyards. Jonas had aroused a tumult of feeling such as she had never before experienced, and she had been exhilarated, astounded, and frightened that any other person could have this profound effect on her.

Then, still in this highly vulnerable state, she had been forced to listen to his conversation with Evadne in

the library, had heard his careless dismissal of their relationship, his declaration that he did not, in fact, love
her, that he had been making use of her. During the days
that followed this she had almost succumbed to despair.
It had taken all the courage of which she was capable
to pull herself together, to paper over the feelings of betrayal and self-contempt and face the world.

Now she could hardly take in the fact that it had all
been unnecessary, that Jonas had loved her all the time.
Whatever he had told her afterwards, however much her
head told her it was reasonable, her deeper feelings
were still numb with shock. But she was slowly coming
to look more and more for Jonas's arrival, to hear his
deep voice, to see his tall figure coming up the path, to
feel that the world was right when Jonas was there.

The three of them—Jonas, Eleanor and Mrs Southeran—had a pleasant meal, which had been carefully
prepared early that morning before Betty and the others
had departed. They were still sitting at the table when
the sound of a horse coming up to the Dower House put
Jonas instantly on the alert. He got up and walked calmly
to the door. As he had thought, it was Nathaniel Oliver.

'Don't bother getting off your horse, Oliver. You're
not coming in here,' Jonas said grimly.

Oliver stayed where he was, but called out, 'I've
come to make peace, Guthrie. Evadne tells me that she
won't wait any longer before she goes back to Boston,
and I've decided to give it up. Miss Southeran is safe. I
was…overwrought and made threats which I now
withdraw. May I come in to discuss it?'

Jonas made no move to welcome him, but stood like
a rock in front of the door. He said coldly, 'And London?'

'That was a mistake. I've had a talk with Evadne since. She tells me you have offered her money to return. I... We should like to take you up on the offer. May I come in?'

'Of course you may, Mr Oliver,' said a voice behind Jonas. It was Mrs Southeran. 'Is anyone else with you?'

'No, I am alone.'

'In that case—'

'No, ma'am! Pray do not invite him into your house! You do not know him as I do. He is dangerous and untrustworthy,' said Jonas with urgency.

'Nonsense! He will surely not attack all three of us at once. Take off your coat, Mr Oliver, and come inside.'

'My coat?'

'I will give it back to you once Jonas has made sure you are not armed.' As Mr Oliver dismounted and busied himself with the coat, Mrs Southeran murmured, 'Sam Carver is not far away, I take it, Jonas?'

He smiled unwillingly. 'You are a witch, ma'am! But I still cannot like exposing Eleanor to this man.'

'I sent Eleanor upstairs.' She turned as Oliver came up the steps. 'Come in, Mr Oliver.' Jonas waited at the door with Mr Oliver's coat until the gentleman had passed into the hall. Then, having checked that Sam Carver was now in the yard and coming towards the house, he closed the door to, without actually shutting it. He was taking no risks.

'Would you like your coat back, Mr Oliver? Now, what can we do for you?' said Mrs Southeran, once they were in the sitting-room.

Mr Oliver put on his coat and settled back in the chair she had indicated. Jonas stood with his back to the window, looking watchful.

'If you could persuade Guthrie that I am sincere in my wish to forget the whole matter and return to Boston, I should be obliged to you, Mrs Southeran. I have lost one very dear friend and I do not wish to risk losing my wife as well—as I shall if I don't give up this…vendetta. She has set her heart on leaving England within the week, and I have told her we shall do so. Unfortunately…'

'You're short of money,' said Jonas sardonically.

'Well, yes.'

'But even supposing Mr Guthrie were generous enough to give you some money, what will you do when you get to America, Mr Oliver? The firm of Anstey and Oliver is finished, is it not?'

Oliver sighed. 'I shall have to look for something else to do. It will not be easy. I was hoping that Guthrie here…?'

'What? Give you enough to live on for the rest of your misbegotten existence? Or did you think I would give you an introduction to my unsuspecting business acquaintances? Not on your life, Oliver!'

'Let us not be too hasty, Jonas,' murmured Mrs Southeran. 'Mr Oliver must be left with some prospect of a future.' She turned to Oliver. 'I have a letter here from a Mr Bitteridge of Tremont Street in Boston. I believe you know him?'

'He was a friend of my father's,' said Oliver sullenly.

'What are you up to, ma'am?' asked Jonas suspiciously. 'And how is it that you have suddenly had a communication from Bitteridge? He's an important man in Boston—one of the town's most worthy citizens.'

'Then why are you surprised that I have correspondence with him? He was a friend of my husband, a fellow bibliophile.'

'Ah, yes! I had forgotten his hobby. I only came across him by way of our trading connections.'

'But I actually wrote to him to ask about the Ansteys and you. I found what he has to say extremely interesting.' She turned to Oliver. 'He seems to think that the part you and your wife played in the Anstey story was, to say the least, dubious, Mr Oliver.'

He started to protest, but Mrs Southeran overrode him. 'However, his friendship with your father inclines him to take a more tolerant view of your conduct than others might. He mentions that he has plans to expand his trading interests westwards. I think you might well profit from a visit to your father's old friend when you get back to Boston, don't you?'

Mr Oliver got up. Almost without appearing to move, Jonas was at Mrs Southeran's side, between her and her guest.

'Really, Guthrie!' Mr Oliver exclaimed. 'What do you suppose I am about to do? I object to your excessive suspicion of me! I find it offensive.'

'Object away,' said Jonas curtly. 'I am not concerned with your feelings. What are you about to do?'

'I would like to thank Mrs Southeran for her interest in my future.'

'It is my daughter's continuing future with which I am concerned, Mr Oliver. I would like you to go back to America and not return. I am willing to intercede for you with Mr Bitteridge, if you think it would help.'

'I think it would, ma'am, indeed I do. Meanwhile…'

'Meanwhile you need some money,' said Jonas. 'I am prepared to make good my promise to Evadne, in spite of your activities since.'

'Too good, too kind,' said Mr Oliver with mock-humility. 'Though a more sensitive soul might find this haste to have me gone a touch hurtful. Still…shall I return here later this evening? I should like to leave as soon as possible. Letters of credit would do.'

'I don't have the necessary papers here—nor do I wish you near this house again. I will give you what you need at Stanyards. Shall we say five o'clock?'

'In the library?'

'Right! And now go!'

'So unpolished,' murmured Mr Oliver. 'I shall take leave of my hostess first. And Miss Southeran?'

'I shall give her your good wishes myself, Oliver. She is not available.'

'Goodbye, Mr Oliver. Do not disappoint Mr Bitteridge.'

After Oliver had gone, Mrs Southeran looked anxiously at Jonas. 'Do you think it will work? Will he leave?'

'I don't know, but I won't take any chances. I'll be with Eleanor for the rest of the day until I go to Stanyards to meet Oliver, and Sam will be on guard while I am up there.'

'He seemed to be interested in Mr Bitteridge's offer, but…'

'I know. He didn't mention consulting Evadne, and leaving Boston would be a major step—he'd never take it without first talking it over with her. On the other hand, she is apparently eager to go back without further action. Perhaps he thinks she would approve. They must be finished as far as the Boston people are concerned. All the same…'

'Take care when you're up at Stanyards, Jonas.'

'It isn't my skin he is after, Mrs Southeran. He wants me to suffer, and he knows it would hurt me far more if Eleanor were hurt. I'm safe as long as Eleanor isn't with me. I haven't told her about Sam, by the way. I didn't want her to know how worried I was.'

Mrs Southeran understood and agreed with him on this. Eleanor's equilibrium was still in a fragile state.

The rest of the afternoon passed pleasantly, and no one would have guessed, as Jonas chatted with Mrs Southeran and played a game of croquet with Eleanor, how heartily he was wishing that the time to leave for Stanyards would come. Eventually he set off at four o'clock, having first extracted from Eleanor a promise that she would stay with her mother, without actually telling her why. On his way to the house he called in at the stables and warned Sam to have extra care.

He had given himself the extra time to write out the necessary instructions to his bank, and prepare for Oliver's visit. He was fairly certain that the house would be safe as yet, for Sam had kept a look-out along the drive and had seen no one. As Jonas walked up the path to the house he was considering what Oliver might do. It could be that the man had concluded that enough was enough, had decided to take the money and go. But Jonas somehow didn't think that this was the case. There had been something about that conversation this morning...

Still, it was worth a risk just to see whether matters could be settled by negotiation. There had been no reports of strangers in the district, so Oliver was on his own. Jonas decided that the danger was not great, once he had removed any weapons Oliver might bring with him—he must remember to search him for a knife...

Once inside the house he checked the library carefully and then locked the door. He wrote out his intrucions to the bank and laid them out ready for Oliver to see. Then he went into the secret room, which he had taken to using for valuables since being shown where it was, and counted out some money. This he put into a small bag, came back into the library and set it beside the envelope on the desk. It was nearly five o'clock. He unlocked the library door and waited by it. Someone was coming up the stairs...

Nathaniel Oliver came into the room, and Jonas seized him from behind, searched him, and removed a pistol from the side-pocket of his coat. There were no other weapons. Only then did he release his guest and invite him to sit down to read the letters.

'Well, I will, though I have a damn good mind to call off the truce, Guthrie. Is this the way you treat your other business associates?'

'It's the only way to treat you, Oliver. And you are no associate of mine, not in any sense. Read the letters and go!'

'I see you are making it a condition that I leave Combe St James by eight o'clock tomorrow morning?'

'You will need to leave immediately if you are to catch the October packet to New York. My carriage will take you both as far as Axminster. You can pick up the London mail from there. You will also observe that the payments are in instalments, and are conditional on the fact that you collect them in person on certain dates and in certain places.'

'An unnecessary complication, surely?'

'It's the only way I can be sure that you actually do travel back in the way you say you will.'

'Such a suspicious nature,' mocked Oliver, but he seemed to be satisfied.

'What about Evadne?' asked Jonas abruptly.

'Oh, she'll be pleased,' said Oliver with a smile.

'She'll be impressed.' Jonas frowned at his tone and Oliver explained smoothly, 'It's a handsome sum of money altogether.'

'Right, I'll just have your signature…' Oliver signed, and the documents were sealed and packed up. Jonas handed Oliver the bag of guineas, and stood up. 'You're getting away with more than you deserve. But it's worth it, just to be free of you. Don't come back to England in a hurry, Oliver.'

'I shan't, Guthrie, I shan't! I'll bid you farewell, then. No, I don't expect you to shake my hand. I'm really quite a reasonable man…' They were walking out of the door, and Oliver started down the stairs, looking up and giving Jonas a mock-salute as he went. Jonas watched him go. At the last minute he sensed danger, but it was too late. Something came at him from behind. He turned to defend himself, but felt a crashing blow on the head, was dimly aware of a loud voice shouting curses and then fell to the ground unconscious…

'Good,' said Oliver, coming back up the stairs. 'Now help me to drag him back into the library. That's it. Over here, I think, by the window. It'll look as if he was trying to get out. I don't suppose he could, if he did come to before it was too late?'

'Have a look out of that window, Mr Oliver,' said Threlfall. Oliver shuddered as he gazed down. Stanyards was surrounded on this side by a deep moat, now filled with iron spikes. 'Excellent! Now, Threlfall, we want kindling and tinder. Did you get it?'

'I hid it in the barn yesterday. Shall I fetch it?'

'Do so. Did—er—did anyone see you with it?'

'Only Tom Briggs, and he won't think twice about it.'

'Right! Fetch the stuff and we'll build a little bonfire

for our dear friend here. I'll just see if there's anything worth keeping…'

'I'm not a thief, Mr Oliver. You do what you please, but I don't want anything but the money you promised me.'

'You are right, Threlfall. Now hurry!'

Threlfall went away while Oliver stood in the centre of the library, deciding how best to arrange the straw and tinder for maximum effect. But once his accomplice had gone he hurried to the desk and searched the drawers. Nothing but the pistol Guthrie had taken from him a few moments before, which he pocketed. Damn Guthrie and his careful ways!

Then he smiled. He had his passage and the letters. He and Evadne could leave tonight for London and go back satisfied to America, while poor old Threlfall took the blame for the fire. A piece of luck that this Tom, whoever he was, had seen the kindling in Threlfall's possession…

As if on cue Threlfall came in carrying a huge bundle of straw and other combustible material.

'I'll fetch some more,' he said. 'You could start laying a trail, if you would, Mr Oliver.' With his experience of burning off the stubble in the fields, he showed Oliver how to set the fire, then went to fetch more straw. 'It's going to be a right good blaze. That'll finish Mr Bloody Know-all Guthrie!' he said as he went.

Meanwhile Eleanor sat in the sitting-room at the Dower House in the fever of suspense. She had listened to the conversation between Oliver and Jonas, though she had remained unseen. She, too, had heard undertones in Oliver's voice. Jonas was in danger, she was sure, and she could suddenly no longer bear to sit there doing nothing.

'Mama, I think I shall just go out for a little air,' she said.

'You promised to stay with me, Nell.'

'But—'

'You will stay, Eleanor.'

Jonas, too, had known there was danger, and had obviously asked her mother to make sure that Eleanor remained in the Dower House. Mrs Southeran very seldom used such a tone, but when she did there was no disobeying it. Or, at least, not overtly.

Eleanor eyed her mother, who was working on a poem at her desk. A little guile was necessary, a little patience. She must go to Jonas, she must... But she would have to wait a while.

Eleanor got up.

'Where are you going, Nell?'

'To open the doors on to the terrace, Mama. Since I cannot go out, I'll sit by them, just round the corner from you, and read.'

The book was fetched, and the two women sat in silence, Eleanor apparently absorbed in her book and Mrs Southeran concentrating on her poem. In a few minutes, as Eleanor knew she would be, Mrs Southeran was lost to the world. She would not notice what was happening for a minute or two. It would be enough.

Eleanor laid her book down and silently crept along the terrace, ducking under the window by her mother's desk as she went. She avoided the steps at the end of the terrace which led down into the yard, instead crossing the lawn and scrambling through the hedge on to the path to Stanyards. Here she took to her heels and ran swiftly along it, driven by a single aim—to get to Jonas. The scent of danger was getting stronger all the time.

She met Threlfall at the foot of the stairs up to the

library, and her heart gave a thump when she saw the consternation on his face as he caught sight of her. He was covered in pieces of straw.

'Where is he?' she cried. 'What have you done with him?'

'Miss Nell! Don't go up there, Miss Nell!'

But Eleanor was already halfway up the steps. She burst into the library, and was horrified to see Jonas's body lying under the window at the far end of the room.

'Jonas,' she screamed. 'Jonas!' She did not see Oliver, pouring oil from the lamp over a bundle of wood and straw, as she ran forward and knelt down beside the figure on the floor. A trickle of blood had dried on Jonas's face. It came from an ugly wound on the side of his head, and as she gently touched it he groaned. He was alive! She got to her feet and looked for Threlfall, but was stunned when she saw Oliver standing by the door, smiling at her. In his hand was a lighted brand.

'Miss Southeran,' he said. 'An unexpected but wholly delightful pleasure to see you here. But I am afraid you will never now marry—either of you!'

Eleanor screamed again as Oliver threw the flaming piece of wood on to the nearest bundle of straw, then slammed the library door shut and locked it. The straw caught immediately, blazing up in a great fan of flame…

Outside the library door Threlfall and Oliver were struggling for possession of the key. Threlfall was beside himself, shouting, 'Let me have it! Give it to me, you bastard! Oh, God, not Miss Nell; you're not going to kill Miss Nell! Give it to me, I say!'

He caught the hand which held the key, but Oliver was holding a pistol in the other, and he pulled the trigger. Threlfall staggered back, then with a roar he attacked Oliver like a maddened bull. Oliver did not stand a chance. He went crashing down the stairs, the key slipping from his fingers as he fell. It tinkled down the steps behind him, finally coming to rest next to his body at the foot of the stairs.

Gasping and groaning, Threlfall lurched down the steps, his eyes only on the key. Oliver was lying with his head at an unnatural angle, his neck clearly broken, but Threlfall didn't wait to look. He climbed the stairs again, slowly, agonisingly slowly, his brow covered in sweat. He gave forth little grunts as he went, as if he had no breath for more than that.

When he reached the door he fumbled with the key for several moments, unable to see the lock, only feeling for it with fingers that were growing numb. Finally the door swung open and he fell into the room. A sheet of flame engulfed him, but he was already dead. His last words, heard by no one, had been a desperate cry to Eleanor.

At the far end of the room Eleanor was huddled over Jonas, her eyes wide with terror at the noise and power of the blaze in front of them. She rose to look out of the window. If only she could open it…

'Don't do that, Eleanor! It'll be the end if you do!'

Jonas was sitting up, holding his head. For a mad moment she thought she was back in the park, so many months ago…

'Eleanor! For God's sake, pull yourself together!' he whispered hoarsely. 'If we are to stay alive you've got to help me. We must get into that room—it's stone and our only chance!'

'The room? Of course!' Quickly she pressed the knob

and the wall beside the window slowly opened, revealing the stone passage. 'I'll help you, Jonas,' she said as he got painfully to his feet. He was sheet-white, and it was clear that he was exerting every ounce of his strength to control his limbs. He was frowning with concentration.

'Quickly!' said Eleanor, trying not to sound as panic-stricken as she felt. 'You go first; I'll close the door behind us. Don't argue—save your strength.' Her voice wobbled and she cleared her throat. 'We'll be fine in there.'

They made their way into the passage.

'Make certain the door is shut tight!'

'I have, I have! Now hurry!'

A breath of cool air met them as they made their way into the little room, and sank gratefully to the floor. Eleanor snatched the cushion she had left there in her precipitate flight almost a month before and put it under Jonas's head. He was lying with his eyes shut, still frowning. Eleanor sat by him, holding his hand and listening to the roar in the library. A sudden crash made her jump.

'The beams in the ceiling? Or the floor?' said Jonas.

'Don't talk. Try to stay perfectly still.'

'It's difficult to do anything else! There isn't room for it,' he said, with a hint of his smile. Eleanor tried to smile back, and for a while there was silence again, during which Jonas gradually relaxed and his face regained a little of its colour.

'I thought you were dead, Jonas,' said Eleanor, her voice trembling. 'For a moment I thought you were dead. And all I could think was that I had never told you...'

'Told me what?' he asked, his eyes still shut. He was hardly daring to breathe.

'That I love you,' she said, quite simply. 'I never realised how much.'

He let out his breath in a long sigh, then said slowly, but with a hint of his old, quizzical tone, 'It takes a lot to persuade you to be kind to me, Eleanor Southeran! It needs an ambassador to get you to dance with me, a fire before you'll come looking for me, and you have to think I am dead before you realise that you love me after all! I can see an eventful life ahead. What do you demand before you will marry me? Carlton House? A visit to the moon? Immortal life?'

'An assurance of your love,' she said. 'That's all I have ever wanted.'

'Oh, my love, my very dearest, most precious love, you have that and to spare,' he said, rolling over and taking her into his arms.

'Jonas, be careful…' Eleanor's protest died away as he kissed her gently, but at great length…

The sound of another crash brought them to their senses, and they realised that the stones on the library side of the little room were growing warm. Jonas got up and went into the passage. When he came back he said tersely, 'I expect that was the floor in the library giving way. Don't look like that, Eleanor, we'll be all right. The stones here are part of the tower and very thick; they're not going to crack unless the fire burns for longer than I think it will. Oliver had put down straw and wood, you say?'

When Eleanor described to him what little she had seen, he said thoughtfully, 'He set out to create a sudden, overwhelming blaze—which he obviously did. The bookcases, ceiling and floor are all of wood—they'll go. The roof might, too. But the walls will hold. They are all of stone. Thank God for your ancestors' distrust of their neighbours, Eleanor! This house was built with the strength of a fortress.'

'I suppose the books will all have been destroyed,' she said sadly. 'My father's treasures.'

'I'm afraid so. But the best are still with Wilkes. That's one consolation.' He saw that tears were rolling down her cheeks. 'Don't cry, my love. We'll build it all up again—Stanyards, the collection, the lot! Together.'

'Yes, Jonas,' she said, trying to smile. 'Yes, I know.'

'We'll assess the damage and start on the repairs right away. You'll see. Stanyards will soon be itself again.'

'I'm not sure that is what I want any more. Perhaps we should plan something new, for a new age?'

'I'd like that! But we could build the new alongside the old—why shouldn't they mix?'

He saw that this subject intrigued her and encouraged her to talk of her ideas. But suddenly she said, 'We are going to get out, aren't we?'

'Oh, yes! The fire will burn itself out soon enough. Meanwhile, we shall have to stay here—we might get warm, but we won't burn.'

'How long, Jonas?'

'I should think it might be all right by morning.'

'Morning!'

'The fire will die down pretty soon now, I should think, but the wood and stone and rubble will be hot for some hours. We're stuck here till tomorrow. Are you afraid that you're ruined, spending the night with me? There's no danger to your virtue. I regret to say that I'm not capable of attacking you—I'm as weak as a kitten. And anyway, I'll make an honest woman of you just as soon as you'll allow me—I'll marry you.'

Eleanor smiled at this sally, but shook her head. 'It's my mother,' she said. 'She'll be frantic.'

He grew grave immediately. 'I'm sorry. I hadn't thought of that aspect; I was just relieved to find that we were not about to be roasted alive. What about Threlfall? Won't he…? No, I suppose not. It would be tantamount to admitting his own guilt. Oliver certainly won't tell anyone. If I know him, he and Evadne will have left the area by nightfall. He has all the necessary funds, and he'll be anxious to exchange the letters I gave him for cash. Sam and your mother will see the smoke, of course…' Jonas put his arm round Eleanor. 'We'll have to sit it out, and so will they, my darling.'

Chapter Sixteen

They made themselves as comfortable as they could. The floor was hard, the atmosphere stifling, and they were hungry and, above all, thirsty. Jonas was obviously still in some pain, but he insisted on giving Eleanor the cushion to rest on. In turn, she made him sit next to the window slit. At least the air coming in was cool and fresh.

The noises in the library were dying down. Before long they heard calls and shouts. Mrs Southeran and Sam were frantically circling the building, shouting and calling. Eleanor leapt up and leaned over Jonas till she could get her hand out of the slit. She waved, but there was no response. The old builders had done their job too well. The window was completely invisible from the ground.

'Here,' said Jonas. She was astonished to see him rip off his shirt and tear it into one long strip. 'Wave that,' he said.

Eleanor waved again and eventually heard an excited exclamation under the window. 'Mrs Southeran, Mrs Southeran! Ma'am! Look at this!' It was Sam.

They heard Mrs Southeran call tremulously, 'Eleanor? Are you there? In the room?'

'Yes,' shouted Jonas. 'We're both here. We're safe enough, but I doubt we'll be able to get out for some time. Don't worry. Have you seen Oliver?'

'Oh, thank God, thank God! Eleanor, say something—I shan't believe you're safe till I hear you.'

Eleanor put her face to the slit and shouted as best she could. 'Mama? I'm sorry. But I had to find Jonas.'

'Have you seen Oliver?' shouted Jonas.

'Yes. Was it you?' shouted Sam. His voice echoed round the little room.

'What do you mean?'

'He's dead. Neck broken,' bellowed Sam. 'We'll tell you about it later. I'll have a look at the stairs again. See if we can get you out.' He was gone.

'Is there nothing we can do?' asked Mrs Southeran.

'I don't think so. We're trapped till it's cooled off a bit. What is that about Oliver?'

'He was at the bottom of the stairs. Jonas, I cannot shout much more; my voice is going. Here's Sam again. Eleanor, take care!'

'She'll be all right, ma'am,' they heard Sam say. 'She's with Mr Guthrie.'

Jonas smiled. 'I wish I had his confidence!'

'Well, I have. Listen!'

A sound of singing and laughter came thinly on the air. The merrymakers were returning. But as they aproached their songs died down and exclamations of horror took their place. Soon Stanyards was surrounded by a throng of worried people. Sam took charge, ordering some to fetch water to make an attempt to put out the last remnants of flame, some to take Mrs Southeran back to the Dower House, and others to start getting rooms ready for those who had lost their sleeping quarters. The best men he kept with him to make an attempt to reach the window slit. Eleanor and Jonas were going to need water and perhaps some food soon.

With the aid of some ingenious devices and skilled climbing, Sam got water and some biscuits through the slit. That would have to do till the morning. During the attempts, the two in the room heard that the library was completely gutted, and its floor had collapsed—there was no safe way out through it at the moment. Fortunately the fire had spread in the other direction away from the corner where the secret room lay. But some parts of Stanyards' roof had given in; others were still burning. 'It'll burn itself out very soon, Mr Guthrie. Don't you worry!'

'Is it bad, Sam?'

There was a silence, then Sam said, 'It's not good, sir. You'll see in the morning.'

With that he was gone. By this time it was dark, and it was with difficulty that Eleanor and Jonas ate their rations. Then they settled down for another rest. Eleanor's fingers came into contact with Jonas's bare chest. She let them roam…

'Don't,' said Jonas in a strangled voice.

'But you're cold,' said Eleanor. 'The floor, no shirt…'

'I am not,' said Jonas, 'cold. Not at all.'

'Oh. I just thought…'

'Well, don't!'

'I quite understand,' said Eleanor mournfully. 'And you did say that you were feeling not quite the thing. Weak as a kitten, you said.'

He pulled her into his arms. 'I suddenly find, my

scheming, conniving, tormenting darling, that I am not as weak as I thought. Come here…'

'But Jonas.' Eleanor's voice was muffled againt his chest. 'You said my virtue was in no dang—'

'I lied! Now be quiet and let me seduce you like the villain I am!'

The next morning Eleanor and Jonas were rescued from their prison. Eleanor was swept off to the Dower House, and Jonas was carried away, protesting that he didn't need a damned doctor. When they met later that day in the Dower House, Jonas went straight over to Eleanor and took her into his arms, holding her close, as if he could not bear to be away from her, while Mrs Southeran watched them with a satisfied smile. Then the three of them talked of the events of the previous day, and Jonas added what he had learnt from Sam and the others.

Threlfall's badly burned body had been discovered in the ruins below the library, but it was still possible to see the bullet wound in his chest. Oliver's body was now lying in one of Stanyards' surviving rooms till the coroner should see it. A gun had been found near him.

Eleanor shuddered and hid her face in Jonas's coat. 'Please let us not talk of it any more. I can't bear to think of it. Poor Threlfall!'

'Poor Threlfall indeed! He was trying to murder me, Eleanor!'

'Well, if you hadn't been so hard on him—'

Mrs Southeran intervened. 'Now, now! It would be quite wrong of you to quarrel about Threlfall yet again. Or do you intend to continue after you are married?'

'Mama! You've spoiled my surprise—how do you

know? I haven't mentioned it. Have you?' said Eleanor, turning to Jonas.

Mrs Southeran said severely, 'No one has told me a thing, Eleanor. But I should certainly hope you are getting married—after last night.' Then she watched in amusement as Eleanor's face grew scarlet. 'I thought as much,' she said.

Jonas laughed out loud. 'I shall marry Eleanor as soon as she has something suitable to wear, ma'am.'

'And the licence?'

'That has been in my pocket since before I left London. But we shan't have anywhere to live for some time. May we lodge with you?'

'Well, I too have a surprise for you. I might be going to visit Boston for two months in the spring. And before that I shall be in London.'

Eleanor stared at her mother. 'What do you mean, Mama?'

'Mr Bitteridge is coming over to Europe very soon, and I shall stay in London with your aunt Hetty and show him the sights. He has invited me to go back with him to Boston, and I think I might.'

Eleanor sat down rather suddenly. 'Is he…is he married?'

'Goodness me, what a question! As it happens he's widowed—like me. But pray do not start adding two and two together and making five, Eleanor. I shall return next summer—if I go at all.'

They were interrupted by Betty. Her eyes were round as she said, 'It's Mrs Oliver, ma'am. Shall I…shall I say you're not at home?'

'No, of course not. Come in, Mrs Oliver.'

Evadne Oliver walked in, as composed as ever. She

was dressed in black, and, curiously enough, the clothes suited her. After an awkward few minutes during which everyone except Evadne tried to find something to say, she announced, 'I know what they are saying, and I think it probably true. Nathaniel tried to kill you, and was killed in the process. I knew nothing of his plan, Jonas. I merely wanted to get away as quickly as possible from England. Do you believe me?'

'Let us say for the sake of argument that I do, Evadne. You may have the money and the rest that I gave your husband. Sam will bring them down to you. Is that what you want? I take it that you still hope to take the boat to New York?'

'New York? Certainly not! I shall go to Madras.'

'Madras?' exclaimed Eleanor.

Evadne Oliver smiled. 'Madras,' she said. She went to the door, then turned. 'The late Mr Oliver was not the only member of our…somewhat peculiar household to like both men and women. And Christopher was much nearer to me in age. I shall go to Madras. Goodbye.' She went out, leaving the three people in the room speechless.

Mrs Southeran followed her extraordinary guest out, and Eleanor and Jonas were left alone.

'What about Stanyards, Jonas?'

'It's badly damaged. Parts of it are no longer safe. I should like to build a new house, Eleanor, perhaps incorporating some of the old. Would you live with me there?'

'A mansion, for a great lord with a title?'

'No, a family house—a large family house for our large family! I shall never be a great lord, but the house will have a great lady for its mistress.'

'No, no, no,' said Eleanor, putting her arms around

him and holding him close. 'A pretty little country girl—
one who will help her husband to while away the odd
hour—all of them, for the rest of his villainous life!'

* * * * *

Enjoy a sneak preview of
MATCHMAKING WITH A MISSION
by B.J. Daniels,
part of the WHITEHORSE, MONTANA *miniseries.*
Available from Harlequin Intrigue
in April 2008.

*Nate Dempsey has returned to Whitehorse
to uncover the truth about his past...*

Nate sensed someone watching the house and looked
out in surprise to see a woman astride a paint horse just
on the other side of the fence. He quickly stepped back
from the filthy second-floor window, although he
doubted she could have seen him. Only a little of the
June sun pierced the dirty glass to glow on the dust-
coated floor at his feet as he waited a few heartbeats
before he looked out again.

The place was so isolated he hadn't expected to see
another soul. Like the front yard, the dirt road was
waist-high with weeds. When he'd broken the lock on
the back door, he'd had to kick aside a pile of rotten
leaves that had blown in from last fall.

As he sneaked a look, he saw that she was still
there, staring at the house in a way that unnerved him.
He shielded his eyes from the glare of the sun off the
dirty window and studied her, taking in her head of

long blond hair that feathered out in the breeze from under her Western straw hat.

She wore a tan canvas jacket, jeans and boots. But it was the way she sat astride the brown-and-white horse that nudged the memory.

He felt a chill as he realized he'd seen her before. In that very spot. She'd been just a kid then. A kid on a pretty paint horse. Not this one—the markings were different. Anyway, it couldn't have been the same horse, considering the last time he had seen her was more than twenty years ago. That horse would be dead by now.

His mind argued it probably wasn't even the same girl. But he knew better. It was the way she sat the horse, so at home in a saddle and secure in her world on the other side of that fence.

To the boy he'd been, she and her horse had represented freedom, a freedom he'd known he would never have—even after he escaped this house.

Nate saw her shift in the saddle, and for a moment he feared she planned to dismount and come toward the house. With Ellis Harper in his grave, there would be little to keep her away.

To his relief, she reined her horse around and rode back the way she'd come.

As he watched her ride away, he thought about the way she'd stared at the house—today and years ago. While the smartest thing she could do was to stay clear of this house, he had a feeling she'd be back.

Finding out her name should prove easy, since he figured she must live close by. As for her interest in Harper House… He would just have to make sure it didn't become a problem.

* * * * *

Be sure to look for
MATCHMAKING WITH A MISSION
and other suspenseful Harlequin Intrigue stories,
available in April
wherever books are sold.

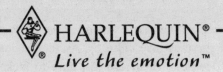

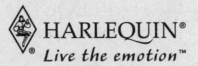

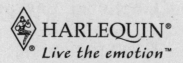

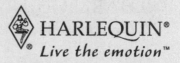